MW00782329

Accomplices IN LOVE

BY

PAT SIMMONS

This novel is a work of fiction. References to real events, organizations, or places are used in a fictional context. Any resemblances to actual persons, living or dead, are entirely coincidental. All Scriptures cited are from the King James Version of the Bible.

Copyright © 2024 Christian Reads Press/Pat Simmons

Developmental Editor: Chandra Sparks Splond
Proofread by Judicious Revisions LLC; Miriam "Cookie" Mitchell
Beta Reader: Evangelist Charlotte Townsend
Interior Design: Kimolisa/Fiverr.com
Cover Design: designerboard18/fiverr.com

To my mother, Johnnie Cole. Happy Birthday!
You're 90 and still going.
Love you, Mama!

ACKNOWLEDGEMENTS

Accomplices in Love was made possible by the following suspects:

First, Developmental Editor Chandra Sparks Splond never fails to challenge me to use my gift and hold me up in prayer with encouraging words as I continue the Jamieson series with the Next Generation of characters. Thank you for juggling my projects this year to help me meet deadlines—lol. Don't retire on me!

Super fans:
Mary Buckner from Chicago. When I told Mary the Jamiesons were coming to Chi-town for a few chapters, she was more than a wealth of information for what I needed. Thank you for being so supportive throughout my writing career.

Evelyn Moseley from Omaha. When I told her the Jamiesons and Robnetts were putting Omaha in the spotlight, she was ready to serve them dinner (lol). Thank you for researching places for my characters to visit, eat, and live. Their cousins, the Robnetts, will take your city by storm.

Beta reader and proofreader:
Beta reader Evangelist Charlotte Townsend and final proofreader Sister Cookie Mitchell. You didn't know what you signed up for as my backup with three-day turnarounds. Your support is priceless.

Husband:
After exposing Kerry to sixteen years of writing deadlines, promotions, and road trips, my husband is the rock in our forty-one years of marriage. He knows more about my characters than he's letting on. Love you dearly.

Praise for Pat Simmons

On the Christmas Takeover, I loved the characters and storyline. The Jamison's Christmas was warm and festive, emphasizing Christ's birth. I enjoyed catching up with all the Jamison family and friends. It was great to see the maturity in Pace and his sisters as they are adults, ready to graduate college. This is an interesting time with several new relationships on the horizon. I look forward to future books about this spirit-filled Christian family. —reader

I loved Stand By Me! The characters became so real to me. I feel like they are friends I know! As always, the story was encouraging and uplifting, with no sexual overtones. It was also educational, as Ms. Simmons included historical facts about African Americans and focused on things that currently concern our community. —Nicole Smith, reader

On the Guilty Generation, Just when I thought that there was no way that Pat Simmons could top her other Jamieson novels, she proved me wrong! This book brought out so many different emotions in me. I laughed at Grandma BB's antics, wanted to snatch Kami up for the way she acted out, and rejoiced when Grandma BB hit Tango with her car & I was in awe of how the Jamiesons showed love & embraced Victoria. This was truly a page turner & I can't wait for the next Jamieson Family Game night!!!!—Ceisha Barrett, reader

On What God Has For Me... Pat Simmons has a way with characters. This story is no exception. From the first page, you are hooked. This is the fourth book of a series and hopefully not the final installment of this family. This is not the first Pat Simmons book that I have read. She has become one of my favorite authors. I look forward to her future work! —Jersey Girl, reader

Accomplices IN LOVE

Chapter One

St. Louis, Missouri

There comes a time in every Jamieson man's life when he knows the woman he wants. Parke Jamieson VIII, aka Pace, knew because he hadn't been able to get Harmony Reed out of his head since Christmas—her brown eyes, thick hair, and smile. She was beautiful, polished, talented, confident, and his sisters' best friend.

Harmony's stay in St. Louis was short as she waited for Chicago's airport to reopen after a snowstorm so she could go home to the Windy City.

Those three days in her presence changed his life.

Pace collapsed on the sofa at his parents' home after visiting his two sisters at Grandma BB's house.

He needed a plan.

Kami, Victoria, and Pace were all seniors in college and on winter break. Victoria was two years younger than Kami and three years younger than Pace, with an IQ that didn't seem possible. God had endowed Victoria with knowledge. His sister was just that smart.

Pace had forfeited a full ride for engineering at Tuskegee University in Alabama to stay at home to keep an eye on his younger sisters, not that they were troublemakers. On the contrary, they could take care of themselves. With three brothers and dozens of male cousins and uncles, no one dared harm a Jamieson woman and live to talk about it.

Instead of appreciating his loyalty, the pair jetted off to Oklahoma City for college after graduating high school while he enrolled at Washington University in St. Louis, Missouri.

Great. They one-upped him. When not away at college, his sisters stayed with Grandma BB, the sassy senior who was the family's unofficial matriarch and grandmother of all the Jamiesons, whether born or yet-to-be-born.

Pace thought staying in touch with Harmony after she left would be simple. Not! As much as he loved his independent, strong-willed sisters, they were just as frustrating in their lack of efforts to convince Harmony to give him her number. He thought it was common courtesy to go through his sisters rather than stalking Harmony on social media. Unfortunately, Pace had resorted to sending Harmony a friend request. She had yet to respond.

Winter break would be over in ten days, so Pace had to take drastic measures to let her know how serious he was about staying connected with her. He searched out his parents in their ridiculously large two-story home. They were relaxing in their master bedroom, sitting on an enclosed sun porch that overlooked the backyard, which opened to a small neighborhood park.

It was their hideout from his younger brothers when Paden, the middle son, practiced on his bass guitar, and Chance banged on the drums to keep the beat. Their father had constructed a music studio to buffer most of the noise for them to practice on the lower level. Pace had to admit his brothers had talents.

He tapped on his parents' door.

"Come in," his father said in a deep voice. Family members said Pace sounded like him, had inherited his dad's good looks, and even had his confident stride.

Pace found his parents in an intense game of chess. When frustrated, his mother tried to play the pieces like checkers.

"What's up, son?"

"Dad, I'm thinking about driving to Chicago for the weekend."

"Oh." Parke turned to his oldest son while watching Cheney's movements on the chessboard. "Don't cheat, wife." He paused and faced Pace. "In January, son? Why?"

"Oh, I want to check out their Black historic sites." He leaned against the doorpost and prayed they didn't want him to elaborate.

Cheney's fingers hovered over the knight, then froze as she glanced up and snickered. "*Ummm-hmmm.* Are you sure that's all you plan to check out?"

"No. There's more I want to see." Pace knew his mother was aware of his attraction to Harmony. He refused to blush in front of her.

"Are your sisters going with you?" Parke asked. "Harmony lives there."

"I think he knows that, honey." She moved her knight.

Pace did not want his sisters to come with him, but he needed them as a go-between to make Harmony comfortable. The problem was Kami and Victoria might try to monopolize her time, even though all three would be back on campus in OKC in a few weeks.

His solution was to take the first step to show Harmony that he wasn't shy about his intentions. Pace's parents stared at him for an answer.

"If they want to, but I won't wait on them."

His father nodded. "Don't blame you with those two sleepy heads. Be safe on the road, son." He dismissed him and turned back to the chess game.

"Well, if the girls don't go, maybe JC can ride with you."

Cheney was overly cautious with all her children, even though Pace was set to graduate this summer. She said there was no age limit when it came to parenting.

That was a thought. Jamison Clark, better known as JC to everyone except Kami, was more than a fellow Wash U student about to graduate. JC had become Pace's brother in Christ when he repented of his sins and received baptism in water and spirit in Jesus' name.

JC was as close as a brother with shared interests and convictions like healthy eating and a lifestyle that included the gym. Both were die-hard Cardinal baseball fans, whether the team won or lost. They shared their love for fresh barbecue pork skins to snack on and played poorly in amateur golf but were determined to conquer the sport. Their family lives were a stark difference: JC didn't have a father in the home. Pace had a loving family, four siblings, and a close-knit extended family.

A crack began in their friendship at the same Christmas Eve dinner table with his sisters and Harmony. Pace's attraction to her was like being enthralled at his first circus performance. He couldn't believe his eyes at her beauty.

Another development was JC's attraction to his sister. It took God to tame Pace's emotions that night, or he risked losing a friend and shaming the Lord. Since then, they had been cool as long as his sister's name stayed out of their conversation.

Kami and Victoria meant the world to him, and as he was taught growing up, the Jamieson men were expected to take care of their Jamieson women. No excuses.

Even his friendship was worth sacrificing to protect Victoria more than Kami from life's hardships—at all costs.

The more Pace considered it, the more he decided this should be a solo trip. He needed to think, strategize his movements, and rehearse the verbiage to win Harmony over.

By the time he made it back to his bedroom, his phone rang. Kami. Pace groaned and answered.

"Mom says you're going up to Chi-town this weekend."

Of course, she did. Cheney Jamieson didn't waste any time. "Yeah. I want to check out some Black historic places of interest." It would be nice if Harmony were his tour guide, he thought. "And I guess you and Victoria want to ride along."

"Can't. We have tickets for a concert, so we'll see her on campus."

Pace froze in his steps. The three friends were inseparable, and Kami wouldn't pass up the chance to visit her. That left him dumbfounded. "Ah, okay. While I'm there, I hope I can see Harmony."

"Right. I'll text you her number."

Since she'd left, he had been asking for Harmony's number, but his sisters had stalled. Now, Kami easily surrendered it. Before he could ask questions, JC called. "Thanks. I'll talk to you later."

"Hey," JC greeted when Pace answered the phone. "Want to ride up to Chi-town with me this weekend?"

"What?" Pace snickered. "I had planned to go myself, hoping to visit with Harmony. What's going on with you?"

"A cousin on my dad's side contacted me on social media and invited me to my great-uncle's birthday party. Since I know very little about that side of the family and we're on break, I thought, why not."

JC and his younger brother had different fathers, and neither was a constant figure in their sons' lives. His mother blamed the men for abandoning her, leaving her broken, low self-esteem, and battling bouts of depression.

"Talk about coincidence. Mom just asked about you. How about I drive? I'm going to need my car for a pretty tour guide."

Chapter Two

Chicago, Illinois

"When did you last speak with your friends in St. Louis?" Lorna Reed asked her only daughter.

Her mother was pretty and so youthful that people often mistook them for sisters. They sipped on morning coffee, crunched on crispy cooked bacon, and indulged in freshly baked cinnamon rolls, dripping with thick white icing.

It was an innocent question.

Harmony had to think about an answer, considering she tried not to think about them. Since Christmas, she had expected the Jamieson sisters to clear up Harmony's confusion about their living arrangements, which didn't include staying home with their parents on Christmas break. Neither Kami nor Victoria had called or texted her as promised after she left for her flight to Chicago.

A nagging thought picked at her. She replayed her conversation with the sisters on their way back to their grandmother's house from the Christmas Eve dinner.

Since Harmony had been stranded in St. Louis, she had helped Kami, Victoria, and their cousins prepare a feast for about forty kinfolks and friends at Grandma BB's house.

Things got strange when the guests left the mansion they had rented for dinner.

Their brothers Pace, Paden, and Chance drove to their parents' house while she, Kami, and Victoria headed to Grandma BB's house. Odd.

Curiosity had gotten the best of her—after all, they were close friends, so Harmony had asked from the backseat. "Hey, I've got a question."

Kami had looked in the rearview mirror. "Yeah, girl?"

"I thought we stayed at Mrs. Beacon's—"

"Uh-uh-uh." Victoria cut her off and wagged her finger. "She told you to call her Grandma BB. That's a privilege denied to many if she doesn't like them. She considers you family, and we do, too."

That sentiment had warmed Harmony's heart. "Then do you mind me asking why you two don't live in the same home with Pace and your parents? I thought we were staying at Grandma BB's while we cooked Christmas Eve dinner for convenience, but it looks like you live there permanently. I saw complete wardrobes and personal items. Why?"

Holding her breath, she watched the sisters exchange what looked like a secret code. Had she overstepped her boundaries? she wondered, as no answer seemed forthcoming.

Kami looked at Victoria again before she glanced at Harmony, upping the suspense. "Do you mind if we talk about that after the holidays so we can enjoy Christmas and focus on getting you home?"

"Right."

Harmony wanted to get home, but she remembered experiencing a sinking feeling in her gut and hoped she wouldn't regret being nosey.

But the holidays had come, and a new year had begun, and she hadn't heard from either of them until she received a text on January first from Kami: **Happy New Year! Enjoy your family. See you back in OKC.**

That was it. There was no hint of a forthcoming answer to last year's question—or maybe they'd forgotten. That bothered her.

Harmony shrugged. "Not since I've been home."

"I guess they're busy enjoying family like you are." Her mother sipped from her cup.

"Or maybe it's something else. I don't know if I trust them anymore." She paused from saying when one of her brothers strolled into the kitchen, sniffing the aroma and rubbing his stomach.

"*Ummm, ummm, ummm.*" Shane grinned. He was three years older at twenty-five, and they were extremely close. "Morn' Mom, Monie," he said, calling Harmony by her childhood nickname as he kissed their cheeks.

Shane headed to the cabinet for a saucer, scooped up two cinnamon rolls and bacon, and poured coffee into a cup. With his hands full, he strolled out of the kitchen.

As the only daughter, Harmony had three older, overbearing brothers. Laurence Junior was the oldest at thirty-one, and Kimbrell was twenty-nine. In her humble opinion, Shane was the most handsome of her brothers.

Only Shane stayed over at their parents' home whenever she came home.

They were quiet while Shane took his time fixing his plate. Once they were alone again, Lorna leaned over with a concerned look. In a hushed tone and with a wrinkled forehead, she asked, "What do you mean you don't trust them? You stayed with them while waiting to catch your flight home. Did something happen that you didn't tell us?"

The face her mom displayed was one meant to instill fear as a child. Her mother, brothers, and dad didn't spare mercy when it came to her.

Harmony needed to shut down whatever retribution her mother was conjuring. She shook her head. "Nope. The family was very cordial. Perfect on the outside." Handsome men and beautiful women. Harmony had been impressed as the adorable young children showed off their musical abilities at the dinner. "But something's not right."

"Like?" Her mother's signature twisting her lips meant Harmony better explain what she meant.

"Well," Harmony said, sighing, "don't you think it's strange that Kami and Victoria stay with their grandmother and their brothers live with their parents? There has to be a reason for those living arrangements, right?"

Lorna frowned, straining her brain to come up with the correct answer, then shrugged. "Maybe there's not enough room at their home."

"Ha! Their house is in historic Ferguson, a suburb of St. Louis, and those homes are gorgeously huge, like in our suburbs. Trust me, there is room."

"I'm sure there's a reason. Have you asked?" Her mother lifted her cup to her lips and sipped.

"I did, Mom, and their body language was suspicious. They never answered. That hurt. I thought all three of us were close, but evidently not."

She and her mother brainstormed different explanations, but none made sense.

"Their hesitation made me feel like an outsider instead of part of a girlfriend-like sister circle. I don't think I want to know anymore."

They had often studied and attended events together and had each other's backs, so when Kami and Victoria invited her to St. Louis to wait out the snowstorm that hit Chicago, she didn't hesitate to accept. That's what friends did. What if it was all an act after four years of a close bond?

"Harmony," her mother said, pulling her out of her musing, "I hope all of this is a misunderstanding. Although I'm curious, too, I hope your imagination isn't running wild. I enjoy chatting with the girls whenever you FaceTime me…"

While her mother rambled on, her brother returned to the kitchen for a second helping as Harmony's phone alerted her of a text. Glancing at the sender, she squinted, then reread it and looked at her mom. "You'll never guess who this is from. Pace, Victoria's and Kami's older brother." She didn't give her a chance to guess. "Kami gave him my number, which wasn't okay, and he and his friend are coming to Chicago for the weekend, and he hopes to see me."

"*Hmmm.* He might have some answers. Strange your friends aren't coming." Lorna frowned, then fanned her hand in the air. "Invite them over for dinner. I want to know what he knows, too."

Conflicting emotions prevented Harmony from responding right away. Her mind drifted to the last time she'd seen him. In the airport, Pace's handsome face snuck into her head as she navigated other passengers to exit the terminal.

Surprisingly and shamefully, Harmony was attracted to Pace. There was nothing not to like about him. Educated, with strong family ties, his handsomeness was well-handcrafted by God. His flawless skin looked smooth—no razor bumps or mishaps. His mustache was trimmed right, not too thick and overgrown like weeds. Judging from his hairline, he never missed a barber appointment.

Pace was tall and buff, evidence that he worked out. JC was nice-looking, too, but Victoria held his attention, although she completely ignored him.

Lastly, Pace's serious expression was betrayed when his eyes lit up, then his lips curved in a slow-cooking smile.

Whew.

Kami texted her on Christmas evening, stating that Pace had asked for her phone number. **Yay or nay?**

Harmony never said either.

Could she blame Kami's or Victoria's odd behavior for not communicating with Pace?

Pace was hard to resist during the family dinner. He was down to earth, possessed irresistible charm, and was blessed with a second helping of handsomeness. Now, he was on his way to Chi-town.

He had gotten up early to drive her to the airport so she wouldn't miss her flight, and then he stayed at the airport on Christmas morning with his sisters to make sure she got on that plane.

That had wowed her.

After taking a deep breath and calming her heartbeat, she texted Pace back. **Mom said you both are invited to dinner when you get in.** She gave them her address.

While her mom planned a dinner menu, Harmony had to leave for her hair appointment. No one kept her from missing it. She wondered why Pace was coming without his sisters. Would he hold the answers, or would the plot thicken?

Chapter Three

The short road trip seemed long to Pace when he wanted to get there to see Harmony. It was a good thing JC was riding with him.

But his friend was unusually quiet, almost guarded, until he turned from the window and faced Pace with a determined expression. "Bro, I need to get this off my chest. I understand that you're overprotective of your sisters, and I respect that, but I make no apologies for my interest."

Hear him out, Pace coaxed himself. Their well-being was the number one priority, although his sisters knew self-defense better than some men. Pace wanted to spare them the matters of the heart. "Well, Kami is a spitfire. I don't know if any man is ready for her," he joked.

"Not her. Victoria."

"Absolutely not!" Pace blurted out as he jammed on the brakes instead of accelerating after the light turned green. "She's not ready for dating."

JC frowned. "Says who? Man to man, brother to brother, you need to step back and let Victoria tell me she's not interested."

Pace huffed. His friend was asking a lot. "My sister would hurt your feelings."

"I'm willing to take my chances, but as my friend and brother, I need you to be okay with that. Just know I could make a good brother-in-law—if it came to that," he joked.

"Getting ahead of yourself, bro." Pace tried to tame the attitude that was building.

"No. I'm saying my intentions are honorable. I'm not out to break hearts. I've lived with a mother with a broken heart since I was born. I know what it looks and feels like."

God whispered, *Whether you agree or not, I control Victoria's destiny.*

"I'm sorry, bro. You're right. You're right."

If Pace were honest with himself, JC had proven to be a good friend and sincere about his walk with Jesus. As protective and nourishing as JC was of his mother, Victoria would be in good hands.

I redeemed Jamison with My blood. Who are you to call him unworthy? God thundered.

Maybe this last-minute road trip wasn't about him seeing Harmony; it could have been about Pace accepting that he couldn't stop his sisters from making their own decisions. He didn't like it, but he had to clear the air with his best friend. "Pray for me because I love them as if they were my sisters."

JC laughed. "They *are* your sisters, but I get it. If you ever see me step out of line against God's will with Victoria or anyone, set me straight."

"Trust me, I will."

The mood shifted as he turned and glanced out the window. "Honestly, I didn't know I had relatives in Chicago." He didn't hide the disappointment in his voice.

"I'm not surprised. Who doesn't have family in Chicago? The first Great Migrations to thc North for Southern Blacks began as early as 1910 and continued into the 1940s. Chicago and Detroit were popular destinations." That information came courtesy of Jamieson Family Game Night 101.

"Ninety-five years old, and I've never met him." JC shook his head and became quiet. I wonder what he can tell me about my father, because I know very little." The hurt in his voice was undeniable. You're invited to come, too." He gave Pace a hopeful expression, reminding him of Chance, his youngest brother, on the first day of school and the fear that he wouldn't make friends in kindergarten.

"Thanks, but I have my own mission. It will be okay for both of us. We're both going into unknown territory. We'll compare notes later."

JC chuckled with a nod.

For the duration of the drive, Pace entertained his doubts about Harmony. An invitation to a family dinner didn't mean Harmony was willing to get to know him personally. He would soon find out.

Harmony had regrets. She should have discouraged her mother from inviting Pace and his friend to dinner. At first sight, Pace was every gradc schoolgirl, woman, or sassy senior's crush. Clearly, she was no different.

She glanced at the time. They should arrive within the hour. When she returned from the salon, her mother had prepared smothered pork chops with extra sides for their guests to choose from: spiraled sweet potato gratin, potato salad, green beans, creamed corn, mac-n-cheese, home-style butterbeans, and buttermilk cornbread. No one could say the Reeds never had enough food.

By the time the doorbell rang, Harmony had prepped herself to blush when she saw Pace again. She opened her door to see him alone, handsome as before. She frowned and peeked around him. "Where is your friend?"

"JC came for a family party in Lake Forest. His great-uncle is turning ninety-five years old, so he won't be joining me. They were waiting for him when we arrived at the hotel…" he rambled. "I was invited, too, but I had dinner plans I wasn't about to cancel." The twinkle in his eyes made her blush as she stared at him. Yep, he still had charm.

"Harmony Reed, please let our guests come inside from out of the cold," her mother fussed, coming to the door. "Oh, where is your friend?" she asked.

"Sorry for being rude." Harmony stepped back, and all the wonderful memories of Christmas Eve dinner in St. Louis came flooding back—the peppermint cheesecake she'd baked, of which he'd gotten seconds, the snowball fight, and him waiting in the airport with her.

He walked in and towered over her but didn't invade her space. She remembered other things she'd rather forget but couldn't—his faint cologne that tickled her nose, a silky black beard and mustache that framed his lips, and intense eyes. His curly hair capped off his looks.

She took his coat and hung it in the hall closet.

"I'm Lorna Reed. Welcome to our home. The food is ready. You can wash your hands in there." She pointed to the powder room.

"Thank you."

He kicked off his riding boots and lined them up against the wall with the other shoes without being asked. Good home training, her mom would say. Harmony couldn't help herself when she spied his socks. Laughter exploded, and she had to hold her stomach. He glanced down and laughed with her.

"More cartoon socks from my young cousins," he explained. "It was a package of three. Believe it or not, these are warm and comfy."

After he washed his hands, he stepped out and smiled at Harmony. "You look pretty."

Harmony exhaled and admired the black-and-blue sweater that complemented his biceps and jeans. "Thank you. Come on. Follow me to the dining room."

The awkwardness was gone. She couldn't believe how comfortable she felt around him—no butterflies or shyness. He reminded her of the relationship she had with his sisters.

Harmony led the way to the dining room. All eyes were on Pace as she made the introductions. "This is Shane, the youngest; Kimbrell, my brother stuck in the middle; and Laurence, the oldest. That's my dad, Laurence Sr. You met my mom. This is Pace Jamieson from St. Louis."

"It looks like a great spread," Pace complimented.

Lorna smiled at their guest. "Thank you. There is plenty."

"Have a seat, young man," her father said. "Since you're our guest, please say grace."

He nodded and reached for her mother's hand on one side and Harmony's on the other and waited for her brothers to follow.

Harmony hid her amusement. This was a Jamieson tradition, she supposed. The Reed household didn't hold hands while praying. Her brothers exchanged bewildered expressions.

"Father, in the name of Jesus, thank You for Your traveling mercies that brought me here. Thank You for the invitation to eat with friends. Bless the hands that prepared this meal and the household. Remove the impurities, and I give thanks, in Jesus' name. Amen."

"Amen," Harmony said loudly while her brothers mumbled.

"I didn't know if that was a prayer meeting or blessing our food," Shane commented as her family began to help themselves, and his mother gave him a warning glare.

"Well, considering we saw a bad accident on the way here, I gave thanks for our safe arrival too."

Good answer. So Pace Jamieson could hold his own with her brothers. Harmony was impressed.

"Tell me about your family," Harmony's mother said.

"I'm the oldest of five—two younger brothers and two sisters, Kami and Victoria, who attend college with Harmony. I'm the oldest of most of my cousins, too."

She and her mother exchanged glances at the mention of his sisters, then Harmony recovered. “And there’s a lot of cousins,” she added, recalling how handsome and talented the Jamieson children were. He turned and smiled at her. No dimples, which were her weakness, but she would rethink that.

“What brings you to Chicago on a cold weekend?” her father asked.

“Believe it or not, I’ve never visited Chicago, although there are Jamiesons in the area. Since it’s only a five-hour drive for a getaway, I hope to tour some Black historic sites, and definitely the DuSable Museum and *The Chicago Defender* building, if Harmony will be my tour guide.”

“That newspaper ceased print publication about five or six years ago, I believe,” her father said, then reached for another hunk of cornbread. After one bite, he smacked his lips.

“You could have booked a tour online,” Shane said, always the instigator.

“I could have,” Pace addressed Shane and then faced her, “but I prefer to pick my own guide.” He didn’t blink.

Her father cleared his throat. “So, Pace, what’s your school major?”

“Mechanical engineering. I’m in the accelerated bachelor’s-to-master’s pathway program at Wash U in St. Louis. The program takes five years. I’ll graduate in the summer.”

“What are your job prospects?” Laurence Sr. chewed as if he was pureeing his food.

“Very good. After my internship at Benson and Frontier Architects last year, I was hired part-time as a mechanical drafter and promised full-time employment once I graduate.”

Her father nodded. “Very good.”

Pace turned to Harmony with a slight smile.

She needed to change the subject because her father would marry her off before Pace drove back to St. Louis. She saw a few empty plates, so she stood to clear the table.

"Want some help?" Pace was poised to stand, but her father stopped him.

"Why your interest in the defunct print newspaper when our city has more profound landmarks?"

Harmony listened from the kitchen. "Our history is documented throughout time through the written word. *The Chicago Defender*'s seeking ads revealed how desperate families were to reunite long after slavery separated them. It also turned ordinary Black townspeople into reporters to talk about the injustices they witnessed across the South. They also reported on Black families building wealth and encouraged folks to migrate to Chicago and the North."

She was impressed with his intellect. Kami mentioned Pace was considered a genealogist understudy because their family was serious about their Jamieson roots and African American history. The Reed family knew four generations of their great-grandparents, then the trail froze.

"Besides taking a glimpse of that building, I would like to check out your museums," Pace said. "I hope I'm not interfering with any plans."

Chapter Four

Pace didn't want to put her on the spot, but they needed privacy. "Harmony, if it's not too cold for you, do you mind taking a walk outside with me for a few minutes?"

"Sure. We'll be back." She walked out of the room.

Pace followed her to the closet to grab his hat, jacket, and scarf, then slipped on his boots. Once they were outside, he studied Harmony and decided she needed his scarf more than him. He removed it from around his neck and gently wrapped it around hers.

"Thank you," she said softly.

"You're welcome." They began their stroll down the idyllic street. "Harmony, I enjoyed getting to know you when you came to St. Louis with my sisters. That wasn't enough time for me." He paused and patted his chest. "I asked my sisters to get your permission for your number."

Harmony lowered her head and glanced away. "They asked, but I didn't give them permission because…" She paused.

"Because of what?"

"Well," she walked ahead, "they told me that you were recovering from a bad breakup."

Pace held his stomach and laughed before catching up with her. "Trust me, I've recovered. My sisters don't know my personal business, and I'm not on the rebound if that's what you think. I'm looking for the real one."

"So you drove here to see me?" She stopped and faced him. Wonder filled her eyes.

"I did." He stared at her.

Expressions played across her face. Although he was man enough to take rejection, Pace wouldn't this time. He would keep pressing because something about her made Pace content.

"The other reason is…well, the dating-your-best-friends' brother trope. You know the scenario where the friendship stalls if there is a fight between the couple, *blah, blah, blah*, but that's changed."

He was about to ask her what she meant when Pace felt the temperature drop. They had only walked about five houses from hers, so he steered her to retrace their steps. "Harmony, please don't overthink this." He wanted to reach for her hand as if they were already a couple but restrained himself. "Listen, I know Chicago has a lot of Black history. I want to check out a few places tomorrow, only if you will be my tour guide."

"Ah, I don't know. This feels like a date somehow." Harmony seemed tortured as she looked away.

"Do you want it to be?" When she didn't answer, he added, "Spend the day with me tomorrow, beginning with the museum, and then decide."

"Decide on a long-distance relationship?" She frowned. "I don't know. We all will graduate soon and go our separate ways to our chosen careers."

This woman was not making it easy. "Harmony, I like you. We connected at my family's Christmas Eve dinner. I sensed the attraction between us, and it's worth exploring, but I won't force myself on you. I'm not into games. If you're not interested in getting to know me, please tell me now, and I'll step back. I'll end my pursuit." He held his breath and prayed for a rebuttal.

She was quiet, clearly considering her next words. The woman's poker face gave no hint of what was coming. Pace braced himself. He could play poker, too.

He wished she'd hurry up because his ears were getting cold.

Harmony tilted her head and lifted a brow. "Catch me if you can!" She took off running toward her house, giggling.

Pace gave pursuit, grinning all the way.

Chapter Five

As they entered the house, all eyes were on them. Harmony sensed Pace wasn't bluffing, so she put him out of his misery.

"I've decided to be Pace's tour guide tomorrow."

"Huh?" Shane twisted his lips.

"You did?" Relief washed over Pace.

Harmony nodded, and not soon after that, he thanked them for the dinner and left. She retreated to her room, her heart pumping with excitement and trepidation. She was curious about Pace.

Were they a match?

Yet, she couldn't dismiss her relationship with his sisters, which seemed to have fizzled without explanation. Harmony was hurt, insulted, and curious about how the Jamiesons could let their brother visit their best friend without them.

You aren't best friends anymore, a voice said and pricked her heart with sadness.

That night, Harmony drifted off to sleep with a tear falling on her pillow.

The next morning, her mother was waiting for her in the kitchen with a hot pot of coffee.

"Hey, Mama." Harmony kissed her cheek and poured herself a cup.

Lorna eyed her. “Well, last night was amusing. Pace is very handsome and very interested in you, and he wasn’t intimidated by your brothers.”

“No, but I saw them peeping out of the window, watching us.”

“You know how protective they are, and we know little about your friends’ brother.”

“Mom.” Harmony twisted her lips in thought. “Is it just me, or do you think it’s odd that Kami and Victoria didn’t come?”

She nodded. “I do, but Pace is not them. That young man is smitten with you.” Lorna giggled. “Do you like him?”

“Attracted—yes. But what if he likes me today and dumps me tomorrow? It could be inherited genes.”

Lorna rubbed Harmony’s shoulders. “You are a smart young woman. Enjoy yourself today while learning more about him and be on the lookout for red flags.”

Harmony jumped when the doorbell rang. “Got it,” Shane said, passing the kitchen to the living room to open the door. She left the kitchen to see Pace and her brother exchange a fist bump.

Pace was about to remove his boots, but Harmony stopped him and smiled. “Good morning. Where’s JC?”

“Spending more time getting to know his extended family.”

“Bummer. I was so looking forward to his company,” she teased.

Pace lifted a brow. “We don’t need a chaperone. God is our witness, and trust me, I drove five hours to make a good impression. I’m not about to mess it up.”

When Harmony sat inside Pace’s SUV the next morning, she sniffed his lingering cologne scent. It brought back warm memories of him driving her to the airport so she would make it home for Christmas. They all had gotten less than four hours of sleep that day after engaging in an impromptu snowball fight after dinner.

Harmony loved every minute with them. Then it went downhill on the way back to Grandma BB's house. She had never seen Kami and Victoria exchange a suspicious look before.

"Thank you," Pace said when they were at a stop light, ceasing her wandering mind.

"For what?" She turned from looking out the window to face him and frowned.

"Choosing me."

Why did everything this man say sound poetic?

And romantic?

And genuine?

Since he waited for her response before driving off, Harmony smiled.

"I'm surprised no one has snagged you on campus."

"Oh, I was snagged alright, but I escaped. She wasn't the one." He nodded at her as if that was all he planned to say. "What about you? I know guys hit on you and my sisters."

"Maybe." She giggled.

"Oh, it's going to be like that, huh? Then maybe I should ask if anyone in Oklahoma City is waiting for you."

Shaking her head, Harmony said, "Nope."

As the GPS guided Pace to the Dan Ryan Expressway, the two chatted about their plans after graduation, hobbies, and family.

"Tell me about your childhood?" Harmony asked.

"You've met my mother, Cheney." She nodded, then he continued. "My biological mother died in a car accident when I was about four."

Harmony's hands flew to her mouth to cover her gasp, but it slipped out anyway. She wanted to hug him. Harmony couldn't imagine life without her mother, dad, or brothers. "Oh, no. I'm sorry."

Pace's expression was tender with a faint smile. "Thank you. Although I was young, I remember she was a beautiful Latina woman who was killed in a car crash. Without a next of kin, I was placed in foster care. It was horrible. One minute, I was loved and secure, and in a flash, I felt like I was in a foreign land with strangers. It could have been worse, like…" He stopped and squeezed his lips together as if a bad memory prevented him from saying more.

"Anyway, I was adopted by a white family." Pace shrugged. "I didn't care. I wanted to feel loved again. Anyway, when my dad found out he had a son, he prayed to God for a shakeup in the legal system to take possession of me. It was a tug-of-war between my adopted parents and my dad. He said with God, no obstacle is too great."

"So Mrs. Jamieson is your stepmom?"

"She's my mother." His tone dared anyone to argue that fact. "Mom acted as if she had given birth to me and nurtured me from a baby. I love her, my younger sisters, and my brothers. We don't do steps and halves in the Jamieson family. I am my father's and mother's son like Paden and Chance."

Stunned at the revelation, Harmony was silent as she processed what Pace had endured as a small child. Her vision blurred with tears. She sniffed. "Wow. Neither Kami nor Victoria ever mentioned that."

"It's not an issue to mention because we're one family."

"I have a family question." If Kami and Victoria wouldn't answer her, maybe Pace would. She fumbled with her fingers. It was worth a shot. "Why don't you and your sisters live in the same house?"

Now, Pace was quiet. He was thinking. It was the same pause that Kami and Victoria gave her. "Grandma BB enjoys their company, and both are girlie girlie and do their thing there. They have bedrooms and are not banned from our house if that's what you think."

Harmony didn't know what she was thinking. However, it was more than what she had gotten from her friends. Still, something didn't seem right. She turned and looked out the window at her surroundings. As the GPS guided them,

Harmony recognized they were close to the Bronzeville Neighborhood in the Washington Park area.

"I think you'll be impressed with our Black History Museum. It has artifacts from Johnson Publishing Company and ever-changing exhibits, like the one of former Mayor Harold Washington. The museum has gone through a couple of name changes since the early 1960s, and it's now known as the DuSable Black History Museum and Education Center."

Pace grinned, then leaned over and slightly elbowed her. "Look at you, a pretty woman who knows her history. See, I couldn't have asked for a more perfect tour guide."

Harmony blushed despite trying not to.

"Did you know that you glow when you blush? And I love your hair. Smells good, too."

Pace was thick with the compliments, and she didn't know what to do with it.

He cleared his throat as she processed his flattery. "I also want to see the historic *Chicago Defender* newspaper building."

"That's on Indiana Avenue." Harmony recalled her local history. "It's in the Douglas Community District in the Black Metropolis-Bronzeville. Even though the *Chicago Defender* is no longer in print production, the building is considered a Chicago landmark."

"Ooh, woman, I'm loving this."

Pace's accolades emboldened her to feel pretty.

"The *Chicago Defender*'s newspaper articles were crucial communication for the Southern states and played a major role in igniting the Great Migration North."

Harmony turned to Pace and grinned. She was equally in awe of his knowledge about her city. Were they a perfect match?

Chapter Six

Pace was in love, not with Harmony—but he could see the possibility of loving Chicago's rich history. He parked, and they stepped out to stroll across the parking lot.

He spied the scarf covering her delicate neck. Pace had no problem sharing his, as he had done last evening if she had forgotten hers. Standing close to Harmony forced her to look at him.

"This building looks majestic compared to the many homes and storefronts converted into African American museums that I've visited," he said, admiring the structure.

"The DuSable Black History Museum and Education Center had its humble beginnings, too, in the home of Margaret Taylor-Burroughs and her husband. This location was formerly a holding facility for the Chicago Police Department."

Pace huffed and stuffed his hands into his pants pocket. "How ironic a former jail becomes a Black history museum."

She stopped, tilted her head, and studied him. "I never thought of it like that, but you're right."

They approached a gray stone one-level building with a cluster of stone stairs, inviting them inside. Pace felt reverence as he opened the door for Harmony to enter. Inside, the space didn't disappoint. The rotunda was grandiose. The walls were covered with mosaic bits that boasted precision artwork.

"Wow."

Harmony grinned and unbuttoned her coat. "Something tells me we're going to be here awhile."

He assisted her, took her coat, and draped it over his arm. "Is that okay? I mean, I know you would have preferred shopping. I promise I won't keep you here all day."

"Pace, I want you to enjoy my city. Whenever you're ready to go, there are more historical places to see."

"*Whew*. Thank you for saying that." He exhaled and then shook off his jacket. They smiled and nodded at other visitors as the two studied one exhibit after another. Their visit was unhurried, and Harmony appeared as interested as him, admitting things she didn't know. They left almost two hours later.

Once they were back in his vehicle, they turned to each other and said, "Where to next?" and laughed that they were thinking the same thing.

"I'm wondering if you would like the Pullman Porter Museum." Harmony tilted her head.

"Right." Pace knew from the many family game nights that African Americans were at the forefront of the labor movement in the country. Philip Randolph, a Pullman porter, organized the Brotherhood of Sleeping Car Porters union. Of course, he wanted to see that. He put in the address, but the building was closed for construction when they arrived. "Bummer. Well, are you hungry?"

"Yup. Let's head to the Mag Mile and eat at The Shops at North Bridge."

Pace followed his GPS to the downtown shopping district. The traffic picked up, and so did the number of pedestrians. "Whew. This looks like New York City."

Harmony laughed as he turned on North Michigan Avenue. "Chicago is sometimes called the Second City behind New York City." She pointed to a parking garage for the Shops at North Bridge.

He eyed the parking fee. It was ridiculously high, but getting to know his beautiful passenger was worth the expense. They parked and walked through the garage to the enclosed skywalk, which overlooked the street below, as they followed other shoppers.

Once they were inside the multi-level mall, Pace shook his head.

"What?"

"We're only five hours apart, but it seems like a world away. Large parking lots surround our malls. This is hidden inside a building."

Harmony shrugged and grinned. "Welcome to Little New York City of the Midwest."

"I'm impressed with this and the company. So, do you want to shop or eat?"

"Let's eat." She slipped her arm through his and dragged him toward the food court.

Her eyes sparkled when they approached Doc B's Fresh Kitchen. They ordered, and within twenty minutes, Pace blessed their food and shared homemade guacamole, chips, and wings.

"This feels like Christmas all over again."

"In what way?" Harmony studied him while munching on sweet potato chips.

"Carefree, no pretense. No agenda—well…I knew I liked you and wanted more time with you." Pace waited for her response. "So, where do we go after this weekend?"

"What do you want to happen? I'll be in Oklahoma City…"

Pace grunted. "I will come to you every month so we can keep getting to know each other." He was serious. His classes were four days a week, and he didn't work on Fridays and the weekends. "Although I could drive the four-and-a-half or five hours, flying would give us more time together, depending on how fast I want to see you."

Harmony blushed. "Wow, you are direct."

"I told you I don't believe in playing games."

She began to pick with her wings and sighed. "I'm like a Crock-Pot—a slow cooker—when it comes to relationships. I need to think this through."

"Fair enough. I texted you, even though you didn't give me your number. Now that I have it, may I call you so we can stay connected?"

"What do Kami and Victoria think about me dating their brother?"

"They gave me your number." Pace thought about the fit his sisters gave him at Grandma BB's pre-funeral service over his ex-girlfriend. Kami and Victoria were upset because they hadn't met Delilah beforehand, and she showed up without warning to the family. "Why would there be a problem? You're the best of friends. You've been our guest in our home—"

"Grandma BB's home," she corrected.

"Same family." Pace refused to backtrack on the progress they'd made. "You were our guest, so I don't see how they would object." She looked away, and he rested his hand on top of hers. "My sisters won't stand in our way. Trust me."

Harmony nodded and twisted her mouth in thought. "Do you mind if we don't discuss what's happening between us in front of them? I don't want them to think my friendship was to meet their brother."

That was ridiculous, but he could tell that Harmony was serious. Pace would agree if that made her comfortable so they could get to know each other.

"Okay. I don't know how this could be a secret, but I will try to keep my sisters out of this. I'm just happy you agreed to be my tour guide."

"Me too."

"What about your brothers?" Pace asked but didn't see them as a threat. They would have to stand down and let Harmony make her own decisions.

Hypocrite, his mind taunted him. He needed to take his own advice.

Chapter Seven

The next morning, Harmony's skin still twinkled from the touch of Pace's short embrace.

Was yesterday the beginning of something wonderful? Harmony wondered as she climbed out of bed, sniffing the aroma of bacon, eggs, and pancakes. Yummy, but for her father's on-and-off-again New Year's resolution diet, her mom probably had a bowl of fruit on the table, too.

As Harmony began her morning regime, she stared at her face in the mirror. She didn't ask for any of what happened this weekend.

In the kitchen, her mother's eyes sparkled. "Good morning, sleepy head. You were gone all day yesterday. Does that mean you had a good time?"

"Surprisingly, amazingly, I did." Harmony smiled.

"Did you find out anything about the sisters' secrecy?"

Harmony wished she hadn't mentioned anything to her mom, whose suspicious mind was unmatched compared to Harmony's. She shrugged. "Pace made it sound like there was nothing unusual. They have bedrooms at home and Grandma BB's, but they stay over there most of the time. Maybe I was overthinking it."

Her mother took the final sip of her coffee and poured the remainder into the sink. "Or maybe not." She kissed Harmony's cheek and walked out of the kitchen.

The road trip back to St. Louis was void of conversation. Pace left at six in the morning, exhausted from packing in as many activities as possible. JC couldn't learn enough about his father's side of the family, and Pace couldn't learn enough about being with Harmony.

JC dozed but came to life at the beginning of a new chapter in Ralph Ellison's *Invisible Man* audiobook. He yawned. "Man, this was a great getaway. I learned so much about my dad's side. He was bad news even as a teenager, but the excitement on my great uncle Willie Earl's face at seeing me brought tears to my eyes. I felt loved."

Pace was happy for his friend. "Now, how are you related again?"

"Uncle Willie Earl had five children—three sons and two daughters. Vivian Tilley married John Matthews—my grandparents—and they had one son, my dad, Wesley. My mom didn't even give me his surname, which didn't seem to matter until I met them."

"So what will you do, legally change your name?"

JC shook his head. "Nope. I'm Jamison Clark, but I have Matthews in my bloodline. I'm good with that. I want what you have with your family—closeness—so I plan to stay in contact with them."

Although JC offered to take the wheel, Pace declined. He was good. They were two hours away from St. Louis.

When Pace pulled to the curb in front of JC's South City home, which he shared with his mother and younger brother when he was not on campus, JC grinned as he got out.

"I'm glad I decided to go."

"I am, too. It turned out to be a good trip for both of us." Pace popped open the trunk so JC could get his overnight bag.

Twenty minutes later, Pace pulled into the driveway of his childhood home. Everyone had already left for church service. “Alone at last.” All through the drive, his eyes were on the road while his mind stayed on Harmony. He grabbed his phone and texted her.

Home. Thank you for everything.

I had fun and look forward to next time, she responded.

There will be a next time.

Pace couldn’t wait to plan that. If left up to him, he would call her, and they would talk for hours, but she needed space to explore their attraction. He had already made a bold move by showing up at her doorstep with little notice.

He walked inside the quiet house. Pace couldn’t wait for his parents to return to talk to them. He put away his things in his bedroom and piled up a few items for laundry. After a quick shower, his stomach alerted him that he hadn’t eaten since the hotel breakfast. He was starving.

Pace was sure his mother had cooked Sunday dinner. All he had to do was warm up his food.

When his family walked through the door, Pace was fixing his plate in the kitchen. Paden and Chance spoke and raced upstairs to their rooms. His parents removed their coats to reveal that his father’s green tie matched his mother’s green suit. It was the norm for them to color coordinate.

He could see why his father married Cheney. She was pretty and could pass as his biological mother. His friends often commented that she didn’t look like she had five children. And she didn’t. Most didn’t know she only gave birth to his younger brothers.

His parents hugged him, then his dad patted his back.

“Welcome home, son,” his mother said. “Looks like we’re just in time to eat with you.”

They walked upstairs to their bedroom and returned in less than five minutes.

Pace heard his father yell for the boys to come down and eat before his parents reappeared in the dining room.

“Can we talk after dinner?” Pace asked them.

"Of course," his father said as Paden and Chance raced down the stairs and leaped off the landing. All horse playing ceased as they walked to the table.

Once Parke said grace to bless their food, his family wanted to hear about his trip.

"The city's historical places were endless. I enjoyed learning about their local history from Harmony."

"Kami and Victoria's friend?" Chance's eyes grew with curiosity. He had developed a crush on her at the Christmas Eve dinner, too.

"Yep." Pace continued to eat. "I can see myself living there."

"I'm sure you can," Cheney mumbled and avoided eye contact as she slid food into her mouth to keep from laughing.

"You missed a great sermon from Pastor Dupree," his father said. "Make sure you watch the replay online."

"Will do. What was the subject?" Pace bit off a piece of corn muffin.

"Repentance over resolution. Only what we do for Christ will last," his father said.

Chance, their young Bible student who liked to memorize Scriptures, straightened his shoulders and quoted the passage. "It's from Romans 14, verses 11 and 12: '*As I live, saith the Lord, every knee shall bow to me, and every tongue shall confess to God. So then every one of us shall give an account of himself to God.*'"

Pace grinned at his brother and exchanged a fist bump. At twelve years old, Chance had a sharp mind and excelled at the gifts God gave him. He liked to match wits with Victoria, who was extremely intelligent in her own right. The youngest girl and the youngest boy were in fierce competition when it came to family game night.

Despite his mother's admonishment to slow down so his brothers could digest their food properly, Paden and Chance seemed to inhale their meatballs and sautéed vegetables.

"Can we go downstairs and practice, Mom?" Chance asked.

She nodded, and Parke sighed. "Go ahead, boys. Just because the sound is somewhat muffled throughout the house doesn't mean you two shouldn't respect that guitar and drum set by testing their durability."

"Yes, sir," the brothers said in unison.

They swiped their plates off the table and rinsed the dishes in the kitchen sink before loading them in the dishwasher. Footsteps disappeared as they escaped to the lower level to their music studio. The game room was on the other side of the spacious area.

Alone at the table with his parents, Pace asked Parke. "Dad, how did you know Mom was right for you?"

His father seemed thoughtful as Cheney and Pace stared at him. Parke rubbed his black mustache sprinkled with gray strands. "When I cared enough about what made her happy or sad, my heart tugged me closer until I was fully invested that I wanted what she wanted."

"It wasn't like that at first." Cheney shook her head. "Let's say we didn't hit it off. Is this about Harmony?"

"Yeah, it is."

"Does she feel the same way?" Parke asked.

"I think she likes me but is hesitant. Plus, she doesn't want Kami and Victoria to know."

Cheney frowned and folded her arms. "That's odd. I can't see your sisters against you dating their best friend."

"I didn't ask them." Pace paused. "She was their friend first. Although I hope that wouldn't complicate their relationship, my sisters are my sisters, and my romance is not their concern."

"Ooh. You are your father's child." Cheney chuckled. "You sound just like the handsome, overconfident, and a bit conceited man I fell in love with. I wouldn't trade him."

Pace could see himself in his father's reflection and held on to what he remembered of his mother, Rachel Lopez, who was pretty with long dark hair. Then he looked at Cheney, who was a mother to him. He reached for her hands. "But I'm your son, too, Mom."

Cheney sniffed. Whatever words she was going to say choked in her throat. His father squeezed her shoulder as if coaching her to breathe as her eyes watered. "You and I both lost. You lost your mother, and I lost our baby boy we named Parke Kokumuo Jamieson VII. You, Parke Kokumuo Jamieson VIII, came as a gift when the doctors said I wouldn't be able to have children because of a bad decision I made in college. You are the son I hold dearly. You are the son any mother would be godly proud to claim, which is why your happiness matters to your father and me."

Pace nodded. He was not about to become sentimental. Parke never discouraged his sons from shedding tears and would hug them afterward. "Now that you've gotten that out of the way, God will give you strength to move on," he always said.

"Thanks, Mom and Dad." He stood and embraced them before going to his bedroom. "I love you and want a love like yours, but I don't want to wait until I'm in my mid-thirties and forties. Too many bad choices could be made before then, and I don't want the temptation. I've begun my search."

As he prepared for bed that evening, Kami FaceTimed him with Victoria in the background. "Welcome back," they said in unison. His sisters were all smiles.

"Thank God for safe travels. JC went with me and met some family members at a relative's ninety-fifth birthday party. It was his great uncle Willie Earl Tilley or Tillman."

"Tilley is Grandma BB's maiden name."

"That's right. I thought it sounded familiar. So what's up, Double Trouble?" he teased them.

"We should ask you," Kami said with a mischievous lift of a brow. "Did you see Harmony?"

"I did." He lifted his brow to match hers as if in a chess move. It was a stare-off.

"Did something happen between you two that Victoria and I should know about?" Kami grinned.

"Nope. Nothing you should know about. Of course, she wondered where her best friends were."

His sisters looked away from the screen.

"Hey, what's going on with you two and Harmony?" He squinted, ready to read between the lines of whatever they were not about to tell him.

Silence, then Victoria asked. "Should best friends have to tell each other their secrets?"

Pace squinted as he held his breath. Victoria had gone through so much in her childhood that the Jamiesons didn't want her past to define her. That was her secret.

"The choice is yours, sis. If you value Harmony's friendship, then one day, you might want to tell her your story. I don't think she's the kind of woman or friend to pass judgment."

"You never know. People are people first before they earn their titles of friend, doctor, lawyer, or whatever."

"Whenever you are ready… If you never are, then that's fine too." Pace meant every word he said.

"You like Harmony a lot," Kami stated as a fact.

"I do." That's all Pace planned to say—nothing about his and Harmony's plans to stay in touch.

"Do you want our approval?" Kami asked.

"Nope. I don't need it. Talk to you two tomorrow." Pace signed off before they picked his brain and pieced together the information they wanted.

Chapter Eight

A week later, Harmony sniffed as she hugged her mom, dad, and Shane in the airport terminal. "I don't think I'm coming home for spring break, so the next time you see me, I'll be a college graduate."

"Yep, and we'll be at that graduation yelling the loudest. We're proud of you." Her mother teared up.

"We sure are. I'm hoping you'll land a job fast here at home." Her father gave her an encouraging smile.

"Me too." Harmony sighed. More pressure.

Once she boarded the plane at O'Hare for Will Rogers World Airport in Oklahoma City, Harmony was nervous about returning to campus. Her life had been simple before the break. Now, three weeks into the new year, and her life had become complicated.

The best of best friends were holding secrets.

Their brother liked her and texted her a Scripture every morning. It felt odd, but it gave her a boost of inspiration with her cup of coffee.

Harmony's response was a simple thank you. She knew God had spoken to her around Christmas. Still, she wasn't ready to attend church every weekend like his sisters, read her Bible regularly, or jump into a relationship. Her future was a frontier waiting for her to explore after graduation.

Pace Jamieson was a nice guy and good-looking. He wasn't the only one with those qualifications for boyfriend material. Well, there weren't as many as a woman would like, but still, she had to focus on her life goals: finish her last semester to graduate with honors and land her first job in Chicago.

This was an exciting year. Harmony had been accepted for her paid internship program at Graphic Original Studio, which would give her experience and boost her hiring ability. That had been a big deal.

Yet sadness seemed to poke at her. She contributed it to the two friends she thought she would be friends with for life.

The flight attendants recited the safety precautions, which snapped Harmony's musing. Minutes after takeoff, she closed her eyes, and her mind drifted again. Pace's explanation about his sisters' living arrangements seemed simple, but a nagging feeling within her wasn't buying it.

Kami and Victoria hurt her feelings by keeping secrets, and to add more injury, they didn't come to visit with Pace. That was a hard slap to the face. *I guess we're not as close as I thought.*

She dozed until she arrived in OKC. **I made it safely**. She sent a group text to her family. She glanced around the terminal for the Jamieson sisters. The three o'clock flight from St. Louis had just landed, and Harmony walked to their gate to see if they were on board. Fifteen minutes later, the door closed. The Jamieson sisters had not come. They'd changed their flight. What was going on with them?

In the past, she, Kami, and Victoria coordinated their arrival for a Sunday afternoon and then split a ride share to their off-campus senior housing units. Harmony's was more like a mini apartment with a kitchen and laundry.

Their hangout was always at Bausher Hall, where they ate or played some of the game machines. Harmony felt alone without them.

It wasn't too late to make new friends. Problem solved.

By the time she arrived on campus, Harmony had given herself a pep talk: This phase, too, would pass.

Her mother called an hour later as she was unpacking. "How's it going, sweetie?"

"It's going okay."

"You sound down," Lorna said.

"I am. I'm trying to adjust to my new norm. Everyone should have a best friend, right?"

"You still haven't spoken to Kami and Victoria, huh?"

"Nope, and I don't know if they've made it back yet. Their classes don't start until Tuesday. If I didn't have to work tomorrow, I would have spent the extra day at home instead of leaving on a Sunday."

"Harmony, you must talk to them and relieve yourself of these suspicions. I'm curious, too, for your sake."

Pushing her clothes to one side, Harmony flopped on the bed and pulled on her hair. "I feel silly, Mom. This isn't a romantic relationship where my boyfriend has done me wrong, and I'm going to confront him. This is friends keeping secrets."

"You need closure in every aspect of your life, whether it's family, friends, or romantic relationships."

"I guess so, but they're the ones who have to initiate it after they closed the door for discussion."

They chatted for a few more minutes, then Harmony ended the call. She wanted emotional peace and to erase the hurt. *Lord, why am I feeling this way over a friendship? It's just a friendship. It doesn't make sense to me.*

God hadn't spoken to her since that day in the kitchen at the Jamieson dinner. She turned on the television to her favorite show, which she didn't watch while pulling clothes out of the closet for the next day.

Bored, Harmony started her nightly regimen to go to bed early when she received a text from Pace. She sighed.

Can I call you?

Her fingers were about to type **No** because she wasn't in the mood to sugarcoat a conversation with Pace. Instead, she typed, **Sure.**

It rang immediately. She answered, trying to sound upbeat.

"What's wrong?" Pace asked as if he knew the internal confusion she was battling.

"Ah…" She tried to come up with anything but the truth.

"Harmony, talk to me. I felt God telling me to reach out. That's why I wanted to hear your voice."

A tear fell that Harmony didn't know was coming. She sniffed. *God, did you tell him that?* "I don't want to talk about it… I don't think your sisters would approve of our relationship anyway."

"They don't have an opinion about this. Anyway, tell me what you want to talk about. There has to be something—graduation, jobs, future…me."

She giggled despite herself. "That wasn't subtle."

"But it made you laugh." He chuckled.

"True, it did. But seriously, I think it's bad timing for a relationship." *With you.* Harmony didn't want to go into details. What was she supposed to say against his sisters? And who would he side with? Harmony was #TeamReed to the core. Nobody could convince her that the Reed brothers were the bad guys.

"Timing is everything, and I told you no pressure." His voice was gentle.

"You did." She climbed up in bed, leaned against the wall, and pulled her knees to her chest. She was comfortable. "Instead of talking about me, talk to me about you."

"I told you I was adopted, and my life centers around family, extended family, and friends like JC. I have a strong sense of who I am as a man of color and a man of God. My hobbies include uncovering historical documents that are treasures and golf."

"I can identify with everything but the last part. Golf?" She smiled. "Are you any good?"

"Let me just say, JC and I have a long way to go before we make pro."

They laughed together.

Pace made her smile.

Pace made her relax.

Pace made her hope for love.

"Now, I won't hold you, but do you feel better?"

"Yes, I do," she admitted softly.

"Then my job is done until the next time. You don't need a reason to talk to me." He paused. "Harmony, call or text me when you need a smile. Since I can't see you, I want to hear your voice unless you FaceTime me."

"Okay, I will."

"Good night."

Pace wouldn't get involved in the disagreement between Kami, Victoria, and Harmony. Although he was a Jamieson through and through, and he always took sides with his siblings, Pace recognized that he and Harmony had to build their trust without compromising his relationship with his sisters.

Good luck with that, his mind taunted him.

"Right."

He would take his sisters to the airport tomorrow. JC asked if he could see them off, and the sisters welcomed his presence. What were the odds that his best friend would be attracted to Victoria? His sisters were too demanding for any man, he mused. But Pace couldn't block the attraction despite his subtle hints.

Although he trusted JC as a friend and brother, he struggled to trust him concerning a romantic relationship with his baby sister.

God whispered, *Watch and pray. Study Matthew 28:41 and pray that you do not enter into temptation; even though your spirit is willing, the flesh is weak. Watch your thoughts and temper.*

On Monday afternoon, Grandma BB waited for Pace when he drove up to get his sisters. Dolled up in a silver multi-color house dress to complement her gray hair and her signature two-tone gray-and-burgundy Stacy Adams shoes, which she wore as house slippers, she sat in a Victorian-style chair near the front door, tapping her shoes on the floor.

"I ought to get a belt to you," she teased, and her eyes sparkled as Pace kissed her cheek.

He did his best to keep a straight face. "What did I do to deserve a spanking?"

"Why didn't you tell me JC and I could be blood kin? Willie Earl is my first cousin, and his folks gave him a ninety-fifth birthday party. He's lyin'. Willie Earl is older than that."

"Huh?" Pace blinked. "Who told you? " Then he paused. Kami and Victoria considered the possibility that a Tilley in Chicago was related to Mrs. Beatrice Tilley Beacon, aka Grandma BB. "It's a small world."

"Yes, your sisters connected the dots before you." She playfully scrunched her nose. "You lose your Black family researcher card for that oversight. Even if we weren't related, you should have wondered."

Pace lifted his hands in surrender. "You're right. I should have been at least curious, so he is your relative?"

"Yep." She nodded. "He left Little Rock for Michigan. When his son, Hermann—my second cousin—moved to Chicago, Willie Earl moved in with him."

"Small world fueled by that great migration from the South," Pace said. "Who knew a random birthday party in Chicago would have roots back to you."

"Sho'nuff JC is Cousin Willie Earl's kinfolks. Wait until I talk to Lily Rae, my busybody cousin who I try not to talk to, about not telling me about it. If I had known, I would have crashed the party." She snapped her fingers for the missed opportunity. "It's not like he's going to turn ninety-five again." She huffed even heavier.

Unlike you. Pace thought of the many birthdays Grandma BB celebrated, boasting the same age every year. It was confusing to him as a boy but shameful as an adult to lie about one's age. Pace folded his arms and squinted. "And how do you know all this about the party because you've never mentioned him?"

"My worrisome little cousin who is old now, too. Lily Rae keeps up with the gossip in the family. The old troublemaker…" She continued her tirade, and Pace was subject to listen. "Did you go?"

He didn't mention Harmony. "Ah, no. I'd rather visit some historical sites."

"*Umm-hmm.* We'll discuss that later. I think your sisters are packed and ready to go." She verified with them over a two-way walkie-talkie. "Secret Service here to pick up two packages. Copy?"

Pace turned around to keep from laughing as he heard Victoria respond, "Roger that."

"Grandma BB, you could have texted them or called A-L-E-X-A." He spelled it so as not to activate the listening monitor. Pace helped her stand, and she patted his back as they hugged.

"Nonsense, grandson. I saw them online and purchased everyone here walkie-talkies for Christmas." She released a whimsical sigh. "Reminds me of yonder years or old school as y'all say today."

Her former Vegas dancers, Chip and Dale, who had become her bodyguards, walked through the front door with their devices in hand and gave Pace fist bumps.

Grandma BB scrutinized them. "Dale, is that gray in your mustache? You better get some Miss Clairol because I need young men on my arms."

The two stepped aside as his sisters appeared with stuffed suitcases, which hadn't looked that plump when they arrived.

"Bye, Grandma BB. See you at our graduation," Kami said and squeezed her tight.

"If I don't be dead by then." She shrugged as if death was no big deal.

"Grandma BB," Victoria said, hugging her. "I need you here for us, so get right with God by repenting so you can stay here longer." She smothered her face into their surrogate god- grandmother's bosom.

"Chile," Grandma BB said, lifting Victoria's chin, "stop fussing about me. I'll be there."

"Let's go, ladies, so you don't miss your flight." Pace lifted their suitcases as if they weighed ten pounds each and ushered his sisters out the door.

The next stop was JC's house, which was twenty minutes away in the opposite direction from the airport.

Both his sisters were glad to see JC and engaged in a lively conversation all the way to the airport. Somehow, JC was winning them over as fast friends. Did Victoria know how much JC was attracted to her? That was the same question Pace wondered for himself with Harmony the night of the Christmas Eve dinner?

Tuesday morning, Pace packed up his suitcase to return to campus living.

That afternoon, he and JC met at the gym. While spotting for each other, JC asked, "You don't voice it, but I sense you still have a problem with my attraction to Victoria. She's beautiful, quiet but observant, and engaging when she's relaxed. Does she fear you won't approve?"

Pace sat on the bench and lifted hand weights. "I'm struggling, man. I mean, I'm the oldest. I'm supposed to set an example. I'm supposed to fall in love first, *blah, blah. blah.*"

"Is it because of my childhood that I don't meet the Jamieson standard with you? Your family seems very welcoming. Although Victoria may be shy to an extent, she doesn't seem to mind I'm around."

"You know that's not it. We're like brothers."

"Then treat me like one. Let Victoria decide if I'm worthy."

Lord, only You are worthy. Please help me step back and not interfere with Your will in Victoria's life—both my sisters. Pace nodded. "You're right."

Chapter Nine

On campus, Harmony confronted the Jamieson sisters one morning during breakfast when she slid into an empty chair at their table.

"What did I say or do to make you two cut me off like I'm an enemy? We've been friends since freshmen year. Whatever it is, tell me. I won't repeat it."

She waited and watched as they communicated silently again. It was becoming annoying and driving Harmony crazy to be left out of the loop, then Victoria slumped her shoulders and shook her head. Her friend's demeanor changed before Harmony's eyes as she studied them.

"Harmony, some things are best left unsaid." Victoria's expression was set and not to be crossed.

"So where does that leave our friendship?" This was not a strained conversation she ever imagined having with these two.

Victoria snapped. "A friendship where we don't have to know everything. Nosey is not a flattering asset."

Kami nudged Victoria and frowned, shaking her head, then faced Harmony. "Sorry. She didn't really mean that."

Harmony stood, fuming from humiliation. "Wrong. My former friend says exactly what she means. Have a good life." She stormed off with as much dignity as she could muster. Whatever was going on with Victoria, let her close-knit family deal with it.

The next few days were mentally draining for Harmony, but she had to bounce back. She came to college for a degree. Friendships were a bonus.

Although their disconnect made her sad, Harmony's bruised pride wouldn't force her to talk to them. As she sat in Bausher Hall to grab a bite before going to her afternoon internship, she stared out the window over campus. It was idyllic. The grounds were inviting for lounging on the plush green manicured lawns. She had no regrets accepting a full-ride scholarship away from home. Oklahoma City University had given her an excellent academic education.

A reflection in the window alerted her to a guest at the table. She turned around. "Oh, hey, Tiffani."

The college junior had taken a handful of classes with Harmony. She was tall—about five feet eleven—and had long black hair. She wore a diamond stud in her nose and reddish-orange lipstick. That's it. Tiffani Mack didn't need much enhancement because she was naturally pretty.

"I see you sitting by your lonesome lately. Want some company?"

How could Harmony turn her away? Hadn't she been asking God to send her some friends that wouldn't hurt her feelings?

"Sure." Once Harmony nodded, Tiffani slid into a chair facing her and made herself comfortable.

"Are you counting down the months? I know you can't wait to graduate," she said between bites of her burger.

"It's a little scary, but I got a solid education that should help me succeed. I'm definitely not the same girl who came here four years ago. I've learned life lessons and made some friends, too." Just not lifelong friends.

"I've seen you hanging with those Jamieson sisters, but not this semester. When I saw you alone at the I Have A Dream celebration and during some mealtimes, I thought maybe you could use a new friend."

Harmony was tight-lipped. If her classmate was fishing for information, she'd picked the wrong one. Harmony didn't gossip. She glanced around the large cafeteria to see if anyone else she knew would join them at the table so it wouldn't be just them.

"Anyway," Tiffani said, shrugging, "do you plan to attend the OCU Got Talent competition?"

That brought back memories. During freshman year, she, Kami, and Victoria had witnessed talent acts and thought they could do better. The trio signed up to sing the following year and learned they harmonized well. They had won first place and split a five-hundred-dollar gift card. After that competition, they would perform impromptu singing duals with friends.

Maybe she should skip the event this year. "I don't know. I guess if you want to go, we could sit together."

"Okay. Let's meet at seven-thirty." Tiffani became chatty, mentioning she was an only child and wished her parents had given her siblings.

"I'm the baby with three brothers. I'm closer in age to the youngest one. What was your major again?" Harmony asked as she saw Kami and Victoria enter the dining hall from the corner of her eye.

Her heart pounded. Would they come and speak or avoid her as they appeared to have been doing? Kami waved. Victoria didn't.

Tiffani looked over her shoulder, then back at her. "Information technology. I want to get into computer forensics."

"Sounds challenging."

"It is. Well, I've got to get to my next class. See you on Saturday." She stood to discard her trash and walked out of the dining hall.

Alone again at the table, Harmony waited to see if the sisters would come to sit with her. They took too long to order their food, so Harmony left for the graphic design studio. It felt awkward being ignored anyway. They had her phone number and knew where she stayed on campus if they wanted to talk.

Life is hard when you don't have friends, she thought.

Pace crammed Black history festivities into his calendar between work and classes. The university held events to honor Black accomplishments. Plus, he attended local civic ceremonies, commemorations with his family, not to mention church programs with his uncle, but he was determined to carve out time for Harmony.

Through persistence, Pace coaxed Harmony to exchange texts each morning during the week. It started with one-way communication: He sent her a Scripture or inspirational thought. His phone revealed she read them, but there was never a reply, until recently when he sent her short prayers.

Pace craved the weekends when he could hear her voice. It would be too distracting during the week with their full class load. Most of the time, he called her, but a few times, she surprised him. He sensed she was lonely. His sisters' names never came up. It was the same with Kami and Victoria when he checked in on them. Pace got it. Relationships were complicated, but this was something in which he refused to intervene. Victoria's emotional healing was still in progress.

Harmony had been on his mind strong for more than a day. His engineering double degree program was intense, so he could use a distraction. Pace texted her after leaving his Friday afternoon class. **Are you anyone's Valentine this year?**

No.

Will you be mine next week if I come and take you to a nice dinner?

She called him. "Pace, that's Wednesday, and you have classes on Thursday, right?"

Pace smiled at her concern. "I do. I'll work it out with my professor and my supervisor at work. I don't want to miss this time with you."

"Then, yes, I'll be your valentine."

Pace exhaled and couldn't stop grinning. "Woman, you have made my day. Now, I can ace this test. Bye."

On his way to the quad, he saw JC. "What's up, man?"

"You look really happy," his friend joked.

"Looks like I have a valentine."

JC adjusted the backpack over his shoulder. "Guess we've been out of the loop. Is it Harmony or someone new on campus?"

The two stepped out of the way of students as they entered the political science building where JC was heading.

"Man, you know Harmony has my attention. This is our last year in school, and I don't want her to feel pressured to invest in a relationship, but I want her to know I'm on the sidelines, ready to step on the field."

In the distance, Pace saw his ex-girlfriend, Delilah, coming out of the medical science building where nursing students attended classes. She was heading toward the parking lot, which meant they would cross paths. He held no harsh feelings against her. Pace couldn't say the same about her, but that was her issue.

She spoke cordially when she saw them, but the glare in her eyes conveyed anything but well wishes.

Pace shrugged. "Anyway, I'm flying to Oklahoma City to take her to dinner, then coming back the next morning straight to class."

JC chuckled, then laughed until Pace joined him. "I know. Crazy, huh? It is because I'm doing almost the same thing."

"What do you mean?" Pace almost stumbled back.

"I'm going to Oklahoma City, too, but on Thursday since I don't have class on Friday. Remember I gave them my number when you dropped them off at the airport." JC smiled. "I texted them, including Kami, to gain an ally and jokingly asked if they had valentines. Kami texted back they didn't, and I told them neither did I. The next thing I knew, we thought being each other's valentines would be fun. You and I might see each other in either airport."

Kami's mastermind idea was stamped all over it, and Pace wasn't all smiles at the new development. His mood plummeted, but he had to recover. Pace couldn't keep reacting this way whenever his friend mentioned his sisters. "I know I said I'm okay with your interest in my sister, but I'm still struggling." He squeezed his lips from saying more, but he couldn't tame the creases on his forehead or his fists from balling. "You free after your next class?"

JC nodded. "Let's meet up in the library, and we can talk."

"I'll be there." Pace shook his head and walked to the library to study—or try to study—and wait. He spoke to his sisters every week. Harmony's name did not come up in his conversation, nor did JC's in theirs. Suddenly, Pace felt overwhelmed.

Let me be God. Cast all your cares on me, God whispered First Peter 5:7. *Know that I not only take care of your sisters, JC, and Harmony, I also take care of you.*

Once he found a secure area, he pulled his tablet from his book bag. Instead of logging on, he bowed his head and began to repent and pray as his soul cried for peace silently. Since he was a boy, he didn't know how not to take care of Kami, and when Victoria became a Jamieson, he took his big brother role to the next level. *Lord, help me. I don't want to lose my friendship with my best friend or my bond with my sisters. I guess I don't want them to grow up—and I don't want to lose the chance to win Harmony over. Those are my personal cares, Lord. Help me to turn them over to You.*

Pace didn't know how long he prayed quietly in his spirit until he felt a nudge on his shoulder.

"Hey, man." JC took the chair near him at the table. "You sleep?"

"Nah." Pace tried to get himself together to have this talk with his best friend. "You're out of class already?"

"Yep. Professor Burns let us out early." He scooted his cushioned gray chair closer to Pace and lowered his voice. "Let me clear the air between us again." He twisted his mouth and gave Pace a dumbfounded expression. "I like your sister—both of them. But Victoria is special, and I sensed early on to get to know her, I have to get past Kami—the gatekeeper, who is worse than you—to accomplish that." He nodded. "She's like a guard dog."

Pace grinned. *Good, I taught her well.* He took credit.

"Victoria is the one who has my interest, and I'm learning to build trust with you and Kami first to have a chance with Victoria. I call and check on them to keep our friendship growing. I didn't think I needed your permission, although I should have told you I planned to visit them and take them out. Sorry I didn't give you a heads-up before now."

"I respect you for that. It's hard being a big brother and letting go. Pray for me."

JC gripped his hand in a shake. "Lord, You know our hearts. Help us walk upright before You and help me and my brother in Christ transition from college students to working adults."

"Amen," Pace mumbled. He needed to hear this prayer. Not only was JC like a brother, but they were also prayer partners. Countless times, Pace had petitioned God on JC's behalf for his family's salvation, especially JC's mother.

"Help us to make the right decisions in our personal and professional relationships."

"Whew." Pace exhaled, looked away, and sniffed.

"You alright, man?"

"Yeah. I needed that." Pace nodded and started to pack up. He didn't get any studying done, but he felt his burden lifted. His mind was clear on acing his test.

JC stood. “Now, if you want a full itinerary of my visit to their campus, I can text you,” he joked.

“Do that.” Pace didn’t smile as they walked outside together. God had lifted his burdens, but Pace would keep his poker face.

Chapter Ten

Harmony and Tiffani had developed a routine. They ate lunch together and attended some campus events, but Harmony wouldn't consider her classmate a bestie.

The woman had an opinion about everything. Many times, Harmony tuned out her drama. *How did I get stuck with her?* she asked herself.

Harmony reasoned that it was better than being alone. As she counted down the months to graduation, she wanted to get back to Chicago with her family and land a job so she could make real friends at a real job.

Stay in the present. Besides, Tiffani would soon jet off to class. She took a deep breath, nodded at her dining companion, and blessed her food.

She was inches from taking her first bite from her club sandwich when Tiffani leaned over and whispered, "One of those Jamieson sisters has a new boyfriend. *Ummm*, he looks yummy. I have to give it to them. They attract all the fine brothers on campus, but I've never seen him."

Annoyed by Tiffani's pestering, Harmony glanced over her shoulder. She blinked so as not to drool.

Breathe, Harmony coaxed herself as she turned back around.

Pace Jamieson was fine. He looked relaxed in his rust-bronze-colored mock turtleneck sweater. Even from a distance, Harmony could zoom in on his dark features, which complemented his silky black curls.

What is Pace doing here a day early? He was supposed to take her to a Valentine's Day dinner tomorrow, so she didn't expect to see him today.

She and Tiffani stared as he gave his sisters flowers. They rewarded him with hugs. There was no doubt the siblings loved and respected each other. Harmony sighed with envy. She could use a hug from Shane, Laurence Jr., or Kimbrell.

"Oh, that's their oldest brother." Harmony masked the longing in her voice.

"Wow-wow. Just think, girl, he could've been your boyfriend if y'all still hung out together." Tiffani grunted, then straightened up and put a smile in place. "Here he comes now."

Harmony steadied her breathing and waited, then she sensed his presence while Tiffani commented on his swagger.

Pace leaned over Harmony's shoulder. "This is for you, beautiful." He nodded at Tiffani, who giggled and then pouted. "It seems I'm the only one who didn't get flowers."

"My apologies." Pace patted his chest but made no promise that any were forthcoming. "Hello. I'm Pace Jamieson. Kami and Victoria are my sisters."

Harmony had questions she dared not ask in front of Tiffani, and her friend didn't appear to be leaving despite her next class.

"Hi, Pace. I'm Tiffani Mack." She batted her lashes. "Your sisters never mentioned you."

He grunted and folded his arms. "I doubt that. Family is all we talk about." Pace glanced at Harmony. "See you tomorrow at dinner." He walked back to the table where his sisters were sitting.

Yes, he does have a confident stride, she thought.

Grinning, Kami and Victoria saluted Harmony by lifting their bouquets. Their smiles seemed genuine. The first in a long time.

Harmony nodded and did the same without a smile. She was sad. Harmony would have loved to be included at their table and share laughs and smiles.

"I am so jealous." Tiffani pouted. "I feel left out, and you've been holding out on me. You two have a date tomorrow? Do tell." She leaned forward for the scoop.

"Considering you'll be late for your class, I'll give you the short version. As you know, Kami, Victoria, and I have been friends for four years. Pace is right. They always talk about their family until you feel like you know them."

Tiffani stood. "*Hmmmph.* If they weren't so snooty, I'd try harder to be friends with them."

Harmony snapped. She might not be close with Kami and Victoria anymore, but they weren't her enemies either. They were good people, and she enjoyed her time with them. "Tiffani, I'm not the one to talk about them, and I don't appreciate you calling them that. They were my first friends here, so don't go there with me." She stood, too, gathered her things, and huffed away.

Note to self: Friendships aren't meant to be long-term. Family is forever.

Pace couldn't stop stealing glances at Harmony's table. Seeing her was refreshing. His memory didn't do her justice. Pace missed her.

Her hair was dark and thick, and every strand was in place.

Her hot pink sweater complemented her brown skin and matched her pink lip gloss.

She was stunning and earned the guys' attention in the dining hall. It was their loss. They had four years to woo her and failed. Harmony would soon be off-limits.

It wasn't their special time yet. This day before Valentine's Day was about his sisters. He had hoped to see Harmony, too. Victoria was amid an emotional storm, and he knew it had to do with her friendship with Harmony. Her struggle was real and seeing her in such a state pained him. Since returning to campus, she'd sought counseling for the abuse she'd suffered. Although her recovery was ongoing, it was a subject that wasn't discussed among the family unless Victoria brought it up. She rarely did.

Harmony being privy to Victoria's past was strictly her decision. The torture of keeping her best friend out of the loop left Victoria in a dilemma of whether to tell or not to tell. This was a decision only she could make, and her family would stand behind her.

He watched Harmony and Tiffani's interaction as he chatted with his sisters. The two didn't seem like a good fit, as Harmony was with his sisters. He witnessed the connection between Harmony and his sisters at Christmas. Their friendship was solid, which attracted him to Harmony in the first place. The trio smiled, glowed, and were in sync.

"So that was nice of you to come in the middle of the week and bring us flowers, plus ones for Harmony," Kami said.

"I figure you all needed some love." He smiled.

"Is something going on with you and Harmony?" Kami tilted her head and studied him with an expression that showed she already knew the answer.

It wasn't going to work on him. "My two sisters introduced me to their best friend at Christmas, and I'm trying to be her best friend now."

Victoria was quiet as she stared at her bouquet, then glanced at Harmony's table. "I do miss the fun times we had. She was like our third sister, but I don't feel safe sharing my past with someone outside our family. I'm not ready." She sighed. "I thought I had moved on and conquered the past… I don't want pity or to be judged."

"Hey," Pace said, placing his hand on hers, and Kami rested hers on Pace's. She was tormented, thinking about it. "You will always be my sister—"

"Mine too." Kami grinned as tears filled her eyes.

"We got you. Mom, Dad, Papa P, and Grandma Charlotte, even our knucklehead brothers."

Victoria chuckled. "Yeah, I like being a big sister. I need more time to decide if this is a secret I want to keep buried forever."

"I believe Harmony is a true friend. Whether you decide to share your past with her or not, you both need to set boundaries in your friendship where some things are off limits." Pace glanced in the direction of Harmony's table. Something was said that made Harmony upset. Before storming out, she picked up her flowers and carried them with her.

One woman at a time, Pace coaxed himself.

Victoria now.

Harmony Reed tomorrow.

Chapter Eleven

Stay out of it, Pace told himself as he listened to his sisters' chatter that night at dinner, which was at their favorite pizza place near campus.

When he asked about their grades, Victoria revealed hers were slipping because she was feeling sad and unmotivated.

Not good. Depression was not going to put his sister in bondage again. Victoria was extremely intelligent and had a God-given ability to process information from classes with little effort. If her grades were slipping, the devil had gotten in her head.

"How are the counseling sessions going?"

"I thought I had graduated from needing them and that Jesus would fix everything." She

shrugged. "I already know the big picture of my life and just can't break through to apply the practices and principles to overcoming it."

"Jesus does fix everything, according to His will." Pace paused when the Lord silenced him with a whisper.

Recall My Word about overcoming.

First John 5:4 came to mind. "Sis, God gave you a strong mind, but the devil wants to weaken it. The Bible talks about us having the victory. *'For whatsoever is born of God overcomes the world: and this is the victory that overcomes the world, even our faith.'* You're going to have triggers, but through prayer and counselors, you can bounce back stronger until you overcome the trauma completely."

Kami and Victoria gave him weak smiles.

"I hate these emotional ambushes," Victoria said with a sigh. "I didn't expect Harmony's question to trigger me."

"It's okay, sis. God has an army of saints to help you fight your battles." Pace reached into his jacket and pulled out the two envelopes. "Here. This is for you two from Mom, Dad, the aunties, and uncles."

Victoria slowly opened the pink envelope that bore their mother's handwriting. It read, "*You Are Loved Today and Every Day*." Every space inside the card was filled with family names, even the toddlers' scribbles. That made Victoria smile. "Wow. I feel loved."

"My turn." Kami ripped open her white envelope. She grinned broadly at the card with glitter and bold colors, whereas Victoria's card was simple and soft, more fitting to her quiet demeanor. "Ooh, this is so me." Kami grinned at the cover, which showed two girls, supposedly sisters, hugging, that read, *When one is weak, the other is strong. Love.* She opened the card to see the same signatures and two one-hundred-dollar bills as Victoria's.

The sisters' hug was more of a chokehold, but Pace didn't protest. This was what family love did. "We are all praying you through this. Mom and Uncle Philip said to finish your sessions with your counselor and don't stop praying."

Victoria grinned. "I feel better knowing that they know what I've endured but they still love me."

The night ended on an upbeat note when Pace drove them back to campus, then he went to his hotel room. "One showing-the-love dinner down, and another one to go."

The next day, Pace was ready to take Harmony to their first Valentine's Day dinner. He wanted to be her comforter and confidant just as he had comforted his sisters.

I am the Comforter. Besides me, there is no other. Draw Harmony to me, the Lord whispered.

Pace gave God a spiritual salute. "Yes, Sir." He wouldn't want Harmony any other way, which was a source of contention between him and his ex. She didn't want God in the picture. Pace had assured Delilah that he was a straight male who would honor God's edict to wait until he married to share a bed with his wife.

He waited outside Harmony's dorm, holding a box of expensive chocolates, reflecting on his conviction. Pace also had a fear of not knowing whether he had fathered a child after a relationship ended. If his dad had known Little Parke existed, Pace wouldn't have been in the foster care system.

Delilah, his ex, thought sex should be a part of the relationship and accused him of not being committed or attracted to her.

Pace shook his head. He didn't take the devil's bait.

Coming. Harmony's text pulled him back to the present. He stared at the night sky as the sun set on the mild winter evening.

The door opened, and a vision of loveliness blinded him. Harmony's long jet-black hair was straight and glossy. Her red dress and heels showed off her legs, but her assets were well-hidden.

Pace stepped closer to assist her with a wool coat to keep her warm, then handed her the box of candy. She whispered her thanks as Pace inhaled her fragrance and beauty. "Thank you for being my beautiful Valentine. Red is your color."

"Any shade is yours and thank you for asking." Her smile made her face glow, emboldening Pace to wrap his arms around Harmony for an embrace.

Did not the Lord tell Pace to bring Harmony to him, and did Pace not have a personal conviction to keep the lust of the flesh at bay? He stepped back, then guided her to his rental.

"It seems like forever since I've seen you," he said, opening the door.

Harmony giggled. "It's been less than twenty-four hours."

"Before that, it's been four-and-a-half weeks, Miss Reed." Pace helped her into the vehicle, then got in himself.

He reached across the seat and took her hand.

Soft and a little cool. The touch was electrifying. They smiled at each other. Did she feel the same contentment as he did?

"It's so sweet of you to come in the middle of the week —"

"That's because I wanted you to be my Valentine." She blushed, and he smiled to himself. "I made reservations at Sparo Little Italy."

"I like that place."

"I wanted to impress you with a more upscale restaurant for the occasion," he explained.

"This is special enough. We're both college students. Usually, your sisters and I have a Galentine dinner, and we buy ourselves a rose, so it was nice to receive a bouquet from you yesterday, although I didn't know you were coming a day early."

"I wanted to check on my sisters. JC is coming, too, and will take them to dinner." Pace chuckled, but deep inside, between him and the Lord, Pace wasn't okay with his sisters dating. The family witnessed Kami's first boyfriend, Tango, trying to lead her astray, first with matching tattoos. Pace knew JC wouldn't do that, but it was a struggle to let go and let God.

"The things you do impress me, Pace Jamieson. Getting up early on Christmas morning to take me to the airport, driving up to Chicago for a weekend, and flying here in the middle of the week for Valentine's Day."

She made him feel appreciated. "Good guys still exist." He followed the GPS's directions to the restaurant nearby.

She faced him as they parked the car and shook her head. "Right now, I'm not sure what I can promise you. We're set to graduate, start our careers in different cities, and make adult decisions. I've been craving that type of freedom since high school. It is scary."

Pace nodded. He understood, but his parents had groomed him and his sisters to make adult decisions today that would impact their future, so they were taught to pray about and be strategic about their life's goals. He and Kami were on board. Victoria was in the slow lane, but she was still trying to figure out her life post-trauma.

"Harmony Reed, if you don't think I know what I want, watch me." Pace stepped out of his car and walked around to help her. She latched onto his hand. Pace wasn't sure if it was because of the high heels that covered her feet or a silent promise to encourage him.

He would take it!

Once they were seated and had ordered, Pace cataloged everything about her to see if anything had changed since he saw her last month. Her lashes were naturally long—his sisters taught him how to spot fake ones—very thick, dark curly; her hair was long and thick, and she had the sweetest face that made Pace want to hide her on an island for only him to admire.

"Why are you staring?"

"I'm admiring. There is a difference."

Tilting her head, she smiled at him. "Gold is your color, but since I've met you, your handsomeness is understated, Mr. Jamieson."

Her compliment caused him to blush and look away. He really liked her and prayed that God would give them both the desires of their hearts.

Then, just like that—a snap of a finger—sadness seemed to wash over her, and she sighed. "I just don't understand what happened between me and your sisters. It's awkward not being close to them while getting close to you. That makes me uncomfortable."

"Don't be. Like there is a separation of church and state, there is separation of girlfriend and sisters."

"I'm unsure if I want to be in the girlfriend status."

That's not what he expected to hear. He reached across the table and covered her hands. "Victoria is just going through something. It will pass—I hope," he added because his family had been praying for her. "Reconciliation is part of friendship. Everything will work out, and all this will be forgotten."

Harmony grunted. "I tried to be the bigger person and ask them what I had done to offend them to be treated as if all of a sudden I was invisible. I'll never forget the way she snapped at me."

Pace didn't know that. Victoria could be combative if she felt cornered. Their food arrived and paused the topic, allowing him to give thanks and ask for the blessing. They were quiet as they ate. Pace's heart was hurting because Victoria's hurt had resurfaced, and she had hurt Harmony. He apologized for his sister's behavior.

"Thank you for saying that, but it's not your offense to apologize for." Harmony shrugged as if it was no big deal, but Pace didn't know how to move past it.

Once he paid the bill and they were leaving, Harmony apologized. "I'm sorry, Pace, if I've ruined your evening and trip. Your sisters are a sore spot with me. As sweet and nice as you are, I can't be with you because of them."

Lord, help me out here. "It's not you," Pace tried to assure her. "Even though my sisters introduced us, the relationship I want us to have is between you and me."

The high of celebrating the day of love was flat-lining.

"Did they tell you what I did or said to cause them to unfriend me?"

Understanding her frustration, Pace hugged her. Helpless to ease her pain, so he prayed for her.

"All I want to do is get through these last three months of school and go back home. The college has educated me in the classroom and taught me life lessons. I've learned about relationships, friendships, and hurt."

Pace felt defeated. "So, you're telling me if you and my sisters reconcile, you're good for us to date?" Stipulations didn't work with him.

"No, I'm not saying that. I'm saying the timing for a relationship between us is off. Couples must be able to talk about anything and everything that bothers them. I can't do that with you because what's hurting me is a friendship that connects us, which isn't solid but fragile."

"Since we're putting our cards on the table," he said, steadying his voice, "I love my sisters, and as an older brother, I can sometimes have the final say, but what my sisters share with you is their business, not mine."

"I can't believe how you can separate the two."

Now, Pace was mad at the world, his sisters, and Harmony.

When he pulled up to the curb, Harmony didn't wait for him to help her out. She stepped out and walked away, not responding to him calling her name. At least, she took her box of candy.

Like the Grinch who stole Christmas, Harmony had ruined Valentine's Day. She cried herself to sleep. She told herself she could have a relationship with Pace, despite not having one with his sisters. That was a lie.

Harmony missed him the next day when his morning text didn't come. She was not in the best mood. As she entered the dining hall, Tiffani was there and couldn't wait to get the details.

"Where did he take you? Is it serious? How do Kami and Victoria feel about it?" The questions were like bullets that never stopped firing.

Massaging her temples to put her headache on pause, Harmony could only stare at Tiffani as she tried to pry out details of her dinner with Pace.

To Harmony's annoyance, Tiffani leaned forward for privacy as she spied Kami and Victoria enter the hall with their arms linked, signaling their contentment. Their dinner with JC had gone better than hers, and they couldn't compare notes.

"So, was last night a big breakup? Please tell me he didn't come all this way to end it—the jerk." Tiffani was merciless with her assumptions.

"Tiffani, I'm not going to say this again: The Jamiesons have been good friends." Past tense. Harmony swallowed the hurt. "I'm not about to badmouth them or let anyone in my presence do so. Friends come and go. It's the circle of life," she said as *The Lion King* came to mind.

Seemingly offended, Tiffani snarled. "You're a fool to defend them."

"I would defend you, too, if I thought you had some good qualities. Now, unless you have something good to say about anybody, maybe we don't have a friendship."

Tiffani stood and *hmmmph*ed. "Why did I waste my time feeling sorry for you? You don't know how to treat real friends." She stormed out of the dining hall without looking back.

Harmony shook her head. *Lord, can You and I be friends?* There didn't seem to be anyone on earth who valued her.

God didn't answer as Harmony waited at the table for the longest time, watching the Jamieson sisters.

I am a Friend who sticks closer than any brother, Jesus whispered.

That made Harmony smile as she gathered her stuff to leave for her internship. She heard her name and looked up. Kami and Victoria waved at her.

She waved back without thinking if it meant the beginning to heal their friendship.

On Sunday evening, a few nights later, she called her mother.

"Hey, sweetie. You sound down."

Yeah, I feel down too. She glanced out her window at the side of the campus where the pathway led to many of the educational buildings. Harmony had been holed up in her place all weekend, opting to eat some of the groceries she had in her apartment and skip the home basketball game. She sighed as she brought her knees to her chest. "Am I overthinking my friendship with Kami and Victoria? I mean, is it natural for me to mourn a friendship because I can't shake the hurt to move on?"

"Yes, it is, and it's called maturing. I liked the sisters for taking care of my baby and making sure you got home for Christmas, but not how they distanced themselves from you for no reason... You'll learn the difference between associates and classmates and not think everyone can be your best friend. I hurt for you, sweetie, because it's happened to me throughout the years."

"So how do I move on, Mom—I mean, really move on—to where I can speak to them and not feel betrayed, used, or put up my guard around them?"

Now, it was her mother who sighed. "Keep living, take one day at a time, and you'll develop thick skin and learn what battles are worth engaging."

I'll fight your battles if you will come to Me, God whispered as she ended the call with her mother.

Chapter Twelve

A few weeks later, Pace still couldn't move past the Valentine's Day fiasco in his heart. He sat in service and listened to his uncle, Pastor Philip Dupree.

"Life happens, saints—happiness to heaviness, rejoicing to mourning—but God is faithful. Are you? Are we consistent when things don't go our way? These are a lot of questions, but God has our answers. In First Peter, chapter five, verses seven through nine, the Bible says, '*Casting all your cares upon him; for he cares for you. Be sober, be vigilant; because your adversary, the devil, as a roaring lion, walking about, seeking whom he may devour: Who resist steadfast in the faith, knowing that the same afflictions are accomplished in your brethren that are in the world.*'"

Pray for her, God whispered.

Pace shifted in his seat, squeezed between his father and JC. He didn't attempt to ask God who. God knew who was on his mind, even though Pace fought hard to dismiss Harmony.

I know your thoughts afar off, God whispered.

Wait a minute. Was Jesus having a personal conversation with him in the middle of a sermon?

"Jesus is concerned about us. God cares about us." Pastor Dupree's voice echoed throughout the sanctuary. "He cares about us. Again, I say He cares about us!" It was a powerful declaration that stirred Pace's spirit.

And Lord, I care about her, Pace spoke quietly to God.

I am God. She needs to know I am there for her. Pray that Satan won't devour her spirit or mind. God's voice was forceful.

Pace got what he came for. God had spoken through the sermon publicly and to him privately.

After service, Pace turned to JC. "If you're hungry, Grandma BB has invited us for Sunday dinner."

JC grinned. "You know I never pass up a free meal with the Jamiesons. Let me check on my mom first to see if she needs anything, and I'll meet you at her house."

They shook hands and parted. JC was a good guy; his sisters seemed to like him, so Pace needed to stand down, and he thought he had—more than once—but God was judging him for not yielding to His words. Plus, he needed to be concerned about Harmony. His hurt feelings caused him not to reach out to her via text. He hurt only her by not drawing her soul to Christ.

He lingered at church and spoke to his parents, brothers, and other family to give JC time to take care of his business. Pace had met his mother a few times and admired how JC doted on her despite her shortcomings, like the Jamiesons respected their elders.

As he was about to exit the sanctuary for the parking lot, his mother stopped him. "Pace Jamieson, ever since you've come back from Oklahoma, you haven't mentioned Harmony over the phone, so look me in the eye, son, and tell me what's going on. How's Harmony, and how are you *and* Harmony?" Her frown didn't hide her concern. "I'm a good listener and prayer warrior."

Frowns never marred his mother's beauty. He suspected Harmony would be just as beautiful as she matured, too. "It's a work in progress."

"Your dad didn't give up on me. If you really care about Harmony, don't give up on her." Cheney kissed his cheek and turned to speak to another church member.

JC arrived at Grandma BB's house minutes after Pace. Before they could officially be dinner guests, she had tasks for them.

"Set the table for three. Pace, you know where the dishes are. JC, you take the serving bowls out of the lower cabinet for each dish. Pile up as much food as you two can eat. I made my famous secret lemonade."

"Boy, it's been a long time since you've made that." Pace couldn't remember when.

"It's a special occasion. I've got more family to enjoy." She made her way to the head of the dining room table unassisted and nodded as they correctly followed her instructions. Soon, Pace and his friend took their seats.

Grandma BB laughed. "Y'all getting free food, so I've got to put you to work for it. Okay, grandson, say grace." She bowed her head but kept one eye open as if making sure they didn't steal her silverware.

"Lord, in the name of Jesus, thank You for one more day of life for us. Thank You for the salvation of the cross…" he prayed, hinting that she needed to submit to Jesus before it was too late. When she cleared her throat, he completed his assignment. "Please bless and sanctify our food and Grandma BB's hands for preparing it and her soul, which You died for. Thank You for Your genuine friendship with my brother in Christ and for reminding me never to take anything for granted. Help us to feed the homeless, in Jesus' name. Amen."

Grandma BB groaned. "If my food gets cold, you're going to warm it up."

"Yes, ma'am." Pace didn't repent. She needed as much prayer as she could get. Stubborn as a youngster, have her tell it, she carried over the bad quality to her old age.

As expected, Grandma BB was her same charming self as she sat regal, decorated with a jewel-encrusted crown and jewels around her neck. Instead of an elegant housedress, she wore a gold-and-black caftan dress and spotless two-tone white-and-black Stacy Adams shoes.

"JC, tell me how Willie Earl is your great uncle. He's my kin, which means you and I are blood." She gave him her full attention, grinning while she listened to JC repeat what he had told Pace. Once JC finished, Grandma BB said, "Goin' to add you to my will."

Pace couldn't contain his laughter. Although Mrs. Beatrice Tilley Beacon was eccentric and wealthy in her own right, she had listed every Jamieson on the document. "JC, by the time her investments are liquidated, we'll get fifty dollars."

"*Humph.* That's what you get for being educated. Trust me, all of you will receive five digits unless you kill me off, then Chip and Dale are instructed to prosecute the suspect to the fullest extent of the law."

"Grandma BB, I don't need any money. Family is more important," his friend told her.

More dots connected JC to Pace's family, blood relatives or not. Pace felt like God was sending him signals to ease his worry.

"Good answer." She pushed back from her chair, crossed one leg over the knee, and began to swing it. "How's Willie Earl?"

Memories seemed to make JC shake his head and chuckle. "I can see the resemblance in personality now. He's a hoot—entertaining like you. I'm glad my cousin found me on social media and invited me. I promised him I would visit again this summer once I graduated."

For the next hour, JC indulged Grandma BB about the birthday party—the guests who attended, what was on the menu, and the type of decorations.

Chip and Dale appeared in the doorway, removing their jackets.

Grandma BB squinted at them. "I left you two greedy pretty boys food, but do you mind serving my guests dessert?"

Dale chuckled. "Guests? Pace and JC are family." Dale disappeared toward the kitchen and returned with a two-tier platter filled with assorted sweets. He grinned as if he had created them himself. "Sharon sent these samples for us to taste test and tell her what we think. She has Chip's and my vote."

"Of course she does." Grandma BB chuckled. "His new girlfriend is starting her bakery business. She's pretty good too. I need a one-year notice before you get married so I can get another bodyguard trained."

"It will be a while. I've got two more children to raise, and then I'll be ready for marriage."

Grandma BB nodded her approval, and when Chip and Dale left, she turned her eyes on Pace and JC. "What I can't understand is why you two don't have girlfriends, and I know you handsome young men are attracted to ladies."

"It's complicated," Pace and JC said in unison, then looked at each other in surprise.

"Well, uncomplicate it." She wagged her recently manicured nail, which she had shaped like a fine-point pencil. "You know I might die tomorrow, and I want to hold my great-great grandbabies in my arms."

Pace rubbed his forehead. Ever since her pre-funeral shenanigans, the pressure was on.

"You remind me of your father when I first met him. Cheney was paying him no mind. She was in bad shape mentally and could take Parke or leave him. I convinced her to give him a chance." She proudly lifted her chin and leaned forward. "Call me an accomplice in love. I'm known for my intervention—legal or under the table."

JC chuckled. "I love her," he said, meaning Grandma BB.

"Please don't encourage her."

"Listen, I invited you two over here because you're graduating soon, and I gave your parents a gift card to eat out today because we need to have the talk." Grandma BB did mock air quotes.

"What kind of talk?" Pace groaned. Whatever she was about to say next probably involved some covert activity, which she was known for throughout the neighborhood, community, and family.

"Parke K. Jamieson the eighth. Never could pronounce that middle name of yours, even with Ebonics. Anyway, Pace, I know you like Harmony. She's a lovely girl who I enjoyed over the brief holiday. I don't know everything about what's going on with my family folks, but I know enough to say some things you just can't fix. Let the good Lord work it out."

This was coming from a woman whose church attendance was holidays—major and minor—even though she loved to hear her nephew-in-law, Pastor Philip Dupree, preach.

"You're right, but you need to come clean, too, Grandma BB. A second mock funeral for you isn't guaranteed."

Grandma BB said nothing as she turned to JC and folded her hands. "Our Jamieson girls are not to be messed with. You either go in wearing gloves, not to throw a punch, but to block their blows. My girls are tough, just like I taught them." She grinned with a perfect set of teeth, still hers. "Now, the next time you two come over for dinner, I expect an update." She yawned and stood with JC's and Pace's assistance. "I'm going for my scheduled power nap now. Remember, I want an update in thirty days."

Staring at JC, Pace gritted his teeth. He had to stay focused on his schoolwork and Harmony and let the Lord take care of his sisters.

Chapter Thirteen

Pace resumed his texts to Harmony like clockwork every morning at about the same time. It thrilled Harmony that he hadn't forgotten about her. Her insecurities hadn't scared him off—yet. However, she never responded because she didn't want to encourage him as if everything was okay, and it wasn't.

But the Scriptures or inspirational quotes might have come too late. Harmony's frustration caused her to withdraw from many activities on campus, except essential ones about graduation.

A double major was no joke, and the pressure was unrelenting this semester. Her college advisor provided seniors with a list of companies that favored upcoming graduates, but she had not received any pending job offers.

Now, Harmony wished to erase all the times she couldn't wait to become an adult. The next morning, after her alarm woke her, a text came seconds later.

Beloved, I wish above all things that thou may prosper and be in good health, even as thy soul prospers. 3 John 2:1

Harmony's vision blurred as she sat on her bed. The words sounded so personal and intimate, like an embrace. She sniffed. It would be a rough day with two exams scheduled, yet that Bible verse made her feel like her problems mattered to Jesus.

"Lord, I don't know what's wrong with me. I feel stuck in time." She jumped in the shower and decided to eat a bagel and drink juice before class. As she crossed campus, Harmony felt alone despite being surrounded by eleven thousand fellow students. Were they as stressed about their future? Her mind was elsewhere when Tiffani walked past her like she was invisible. Harmony didn't care. That battle wasn't worth putting on emotional armor to fight.

She walked into Dreker Hall and hiked the stairs, asking God to allow her to excel on her history of typography exam. After that, she planned to go to the library for two hours to prepare for her computer graphics IV mid-term presentation.

When she couldn't concentrate at the library, she stepped outside and called home. "Hey, Mom."

"How's everything going?"

Harmony flopped on a bench and looked into the sunny blue skies. There seemed to be streaks of clouds for aesthetic accents. The weather wasn't cold but chilly enough to keep her alert. "I'm overwhelmed. I took one exam but have to prepare for my class projects and presentations. I'm doing my best at the studio internship to get a job recommendation. I'm working with my advisor in the career development center about résumé writing and interviewing skills. It's hard to juggle it all."

"You can, Harmony Reed. Take a deep breath. I would say come home for a weekend, but I don't think that will help. You can only do one thing at a time." Her mother made her compile a list and numbered them in order of priority. "Let's do what's doable this month."

That sounded like a plan, but she lacked the strength to calm her nerves. Lorna distracted her with news of what was happening in her three brothers' dating lives, sick neighbors, and the latest art exhibits coming to Chicago. Harmony appreciated that it was anything but school. When they ended the call, Harmony felt energized to take on the world.

Two days later, a large box arrived from Chicago. *Love Mom and Family* was scribbled below the city and state. She hugged it as if it were her family. When she opened it, Harmony cried. Homesickness pierced her on every side. She sniffed the residual fragrance of her mother's perfume, imagining she had lovingly packed every item.

Harmony tugged a stuffed animal that peeped through the treasures. She danced when she discovered a bag of Chicago-style popcorn from Garrett's. As if her mother knew Harmony's appetite was waning, the treasure hunt continued with a carefully wrapped box of Ann Sather's cinnamon rolls, which had been frozen to preserve their freshness during transit. By the end of the day, they would thaw out, and Harmony would feel guiltless eating more than a serving. She sniffed and wiped her tears away. "Thanks, Mom," she whispered.

Other snacks were attached with notes: *Eat while listening to soft music, Munch on popcorn as you stroll through campus*, and more. At the bottom of the box was a large envelope signed by her parents and brothers. Inside was a plane ticket to New Orleans with a note: *Meet us there for spring break.*

Her eyes widened in surprise. Joy filled her space. "Yes!" She had never been to New Orleans and wouldn't want to experience it alone. The tears started again as a stream and flowed like a flood. Despite everything not going as she wanted this semester, Harmony felt at peace in the chaos.

Laurence Jr. had sent her a two-hundred-dollar gift card. Her other two brothers sent cash.

Their generosity was making her an emotional mess. Four hundred dollars was a lot of money. She could spend some on a new wardrobe for spring break and have money left over.

Life was good.

Beloved, I wish above all things that thou may prosper and be in good health, even as thy soul prospers, God whispered.

Pace was happy. His texts to Harmony were marked "read." His heart was concerned about his sister. Kami said Victoria had become quiet and withdrawn, even from her. If her mental state didn't improve, the entire Jamieson clan would descend on campus to give Victoria some tender, loving care. Uncle Philip would turn the campus into a tent meeting for deliverance. Evangelism had been his trademark before he became a pastor.

When he walked out of his engineering class, Pace was in deep thought and prayer. He decided to stop by his parents' house before he head to work. As he was to climb inside his car, JC pulled up beside him and parked.

"Hey, buddy." Pace greeted JC with a smile, fist bump, and pat on the back when he walked up to him. "What's up?"

"You know, man. Preparing for the real world. Everybody good?"

"No" was on the tip of his tongue without thinking, but this was his friend, brother, and confidant. Pace leaned against the trunk of his car and folded his arms. "Man," he began with a sigh, "I'm worried about Victoria."

Fear struck JC's eyes. He stood at attention. He mirrored the reaction Pace would concerning any mention of his family. "What do I need to do? What's going on? I can be on the road in an hour…" When he paused, something clicked, and JC's demeanor changed. "She didn't mention anything when I talked to her."

Pace processed the tidbit. He had spoken to his sister? The best Pace could do was hope Harmony read his text. "When did you last talk to her?" He watched his friend, hoping there wouldn't be any signs that he was withholding information.

"We talk a couple of times a week. Of course, I give Kami her five minutes of attention."

The friends chuckled together before Pace said, "Of course. She would not be denied attention."

"We basically talk about our childhood…" JC slipped his hands into his pockets while Pace made himself comfortable because he wasn't going anywhere.

"Let's go to the coffee shop for a sandwich. We need to talk—or maybe, I need to listen," The two drove their separate cars a few blocks to the spot where most Wash U students hung out. It wasn't as big as the dining hall at his sisters' school, but it was inviting, with soft colors, bold lighting, and comfortable seating for study or group chats.

Once they settled into a booth for two, a fellow college student appeared to take their orders, flirted with them until Pace and JC blushed, then walked away.

Pace leaned across the table and lowered his voice as if the overhead music and the chatter around them wouldn't give them enough privacy. "So things have been progressing with my sister since your visit on Valentine's Day?"

JC nodded, then reached for his glass of water, which the waitress had placed before them. "I like the sound of her giggles. Although she appears to be guarded, we click."

Now, it was Pace's turn to nod. Victoria wasn't open about her past, so he wanted to know what his sister had shared with his best friend without being direct.

"I find myself telling her about my childhood, mistakes my mother made, and how they shaped the convictions in my life."

Pace blinked. "You willingly disclosed that? Wow." He looked away and rubbed the hairs on his chin.

"Victoria is special. She knows that. I can be raw with her without judgment, and I've never, ever felt safe talking about my past with anyone else before."

Speechless, Pace's jaw dropped before he could form his thoughts. "Are…are we talking about the same Victoria Jamieson?"

His friend laughed as their sandwiches were placed on their table. They paused to say grace, and then JC sampled his fries.

"I'm being transparent with her in hopes she can trust me with whatever bothers her."

"*Umm-hmmm.*" Pace's appetite was on hold, depending on the answer to his next question. "Has my sister opened up to you?" He held his breath and waited. If Victoria had, that would be healing.

"Not really." JC shrugged, and Pace relaxed. "But she listens, and laughs, and teases me. I'm building trust with her, brother, no pressure."

"Thanks." Pace ate his Swiss and ham sandwich with gusto. "I'm glad you're there for her too. I really mean that."

JC lifted his fist for a bump. "I'm glad I have your blessing."

"Not yet, but we're getting there." Pace took another bite of his sandwich.

"I know, and I'm praying on it." The two talked until it was time for Pace to leave for work. He would stop by his parents' house later.

On his way to his part-time job, he called Kami. After she greeted him with all the sisterly love a brother could handle, he asked, "Why did you lead me to believe our sister was regressing into depression?"

"Because she was," Kami answered, then *hmmmph*ed, "then Jamison called and made her laugh, and he challenged her to have hope for the future, which is good. But you know our sister, once she sets her mind on something, she rarely changes it. If Victoria doesn't want to talk about her past with anyone, she won't."

The false hope JC gave Pace was no longer there as he listened to his sister. They were about to cross over to the adult phase of their lives, and all of them would have to decide what part of their childhood they would bring with them.

Pace continued suffering spiritual setbacks. He took a work break at Benson and Frontier Architecture and texted his pastor: **Praise the Lord, Uncle. Do you have time to meet with me after I get off work tonight?**

Ten minutes later, Philip replied, **I always have time for you—always.**

Good. Pace sighed in relief, returned to his station, and refocused on making sure a customer's work order and the tool drawings matched before his supervisor okayed it for production.

His proficiency in the SOLIDWORKS design program allowed him to easily create tool drawings based on the company's clients' requirements. He was also adept at tweaking them based on customer feedback, showcasing his adaptability and commitment to delivering the best results.

That attitude and his father's counsel had taught him to become invaluable, and Pace had done that.

The STEM program he was exposed to in middle and high school gave him the fast track in college, preparing him for the accelerated bachelor/master program in mechanical engineering. It guaranteed him an impressive salary with his choice of companies. Well, he was ready to cash in.

Pace signed off at eight, then headed to the Duprees' home in North County. When he arrived, his aunt, Queen Jamieson Dupree, greeted him at the door with her baby girl in her arms. At six months, Suzette was bright-eyed and curious about Pace's presence, and the child was a carbon copy of her beautiful mother.

"Hey, Auntie." Pace kissed her cheek and then her daughter's before lifting Suzette out of her arms. When the baby began to fuss, Pace handed her over.

They both laughed and then she smothered her daughter with kisses. Queen looked so happy, and Pace wanted to experience that in his life sooner rather than later.

She yelled up the stairs, "Philip, our nephew is here."

Philip peeped over the banister and grinned. "Thanks, babe. Pace, come on up to the pool room. We don't need an office setting to talk."

"There are sandwiches and chips. If you want something heavier, I cooked country fried chicken, mashed potatoes, and green beans in the kitchen."

"This is going to be a quick consultation," Pace said as he hiked the stairs. Philip met him at the landing with a hug, then they walked into the rec room where a pool table was racked for play, snacks were set up on a wet bar, and a pair of pinball machines were in the corner.

Pace helped himself to the snacks but would take a plate home. Philip waited until Pace sighed with contentment, then asked, "What do you want to talk about?"

"Victoria."

He frowned. "Oh? What's going on with my niece?"

The alarmed expression on Philip's face mirrored everyone in the family whenever her name came up. "I'm having a hard time letting go. I know she's smart and grown, but…"

Philip was quiet as Pace struggled to confess his fear. "I wasn't there to protect her as a young girl, but since she became a part of our family, I have been her protector. I won't let anything happen to her or Kami."

"We all feel the same way."

Pace slumped. His shoulders shook with agony. He started to mumble, "God told me not to let my attitude cause me to lose a friend…how can Victoria move on after what she experienced? Who can I trust to take care of her?" He sniffed, and his uncle stood and handed him a ball of tissue, then patted Pace's shoulder.

"Sorry." Pace choked. "I can't remember the last time I cried."

"Jesus wept, David cried, the Israelites cried out, and God heard them. The most important thing is God hears us." Philip gave him an encouraging smile.

"Victoria is a Jamieson today because God rescued her, filled her with His Spirit, and restored her soul."

"I know all that, but still…"

If only his uncle could read his mind so that he wouldn't have to say it. "Will she ever be able to handle a relationship?"

"Pace, I think you're more afraid than her. My niece is living the life God gave her to the fullest. She is happy, grounded, smart, and beautiful inside and out."

Pace twisted his lips. "Yeah, she's all that, and JC likes her."

Philip nodded with a smile that turned into a grin.

"How can you be happy about that?" Pace wanted his pastor-uncle to be offended and concerned like him.

"How can two walk together unless they agree? Victoria and JC have surrendered their lives to the Lord and are walking with Him from what I can see." Philip stood and strolled to the pool table and picked up a stick. He nodded his head for Pace to join him. "I'll let you break."

Pace accepted, broke the pool balls, and began to play. It released some of his tension.

"The last time you were here, it was about Harmony. You even drove to Chi-town to see her in January. Let's talk about you and her walking together with the love of Christ."

"She's not there yet. I don't think Harmony attends church while on campus, but I have been sending her Scriptures. I think our relationship is dependent on hers with Kami and Victoria. That I don't like."

"Sounds like you," he said, pointing before accepting his turn to shoot. "You need to be praying instead of worrying. God has Victoria. Let your heart rest. No one would ever know you're adopted unless you tell them. No one would ever know Victoria's story unless she tells them. The choice is hers."

Pace couldn't argue that as he never got another chance to shoot, and his uncle won.

After pumping his fists in the air, Philip grinned. “Now, I’m going to pray for you. My wife is going to fix you a to-go plate, and you’re going home so my family, and I can go to bed.”

“Yes, Pastor.” Pace accepted that every situation was in God’s hands.

Chapter Fourteen

Harmony left the graphic arts studio, chatting with a fellow student. "I'm meeting my family in the Big Easy for spring break. I've shopped online and at the mall. All I have to do is pack and book a ride-share."

Wade Post, who excelled at illustration, grinned. "Sweet. Me and a couple of friends are going to Dallas to see what trouble we can get into."

"Despite the city's nightlife, I can't get into too much trouble with my brothers and parents around."

"Then why are you going?" He peered through his glasses with a curious expression.

"Because I miss my family."

Wade nodded. "Good enough reason. Don't worry about a rideshare driver. I'll drop you off at the airport."

"You sure? I don't want to inconvenience you." Either way, Harmony wasn't going to miss her flight.

"Yep. But here's the deal: If you land a job before I do, you've got to put in a good word for me."

Harmony grinned. "Same goes for you."

"Ha. You're the master of artistic drawings. Text me your flight info. Can't say I'll be here to pick you up—"

"Your offer to take me is enough." They said their goodbyes.

That night, Harmony was in the best mood. "New Orleans, here I come," Harmony said as she packed her suitcase with shorts, tops, and other cute outfits for spring weather. For the past two weeks, she'd reminded herself that the spring break trip was her reward for the semester. She'd stayed focused and passed her mid-terms.

Harmony was also learning valuable lessons. She didn't need besties to hang out with but enjoyed the company of whoever was around her.

The next day, Wade helped her with the luggage from her apartment. "How long are you going to be gone, girl? Spring break is only eight days."

She laughed. "I've got to be cute at all times."

"Done. You've been cute since our first day in design foundation class."

Was he flirting? Harmony didn't know but didn't respond. She only wanted a ride to the airport, not a relationship so close to graduation. Wasn't that what she had told Pace? Wade had always been so intense in his work, she considered him a loner.

Half an hour later, he dropped her off at the Will Roger Airport departing flights terminal.

She had just cleared security when Pace sent another text—the second for the day—and that was unusual: **The peace of God, which passes all understanding, shall keep your hearts and minds through Christ Jesus. Philippians 4:7**

Harmony almost smiled. Peace seemed to elude her. She hoped to get it back in New Orleans.

"God is calling for us to trust Him and stop micro-managing our lives," Pastor Dupree said, closing out his Sunday morning service. "Jesus doesn't need your help. He demands your faith. Take that with you throughout the week."

Pace nodded as he and the others stood for the altar call for discipleship. He had been guilty of trying to micro-manage his sister's life, but God was showing Pace He was in control every step of the way. He smiled.

It wasn't lost on Pace that many of the people who went to the altar for prayer or salvation were young children who didn't seem old enough to know the difference between right and wrong, yet many of them were victims of criminal acts or perpetrators of them.

Lord, keep them all safe, whether at home or in foster care, he silently prayed.

After the benediction, he and JC discussed what had happened in each other's lives the past week.

"Man, do you realize that this is our last year in college, and we have to say we went somewhere on spring break? Got any plans for the upcoming week?"

"Work." Pace laughed. "I would love to drive back up to Chicago and explore more of the city's culture, but it wouldn't be the same without Harmony as my tour guide."

"I guess not." JC slipped his hand into his pants pocket and pulled out his car keys. "Are your sisters coming home for break?"

"You don't know? You talk to them more than me." Pace chuckled.

JC shrugged. "Victoria mentioned some students were going to Dallas, but she and Kami hadn't decided to go yet."

Pace resisted the urge to call them for an update. Didn't his uncle preach on essentially butting out of others' business and trusting God with it? "I think I'll use my free time to work extra hours and chill at Mom and Dad's house." His two-to-three-day work week paid his car note, insurance, and minor incidentals, and he hoped it would keep his mind off Harmony. How could she shut him out when there was a connection? He had hoped the Valentine's Day dinner would have been the first of many trips to her campus to visit. That was two months ago, and nothing.

To keep his mind from drifting, he refocused and asked JC, “You?”

He shrugged. “I’m considering booking a hotel suite for my mom and treating her to a day spa. Something nice.”

Pace smiled. “A brother after my own heart. Okay, I’ll touch base with you later.”

The next day, Pace’s supervisor at Benson and Frontier Architecture was happy to have him work on more projects. They considered him a regular employee as if he was already full-time.

But Pace was starting to become restless living in St. Louis. It was time to consider other cities for relocation. Chicago was at the top of his list.

His spring break was uneventful—until his parents received a call that Kami and Victoria had been involved in a car accident in Dallas.

Chapter Fifteen

Spring break in New Orleans had turned into a Reed family vacation. It was an eight-day escape from Harmony's reality.

She fell in love with the charm of the French Quarter. Colorful two-story buildings with black cast-iron balconies transported her to a historic period in American history. Blacks were classified as quadroons, Black Creoles, and other terms depending on how much African blood was in their DNA. It seemed like a different world from other parts of the South during slavery.

The first night, the Reeds attended a jazz club on Bourbon Street. Shane commented on the thriving nightlife. "This is so me." He bobbed his head.

The next day, the siblings split up from their parents, who planned to visit New Orleans' Jazz Museum while Harmony and her brothers checked out the cemetery tours. That's when she learned that the Big Easy was considered a top destination for ghost tours and voodoo.

It was hard for her to stomach the details of Madame Delphine LaLaurie's heinous torture of those she enslaved at her mansion. Because of that, the locales refer to 1140 Royal Street as the Haunted House.

Aside from the dark past, Harmony enjoyed the history. She slept late every morning and woke with excitement to see more sights and sounds of New Orleans. They had a full day: tour neighborhoods that Hurricane Katrina destroyed, the three historically Black college campuses, sampled local cuisine and admired the Spanish- and French-influenced architecture.

Her eyes soaked up the vibrant colors, inspiring her to interpret them in her own graphic artwork. Harmony captured the experience with photos and videos. “This place is a haven for graphic artists. I could see me working here.”

On the final night, her family dined at one of the city’s top restaurants. The ambiance was relaxing, so they lingered and enjoyed each other’s company. It was late when they returned to their hotel, but Harmony packed the cute outfits and souvenirs she had purchased on the trip. It was one of the best vacations she had experienced in a long time.

The next morning, Harmony met the rest of their family in the lobby, waiting for the driver to take them the short distance to the Louis Armstrong New Orleans International Airport.

After checking the departure board, they noticed Harmony’s gate was in the opposite direction. Since her flight was an hour earlier than theirs, they tagged along with her.

“You look better.” Her mother seemed relieved as she sat next to Harmony.

“I didn’t realize how much this getaway would recharge me for the last stretch of college. Thank you, Mama, for thinking of this.” She squeezed her tight and didn’t want to let go. Being an adult was overrated. Harmony craved to remain in her parents’ cocoon and never leave the nest.

She choked back a sob when she looked at her brothers, who had put their lives on hold for a week to dote on her. When the boarding for her flight was called, Harmony stood and hugged each of them. “I couldn’t ask for a better family.”

Her father opened his arms. "One month to go until you graduate," Laurence Sr. said. "Hang in there. We're proud of you. When you have your degree, the sky is the limit, and you can get the job you want."

"Thanks, Dad." He hugged her twice as long and kissed her cheeks.

She gathered her suitcase and purse, then hurried to get in line as they stood on the sidelines. Harmony waved through misty eyes. She missed them already.

"Is that your family?" a young woman on the other side of Harmony asked.

She turned around and smiled at the woman who looked like a college student, too. "Yep."

"Your brothers are fine. We definitely need to exchange numbers and be besties," the girl said, lifting her phone, poised to do just that.

Harmony played it off and followed her line to the ticket agent. She should write a book on how to spot fake friends.

The flight and landing at Will Rogers Airport were smooth. She ordered a ride share and was back on campus sooner than she wanted to be.

As she walked into her apartment, something seemed off. Had some of the evil spirits from New Orleans beat her there, waiting to remind her of all the woes she'd tried to forget—all the things that weren't right in her world?

Despite Harmony not wanting to be sucked back into bouts of depression, it was an overpowering sensation.

Harmony exhaled, flopped on the bed, and grabbed her phone. She needed the photos and videos to take her back to a happy place. For the first time since she'd left for spring break, she noticed she had many unread texts. They had been from Pace. Funny how she didn't need his inspiration, and now, she craved it.

Morning, beautiful. God so loved the World that He gave His only begotten Son that whoever believes in Him shall not perish. John 3:16

That was sent the first day she was in New Orleans. More followed.

When you are weak, God gives you strength. 2 Corinthians 12:9-10

Jesus will never leave nor forsake you. You're never alone, Harmony. Hebrews 13:6

Greater is He that is in you than he that is in the world. 1 John 4:4

May all your thoughts today be beautiful. Think about all good things. Philippians 4:8-9

You need My power, Harmony. You need Me for your peace, God whispered, and Harmony realized that the anxiety that was ready to take her hostage had disappeared.

Suddenly, an intense craving stirred inside Harmony and caught her off guard, considering she wasn't hungry. She had never experienced it before, and snacks couldn't fill it.

Seek Me while I can be found, God whispered.

Harmony's heart pumped faster. "How?"

Her frustration built when God didn't give her any further instructions, even though she pleaded until she found herself crying uncontrollably. Then she remembered the church near campus that Kami and Victoria had attended.

Redemption Temple.

She had to go. Nothing and no one could keep her away. Maybe God would answer her there.

Chapter Sixteen

Life is not promised. The car crash in Dallas last week brought that home.

Pace was glad his sisters were safe. A classmate called his parents from Victoria's phone, saying they had been involved in a bad accident. They made it seem like it was fatal.

His mother prayed and made frantic calls to the Texas Highway Patrol for more details. Jamieson households were alerted to pray after calling Kami's phone and getting her voicemail. Cheney endured a chain of phone calls before she was actually connected to an officer who worked the scene.

Pace and JC had made it to his parents' home by this time. On speakerphone, Officer Giles confirmed it was a serious three-car pileup. "Those kids were lucky no one was killed or critically injured."

While his family praised God in the background, his mother corrected the officer. "Our children were blessed and rescued out of the jaws of death."

"Yes, ma'am."

"Where are they now?" she asked.

"All were transported to Baylor University Medical Center for evaluation."

Cheney ended that call, located the ER number, and after a series of transfers, they all heard Kami's voice. She seemed dazed but thankful.

"Mom!" The relief in her voice was unmistakable. "If you could see that car…" She sniffed. "There is no way we should have escaped and be alive." Heavenly tongues filled her voice, and then Victoria came on the line.

"We're alive, Mom and Dad. We shouldn't be. There were a lot of ambulances because the police thought we were dead by the looks of the wreck, but Jesus said no!"

"We praise You, Jesus, for sparing our daughters' lives." Parke hugged his wife and swallowed back his emotions. "Do you need us to come and get you?"

"No, Dad. The hospital is coordinating with someone so we can spend the night at a hotel and pay for our tickets to fly back to Oklahoma in the morning," Kami said after some composure.

"We're going to book our flights—" Parke said.

"Dad, please don't. Jesus covered us. Let us be grownups," Kami pleaded.

"Do you think I care whether you're six, sixteen, or twenty-six? You and Victoria are my babies, and you can't tell me not—"

Pace patted his father's shoulder and took the phone. "Sis, the only way none of us are coming is if you check back with us regularly and then let us know when you're flying out in the morning. Otherwise, you know you can't stop us."

Kami huffed and exhaled. "Yes, I remember when Aunt Queen had her car accident. We flew in and took shifts taking care of her, but none of us in either car had broken bones. We're good, and we'll call with updates."

That seemed to placate his parents and his aunts and uncles, who had arrived moments earlier.

JC nudged Pace. "Mind if I speak with Victoria?"

Pace mouthed okay. "Hey, Kami, put Victoria on the phone. JC wants to talk to her."

All eyes were on JC as he accepted the phone and turned off the speaker. He lowered his voice as he put some distance between himself and her family, but Pace heard him double-check that his sister was okay." He nodded a few times. "See you soon."

"You will?" Pace asked when he turned around and handed him the phone.

"Yep. They graduate next month," JC reminded him.

"Right." How could Pace forget that? So would Harmony.

The next morning, Harmony woke early and dressed for Sunday service. Ironically, she had planned to attend Redemption Church, which was Apostolic, after God spoke to her during the Jamiesons' Christmas Eve dinner.

But with so much going on, she had forgotten about that experience and her desire to start reading her Bible with Kami and Victoria and to go to church with them.

Funny how that spiritual encounter had frizzled from her mind. She didn't even know whether Kami and Victoria still attended there.

She smiled at one of the sundresses she had purchased for New Orleans. It was a spring day, and the sun's rays fed her excitement.

Although the church was a short bus ride, Harmony decided to splurge on a ride-share. She grabbed her purse and a Bible whose pages had stuck together from lack of use.

Twenty minutes later, she arrived at her location. It reminded her of an island, and the cars in the parking lot pointed toward a gray stone building. She stepped out, steadied herself in the heels she wore on special occasions, and took a deep breath. A large black awning provided cover for the entrance. Two young boys in blue suits and bow ties opened the doors and greeted her.

She felt welcome. Despite that, Harmony only wanted to be an observer in the back row.

When she entered the sanctuary, Harmony experienced a rush of wind like she had walked into a deep freezer, except there was no chill. “A back seat, please,” she whispered to a young woman who appeared to be her age.

The usher complied and allowed Harmony to slide into a pew three rows from the back. She smiled at the other person on the pew, who nodded a greeting to her, then glanced around. Harmony was surprised there were so many who looked her age, unlike the older people at the church she sometimes attended with her parents.

A boy behind the drums seemed comfortable as he clicked his sticks, and the musicians followed his lead. Harmony rocked in her seat when another young woman took the microphone and belted out a song. She bobbed to the beat, and the words began to penetrate her soul: *I am available...*

“I love this song,” someone behind her said.

Harmony closed her eyes, and the words serenaded her: “*You gave me my voice to sing your praises...*” Yes, Harmony could sing and carry a note since childhood. Her parents said she had a gift.

Glorify Me with your voice. God’s whisper sliced through the music, and she heard Him clearly.

She opened her mouth and allowed God to fill it with the words of the song. “*My storage is empty...*” over and over. Tears streamed down her cheeks as she surrendered to God. Another song, “Holy Spirit You Are Welcome Here,” followed, but Harmony kept repeating, “*My storage is empty.*”

When the music ended, a calm settled over her. It was as if she had shed layers of burdens. Harmony exhaled. “Whew.” She was ready for what was yet to come.

“Good morning, saints and friends. I’m Pastor Gary Moore, and together with Redemption Church, we’re delighted you've come to worship with us. If you are a first-time visitor, do you mind standing so we can acknowledge your presence?"

Harmony complied and was surprised she was among a large number of visitors. Wade Post and four classmates stood in a pew where Kami and Victoria sat.

Minutes later, the pastor instructed everyone to open their Bibles to First Peter chapter five. Embarrassment began to creep up her spine as she flipped through sections, trying to find the passage.

A woman sitting next to her leaned over. She smiled at Harmony. "Sometimes, these pages stick. Do you mind if I help you?"

"Please. Thank you." The woman's kindness made Harmony tear up. With the chapter opened on her lap, Harmony smiled in victory.

"Let's read verses seven and eight: '*Casting all your cares upon him; for he cares for you. Be sober, be vigilant, because your adversary, the devil, as a roaring lion, walks about, seeking whom he may devour.*' If you don't think you have enemies, think again, and the mastermind behind all of them is Satan. He's a spiritual demon that uses flesh-and-blood people to do his dirty work. Ephesians six and twelve says, '*For we wrestle not against flesh and blood, but against principalities, against powers, against the rulers of the darkness of this world, against spiritual wickedness in high places.*'"

Harmony thought about the ghost stories she'd heard in New Orleans and what she sensed when she arrived at her apartment.

"The devil wants to take you down by any means necessary—drugs, depression, crashes. His ultimate goal is the loss of your soul—in hell. Cast your cares on God, for He died on the cross to fight your battles…" the pastor preached, and every word riveted Harmony.

The sermon wasn't long, but Harmony wanted an encore. She wasn't full yet.

"God will save you from all the heartache the world wants to give you. Will you surrender today?" he asked the congregation.

Harmony heard herself say, "Yes."

"Amen." The woman beside her patted her hand. "I was about your age when I surrendered to Jesus."

Wow. Harmony blinked, and before she realized it, she joined others on the journey to the altar, where the pastor invited anyone who needed prayer or salvation to come.

A minister beckoned her closer. "What do you seek of the Lord today?"

"I want to be saved," Harmony heard herself say as if her spirit was taking charge of her life.

"Then repent. Be sorry for your thoughts and deeds you've committed against others, including Him. Tell God you're sorry and consent to be baptized in water in Jesus' name."

Immediately, Harmony began to cry as the Lord flashed people she had wronged, situations she had mishandled, and evil thoughts she had entertained. Harmony bawled as she felt a hand on each shoulder. She opened her eyes and through blurred vision, recognized Kami and Victoria at her side, also crying. Wade and other classmates were nearby.

"I want my sins washed away," Harmony murmured.

The minister waved for an elderly woman to guide Harmony through a door to a small room where she changed out of her pretty dress and shoes into a white T-shirt and long cotton gown. She was given a white swim cap for her hair, but Harmony didn't care if it got wet. That had to be God.

Harmony wanted salvation!

She stepped into the pool, which reached her chest. Another woman entered the water behind her. Two ministers waited for Harmony and the other woman to cross their arms on their chests.

"Ready for a new life?" the minister asked before gripping the back of her garment with one hand and lifting his other. With a loud voice, he declared, "My dear sister, upon the confession of your faith and the confidence we have in the blessed Word of God concerning His death, burial, and grand resurrection, I now indeed baptize you in the only name on Earth given to man to be saved, and that is Jesus Christ our Lord."

Even though the minister had a hold on Harmony's garment, she seemed to float down to the bottom and then sprang up like the majestic power of a whale.

Harmony wondered if she was in another dimension as she heard herself speak in a heavenly language. It was terrifying and exhilarating at the same time. The emotional and mental burdens were lifted. Tears flowed, and she didn't care how she looked or who saw her. The experience was too awesome.

Still worshipping Jesus, Harmony was guided back into the room to dry off and put on her clothes. Harmony didn't want to let go of what she was experiencing—ever. She could talk to God all night.

Physically exhausted but mentally recharged, Harmony opened her eyes to see Kami and Victoria praying nearby. Her classmates, along with two older women in white, were praising and worshipping God, and they were crying, too.

At that moment, nothing mattered…nothing but Jesus.

Sunday afternoon, Kami called Pace, speaking so fast that Pace had to slow her down to understand what she was saying and brace himself for more bad news. "What's wrong?"

"Just listen."

The background noise grew louder. Pace recognized the voices of heavenly worship. There was high praise wherever his sisters were. "Okay. So what's going on?"

"That's Harmony. Can you believe she repented and was baptized in Jesus' name this morning, and the Lord spoke to her in heavenly tongues?"

His spirit quickened as if God's finger touched him like lightning. Tears fell down his cheeks as his arms lifted to the Lord in praise that Harmony had been rescued from hell. Now, he understood his sister's excitement, and they began to worship God together until the Holy Ghost released them.

When a new soul repented, it was one less casualty and win for Satan. "Whew. That is good news, sis. Good news." He briefly wondered if sending his daily Scriptures had helped.

I am God. I died on the cross for her sins and yours. You work in My Vineyard, God thundered.

And Pace repented as he tried to take any credit for Harmony's salvation. "Lord, I just thank You for saving her."

"Me, too, bro," Kami said as if Pace was speaking to her, "and there's more. Some of my friends who rode with us to Dallas last week attended church with Victoria and me this morning. They also surrendered to Jesus because the accident shook them up. Wade, Fred, and Justina said there was no way they should be alive when they looked at the cars."

God was busy. Pace shook his head in awe. "The devil meant to take you all out in that accident, but the Lord said no. And Harmony just showed up at church on her own?"

"Yep."

Pace grinned. "So, what does this mean for your friendship with Harmony?"

"Well, I'll let you talk to Victoria," Kami said.

"Hey, big brother." Victoria sounded upbeat.

"Hey, sis." Pace grinned whenever Victoria addressed him as big brother. Headstrong, Kami refused to use the endearment growing up because they were so close in age.

"I think I'm ready to confide in Harmony. Kami and I miss our closeness."

"I'm sure she'll understand your hesitation once you explain everything," Pace encouraged her.

"Yeah." Victoria sounded unsure. "At least, now that she has the Holy Ghost, she has the ability to forgive me."

"Amen." Pace was filled with happiness but knew he had to tread lightly when bringing up the topic of a relationship with her, and it had nothing to do with graduation stress. He had to remove his intentions so God could shape her for His purpose.

One thing was for sure, Pace would have to stay on the sidelines until God gave him the precede signal.

Chapter Seventeen

Harmony was happy. Her family attributed her newfound joy to their trip to New Orleans.

When she tried to explain her salvation through the Pentecost experience, she couldn't do it justice.

Since Sunday, she had woken early to pray. Harmony wanted to feel God's presence again and hear Him speak to her. She felt important, handpicked out of the billions of people in the world for Jesus to save.

Many are called, but few are chosen because I am not their priority. Make me your priority, God whispered. *Read Matthew the twenty-second chapter*.

"Lord, thank You for calling me," Harmony said in her prayer, scribbling the Scripture on a pad on her desk.

You accepted, the Lord whispered.

Harmony couldn't wait to return home from class or work in the evenings. She craved time with the Lord in prayer or Bible reading. The stress and worry that had oppressed her were gone. Knowing God had an eye on her gave her peace.

After their graphic design class, she and Wade chatted about the awesomeness of their experience with the Lord, and they couldn't wait to return to Redemption Church on Sunday.

Now, she understood Kami and Victoria's commitment to God. Midweek, Harmony sat at her usual table in the dining hall, eating and looking out the window over the campus courtyard. Although it was a rainy spring day, she searched the sky for the seven colors of the rainbow God created, which she learned was different from what the LBGTQ community used.

Harmony noticed two reflections in the window and looked over her shoulder to see the Jamieson sisters. The loss she felt as they distanced themselves from her over the holiday was gone. They and she had moved on. Harmony had peace. There were no worries too big for God to handle.

"Hey."

Victoria slid into a chair across from her, and Kami took one from a nearby table and dragged it to Harmony's. They both smiled at her, and Harmony smiled back.

"I'm glad you surrendered to Jesus," Victoria said.

"Me too." Harmony was on a spiritual high. She was ready to go to heaven. "The peace I have is amazing."

"We know," the sisters said almost in unison, then Victoria's expression turned somber. "Ah, do you mind if we talk? You asked me a question over the Christmas break, and I wasn't willing to answer until now."

Harmony rested her hand over Victoria's. "It's okay. You owe me nothing. Our slates are wiped clean." She smiled to show Victoria that she had no hurt feelings. She had been set free from the torment of their broken friendship.

Tears filled Victoria's eyes. "Harmony, please. Can we talk? But not here." She looked tortured, and Harmony ached for her old friend.

She reached across the table and hugged Victoria. "Sis, we are talking. We're cool. Really." Harmony glanced at her watch. "I've got to get to the studio."

"We know when you get off, so we'll be at your place at eight-thirty. We'll bring pizza," Kami said, determined to talk.

Harmony laughed. Her friends hadn't changed. Kami was the take-charge sister and was still as bossy as ever. "Okay. See you two later."

Outside, she opened her umbrella and hurried to the school shuttle to take her to the studio. She exhaled, thinking about what took place. *Lord, I never thought I could forgive so easily, but I don't want to rehash anything with them again.* She had a mind to take her time to get home, but that would be petty.

God didn't do petty.

At the studio, Harmony refused to let frustration overwhelm her on this project. Since when did dolphin blue look soft gray? She entered color code after code until it matched the specifications for the project.

Harmony arrived at her apartment later than expected, and Kami and Victoria were camped out on the floor in front of her door, heads together. Kami dozed while Victoria's beautiful face looked tortured, staring at nothing. A massive white paper-wrapped bouquet in a vase was anchored between them, along with a large pizza box.

A peace offering? These two were going to the extreme. She studied her friends. At another time, the two would have used their key to let themselves in. Harmony had a swipe key to their place, too.

She called their names softly until they stirred. "Sorry, I'm late." Harmony was too exhausted for company but had enough energy to pray. But she agreed to hear Victoria.

Kami woke and stretched. Victoria snapped out of her trance-like state. They scrambled to their feet, then the three exchanged hugs like old times.

"You're here now." Victoria sighed in relief. "We weren't going back to our place without getting this talk out of the way," Victoria said.

"What's with the flowers?" Harmony pointed.

Kami and Victoria shrugged.

"They were here when we arrived," Kami said.

Harmony opened her door and attempted to scoop up the vase, but it was too heavy, so Kami helped her bring it inside and set it on her counter in the kitchenette. She didn't want to rush them, but everything between them was fine.

Victoria began to pace the floor, twisting her fingers. Harmony sat on her bed and watched her. Kami's expression gave nothing away.

"Okay, you two, what's up?" Harmony's friends were so dramatic.

Victoria stopped, exhaled, and said, "Kami and I are half-sisters."

"W-What?" Harmony's jaw dropped.

She squinted between the two and didn't believe it. Pace had mentioned his father adopted him after his mother had died. Now, what was their story?

"We both were in foster care," Victoria continued, watching Harmony's reaction. "Kami and I have the same mother. Parke adopted her when she was four. I wasn't adopted until I was sixteen."

Now, Harmony's heart ached for two sisters who had been separated for so long. She stood and hugged Victoria.

"I was molested while I was in the system," Victoria mumbled.

Harmony stepped back and stared at her friend. The sad truth rested in Victoria's eyes. "What! Oh no." Shocked at the revelation, Harmony sobbed. "I'm so sorry you had to go through this."

"Me too." Kami's nostrils flared.

"It happened more than once with two families. I was done being a victim. I used hate to fight back. I was labeled as a problem child and hard to place. I didn't care." She huffed. "While in the system, I attended a school where I was bullied. Kami was going to that school, too, and people kept saying we looked alike."

"And we do," Kami said proudly. "When I learned what she had gone through, I asked my mom and dad—"

"Now, is Parke your birth dad?" Harmony asked.

"No, but he's the only dad I know," Kami said. "Anyway, I asked my dad to adopt Victoria once I told my parents about her, and with no questions asked, they started the process."

"To answer the question you asked about why I live with Grandma BB, it's because although they adopted me, because of my trauma, I didn't want to live in the same house where there were boys or men. Grandma BB offered me a safe haven in her home, so Kami moved in with me. No one else knows this, and when you asked, I wasn't ready to relive the ugliest part of my past. I've been in counseling since I came back to campus."

Emotions unchecked, Harmony cried on her shoulder. "Victoria, I'm so sorry I put pressure on you. I didn't know what to think. I just knew something wasn't right. Please forgive me."

"Forgive us," Kami said as they continued to cling to each other, "for shutting you out, but it was Victoria's decision to tell you."

The thought of what her friend endured sickened Harmony. She didn't want to imagine the abuse any girl or boy would suffer from adults who were supposed to take care of them.

"When Pastor Giles preached casting our cares on Jesus, I was set free," Victoria said. "Kami and I have missed you. Can we be friends again?"

"You don't have to ask." Harmony wiped the tears from her eyes and sniffed. "I want to pray for you—and us."

Victoria grinned. Kami nodded, and they held hands and bowed their heads. The trio's prayers transitioned into worship, and the Holy Ghost filled the room, and they began to speak in heavenly tongues.

Soon, their voices softened, and the atmosphere around them stilled. Harmony grinned. "I never thought I would say this, but I like to pray."

Victoria and Harmony cheered. "I'm glad you came home with us and your innocent question forced me to go to God again. Thank you," Victoria said.

"All that praying has made me hungry," Kami said. "The pizza is probably cold."

When they turned toward the microwave, the flowers on the counter became the center of attention.

"You don't know who they're from?" Kami pointed.

"Nope." Harmony began to rip off the paper around the glass vase as Kami and Victoria looked over her shoulder.

Released from confinement, the flowers sprang forth like a peacock's tail. "They're beautiful." Harmony reached for the envelope and pulled out the card. *Congratulations on your new walk with Christ. Pace*

"*Awww.* Our brother sent those?" Victoria said. "Wow. Pace likes you."

"So catch us up." Kami grinned, tore off a couple of slices of hamburger pizza, and opened her cabinet for a plate. She popped it in the microwave and spun around. "What's going on with you two?"

Her friends were back. The buzzer went off, then it was Victoria's turn to reheat her slices while Harmony watched. "Absolutely nothing. Nosey as ever," she teased and changed the subject before reminding them they had exams to study for. "And I have a presentation in the morning."

When they left, Harmony closed her eyes and leaned against the door. "Lord, forgive me for judging my friends."

Harmony called Pace early the next morning and thanked him for the flowers, and he was excited for her salvation report.

"If you have time, I would love to hear every detail."

Giddy, Harmony made time, and when she finished, they had been on the phone for an hour. They even prayed together, and Pace shared Bible passages with her.

"Will you still text me morning meditations or Scriptures?" Harmony asked as she admired her Bible.

"Do you want me to?"

"Yes! Please."

His chuckle was deep, and Harmony imagined the smile accompanying it. "You got it," he said quietly. "My sisters told me they were going to talk to you."

"They did." Dropping her shoulders, Harmony squeezed her lips in shame. "I'm so sorry for believing the worst about them. It was torture not knowing if I had done something wrong. That was hard."

"I know. I could feel your pain and their sorrow whenever we spoke. I've been praying for you and my sisters. This was the first time since Victoria became a Jamieson where she had to decide whether she wanted to disclose her past. I'm glad she opened up to you."

Harmony couldn't get the word *molested* and Victoria out of her head. She knew it happened to young boys and girls, but she'd never had the face of a victim—until now. The thought was making her sick and trying to suck out all the joy God had given her. "I see why Kami fiercely protects Victoria, and I will be, too, from now on."

"You already were. I'm sorry I couldn't say more, but it wasn't my story."

"If I can be honest, it was killing me inside to lose their friendship," she said and blinked back tears at the memories of her weight loss that her mom had mentioned, but Harmony hadn't noticed, some restless nights, and lack of focus as if she had lost a best friend, which she had. Those thoughts she kept to herself because it seemed foolish to be that attached to a friendship.

"I'm sorry, Harmony. I hope you never have to experience that again. Have you heard the song, *What A Friend We Have in Jesus*?"

"I'm not sure." She couldn't remember if she'd heard it as a child in the church she attended with her parents.

"Pull it up online. It's an old song, but one line is on point." He began to sing, "*O what peace we often forfeit, o what needless pain we bear, all because we do not carry everything to God in prayer...*"

Closing her eyes, Harmony admired his singing voice. She hummed along until he finished, then exhaled. "I love that song now."

"I thought you might."

"Well, I'd better go. I got a presentation today that I want to review one more time. Guess I'll see you in a few weeks at the graduation."

"I pray God shows you favor on your presentation. I'm looking forward to seeing you again."

After their goodbyes from that day forward, Harmony never felt alone, whether in the dining hall or on campus. Besides Kami and Victoria, it was like an impromptu church meeting whenever Harmony was around Wade, Fred, Justina, and other new converts.

Go #TeamJesus.

Pace was amused as he packed for his trip to see Kami, Victoria, and Harmony's college graduation. They both had beaten him to receive their degrees, even though he was the oldest child.

A mix of nervousness heightened his excitement. This would be the first time Pace would see Harmony since the Lord filled her with His Spirit.

Their last face-to-face meeting hadn't ended well. Things had changed with her salvation and her talk with his sisters, but did things change between them, too? He would find out on graduation day.

For the past three weeks, Harmony hadn't given him a morsel of encouragement about a relationship. He continued to send the morning meditations or Scriptures, and she would respond with thank you or ones she'd found.

They rarely talked on the phone. Pace reasoned that they were both busy with their studies.

JC called to say he planned to go to Oklahoma for the Jamieson sisters' graduation, too, even though he was busy with final tasks for his own undergraduate degree. God had been right all along. If someone was interested in his sister, Pace couldn't go wrong with his best friend.

"What's up, man?"

"Busy getting ready to walk across the stage. My mom is so happy she can't stop crying." JC chuckled.

"I think my parents are just as sentimental. You sure you don't want to ride with us? Mom and Dad rented a fifteen-seat passenger van. Uncle Malcolm and Cameron and their families will be on board. Uncle Kidd is coming, too, with his family, so that leaves two open seats."

"Nah, I'd rather drive so I can head back sooner to take care of last-minute things."

Pace rubbed his hair. "With all this excitement, you all are making me wish I was graduating now."

"Bro, you're doing it right being in a dual-degree program. In August, you will have an undergraduate and master's degree."

"Thanks, man, for reminding me." They chatted about when they would leave, prayed for each other's safe travels, and ended the call.

The next morning, the Jamieson travel bus, as his father dubbed it, was on the road toward Oklahoma. Pace and his dad were the designated drivers. Chip and Dale trailed behind them, chauffeuring Grandma BB in her Cadillac sedan. It was decked out with new graduate signs and balloons as if she was joining a local parade instead of a seven-hour road trip.

Even though only four families were represented in the van, it felt like a family game night. His younger brothers were happy to miss a day of school and were playing video games. The younger cousins filled the interior with chatter loud enough for outsiders to hear. His aunt constantly reminded the children to use their inside voices.

Once they exited I-44, the route was picturesque, with plush green hills his young cousins called mountains. As soon as Pace drove past Six Flags in Eureka, the children wanted to stop and go play.

Family. Pace couldn't get enough of them. Four hours later, halfway through the trip, they stopped for lunch, and his father took the wheel for the remaining three-and-a-half-hour drive.

The closer they got, the more Kami and Victoria called. This time, it was Victoria's ringtone. "What's your ETA?" she asked through the speakerphone. "I think our app is broken because it doesn't look like you are moving."

Now in the front passenger seat, Cheney leaned over and looked at the navigation screen. She and their dad said simultaneously, "We're an hour and forty-five minutes out. Reboot your phone."

"How slow are you driving?" Kami demanded.

"Five miles over the speed limit," Parke said to their daughter. "Now, we will call you when we're within the city limits." He pushed End, and the sisters were gone.

Soon, they made it right on schedule. His father parked the van at the curb of the address of the Airbnb they had booked.

"Mom, Dad!"

Turning around, he saw his sisters...and Harmony. His heart bounced within his chest, then settled as he walked closer to them.

Harmony glowed, and Pace hoped her smile was for him. Pace hugged and kissed his sisters on autopilot, but appraised Harmony. From the curls in her hair to the gloss on her lips to the pink sundress that stopped at her knees. She was thinncr but it took nothing away from hcr bcauty and glow. His heart raced, waiting for Harmony's acknowledgment.

His blood pressure seemed to drop from her very platonic greeting.

"Hi, Pace. It's good to see you again."

"You have no idea how good it is to see you."

Pace was dismissed when his parents and family members, who had met her at the Christmas Eve dinner, vied for their turns to greet Harmony with 'Praise the Lord' and congratulated her on her newfound salvation.

The women chatted excitedly about the power of the Holy Ghost in their lives as the men gathered their luggage and headed to check out the home they rented for the weekend.

After everything was settled inside, Pace returned to find Harmony gone and JC parking his car. He had booked a hotel room near the campus since their Airbnb was packed with Jamiesons. "Where's Harmony?" Pace asked.

"Oh, her family's flight landed early, so she called a ride share to the airport to meet them," Victoria said.

Pace nodded, reminding himself that this was not about him. Patience.

Chapter Eighteen

Wow was Harmony's first thought as she watched Pace Jamieson approach her. His lips curved upward, touching the silky black hair of his mustache. He was one fine man! His jeans fit, and his tan shirt didn't disappoint in showcasing his muscles. Pace continued to be swoon-worthy.

Without knowing it, Pace had been Harmony's constant inspiration during the mental turmoil with his sisters and her new salvation walk with Christ.

Now, seeing him again after a few months made her nervous.

She had to answer the question of what he meant to her. She had overnight to find out.

For sentimental reasons, Harmony's family wanted to see her apartment, tour the campus for the last time, and visit the graphic studio where she had interned.

They had insisted they wanted to do this before checking into the hotel and having a celebration dinner.

"I was hoping to meet your friends' family," Lorna Reed said at dinner. She was at peace since Harmony had reconciled her friendship with Kami and Victoria.

All her mother knew was that something bad had happened to Victoria as a child that had nothing to do with the Jamiesons and she hadn't been ready to disclose it.

Harmony was sure her mother read between the lines and never mentioned it again.

Toasts went around the table, saluting Harmony's accomplishments and three-point-seven GPA. "So, have you started applying for jobs?" Kimbrell asked. As a television producer, he offered to put a word in for her at the station.

"She has all summer to recharge," her mother said.

Everyone had an opinion on Harmony's career path. "I plan to enjoy the first few weeks at home, then start applying to some companies I've been eyeing."

"Well, I've seen your portfolio, so you shouldn't have any problems, but," her father paused. "People don't get hired on the spot these days. You can still enjoy your summer while applying."

Harmony wasn't ready for adult logic, but if anything, she could prove them wrong, and a job offer would delight her.

The night ended early without Harmony seeing any more of the Jamiesons.

The next day, the graduates lined up for the ceremony at the Hamilton Field House based on their majors. "This is it," she mumbled.

"Yes," Wade Post said. He had secured a paid summer internship in creating illustration specs for a company back home in Nashville with a verbal promise of an entry-level position after six months.

Lord, I know You have something for me, Harmony prayed, fighting back the envious spirit that Satan was taunting her with against her brother in Christ.

The band began the chords of "Pomp and Circumstance," cuing the grand marshal, banner marshals, faculty marshals, and general faculty to start the procession, leading Harmony and fourteen hundred fellow graduates down the pathway to their designated seats.

The moment was exhilarating.

Surreal.

Scary because she would officially be an unemployed college graduate until an opportunity came her way.

Harmony was the last sibling to earn her degree, and she dreamed of becoming successful like her older brothers. As fear tried to creep in at the realization, faith shut it out. She had God on her side, and He was navigating her future.

College President Todd Hill stood at the podium in his formal graduation attire, a black robe with matching tam and a yellow tassel like all the graduates. He congratulated them in his opening message. "Perseverance has gotten you to this day. You fought for it, studied, and learned about life's challenges. You're leaving here today with more than book knowledge, but wisdom…"

Next, he thanked the parents, family, and friends for supporting the students. "Rest assured, OCU has successfully equipped these graduates to achieve their life's goals. What would college life be without learning life's lessons?" He looked out into the crowd. "They were educated on that, too."

She totally agreed with that statement. Harmony nodded to herself, then her mind drifted, imagining God looking down on her. Harmony glanced up at the sky—no clouds. The Lord had a clear view of where she sat and set the perfect temperature for the sun to shine. The gentle breeze reminded her of His presence.

Next, she scanned the stadium seating for her family and squinted. Her phone buzzed a text.

Pace.

I'm looking right at you. I'm going to cheer the loudest.

Harmony bowed her head to hide her blush.

President Hill introduced guests on the platform before welcoming the speaker. "Alumni Adam Podner is no stranger to those on social media. His startup company seems to be the talk everywhere." The two shook hands. Adam took the podium and cleared his throat.

"This is it, graduates!" he shouted and was met with cheers. "I am a success story by accident. My education as a liberal arts major at OCU prepared me for a world that was light-years behind my thinking. I didn't seem to fit in their box. So, even after I graduated, I had to study the market trends and get a pulse on what others wanted…"

His message resonated with Harmony. She would have to create her path.

"Don't be ashamed of making mistakes and taking every opportunity to advance your career. Nothing is too small or unimportant for your success."

Harmony felt pumped that she could navigate her future with God helping to direct her.

"In conclusion," Adam said, "this day is the beginning of the rest of your life. Celebrate it, remember your struggles and triumphs here, then take them with you through life to become your best. Thank you."

"Now," President Hill said after patting Adam on the back, "what you came for, the token of your achievement." He called each school of study. Soon, it was time for the business school candidates to stand. Kami was all smiles as she strutted in her heels to the stage to the roar and whistles of her family.

Harmony chuckled. The Reeds were loud, too, but not as long-winded as the Jamiesons. She and Victoria, along with classmates in the School of Liberal Arts Program, were called and stood.

The cheers Victoria received were louder and longer. She waved at them. Knowing what her friend had endured made this moment bittersweet and the accolades more meaningful. Victoria was a survivor, and she would conquer the world. Harmony's heart beat faster as she walked out into the aisle, seconds away from getting her degree.

The noise was deafening, coming from opposite directions. She spied the Jamiesons, and the Reeds were on the other side. Harmony couldn't believe how the Jamiesons were cheering her on, but knowing what she had learned about them, Harmony felt part of the family.

She was.

Chapter Nineteen

Finally! Pace thought as the graduates moved their tassels from right to left, signifying the completion of their studies, followed by the hat toss.

He hoped Harmony would feel freedom to explore a relationship with Pace during the summer, although he would still be in school. *When a man knows what he wants, multi-tasking seems easy*, he mused.

Family and friends dispersed from the stands in search of their loved ones. Pace had already tracked Harmony's movements. He started his approach, maneuvering through the chaos of the crowd with a bouquet in his hand.

He spotted a huddle of graduates in the distance. Kami pulled Victoria into the group, and she tugged Harmony with her.

As the Reed and Jamieson families stepped closer, they could hear the group singing praises to the Lord.

The sound was sweet to Pace's spirit. He was thankful that Harmony and four others had surrendered to Christ. Now, Pace waited for his turn to vie for their attention.

"Congratulations!" the Jamiesons said in unison as they greeted his sisters.

Pace hugged and kissed Kami and Victoria, then waited his turn to speak with Harmony. "For you." He handed her a dozen yellow roses because the color reminded him of how she seemed to glow the first time he met her.

Then, unexpectedly, Harmony left her family gathering and hugged him like it was normal. The shock wore off quickly, and he responded by trapping her in his arms to savor the moment.

She looked up at him with the sunlight brightening her brown eyes, and he squeezed her tighter. "Thank you for every morning text you sent me with Scripture and motivational thoughts. It kept me going many times."

"You're welcome," he whispered as his lips inched closer to hers. To his surprise, she met him halfway so their lips could touch. The kiss was soft, brief, and tingling. Pace found his voice to say, "Congratulations."

"Well, well…you two are an adorable couple," Mrs. Reed said, beaming then directing them to pose.

Kami and Victoria raced up to them. "When did all this happen?" Kami wanted to know.

Pace looked at Harmony and snickered. "I guess God was working undercover on our behalf."

JC was all smiles. "I see you, man. Happy for you, bro."

The Reed and Jamieson parents introduced themselves while Harmony's brothers folded their arms. They did not look happy.

"I want to know, too. When did all this develop?" Shane asked.

Get over it, Pace thought. *If I had to step aside for my sisters, then you better get in line*. He extended his hand to Shane, who seemed hesitant but accepted it. "Nice to see you again," Pace said.

"Nice if I got an answer because I know nothing about this."

The crowd parted with horn toots and a flag flapping in the wind. Grandma BB was dressed in her finest—a red dress and purple hat. She wore two-tone red-and-black Stacy Adams shoes. Bodyguards Chip and Dale were at her sides.

The pair wore red T-shirts that stretched across their pec muscles, black pants, and black sunglasses.

Security was stamped boldly on their chest.

They garnished as many stares as Grandma BB. Pace and his family masked their amusement at their eccentric matriarch's appearance and let her have her way—like she always did.

His sisters and Harmony raced to give Grandma BB hugs. She soaked up the attention, then pulled out envelopes and handed them out. "You all have the same amount." She looked at Harmony. "You'll be my honorary great-god-granddaughter for life."

Pace held his humor and his patience to steal Harmony away for sixty seconds for himself. How could Grandma BB bestow a title on someone and get it wrong? Harmony sniffed and gave her another hug before waving her family over to meet the Jamieson matriarch.

Victoria slipped away, and Pace saw her and JC taking selfies. He was a special man who could cause his baby sister to push aside her reservations about men outside her family and open up. Pace smiled, suspecting her recent counseling session helped her with that relationship, too.

Slipping his hands into his pockets, Pace continued to bid his time as Harmony posed for pictures with her family and friends. When Harmony made eye contact with him, he smiled, and that was enough for her to come to him.

"So, Miss Graduate, I know someone who is interested in getting to know you."

Harmony tilted her head and gave him a curious stare. "You do?"

"Yep." Pace nodded. "He's college-educated too. Comes from a big family, is a practicing Christian, and respects women. Any idea who that could be?" He lifted a teasing eyebrow.

She playfully scrunched her nose at him. "Sounds like Pace Jamieson."

"I'm glad you think so." He took the liberty to slide his arm around her waist and pull her closer in a hug. "Harmony, I've missed seeing you and hearing your harmonious voice. Now that you've checked off one must-have degree on your bucket list, can you add me to your summer must-do-and-see list?"

"I think I can pencil you in." She giggled, then frowned. "But you're still in school."

"True." Pace nodded. "Only for three more months. I know how to multi-task." He slipped his fingers through hers. *Finally, progress.*

He squeezed.

She smiled.

And it was on!

It had to be fate that the Jamiesons invited the Reed family to their celebration dinner for Kami and Victoria.

"I'm sure you've planned something special for Harmony, but we would like for you to join us, even for a little while," Cheney said to Harmony's mother, who looked at her husband.

Mr. Reed shrugged, conveying it was his wife's call.

"Why not? It will give the girls more time together, and we can celebrate all of them."

The three new graduates seemed pleased. Not as much as Pace. They trailed the Jamiesons to the banquet hall his family had rented, which had seating for up to thirty-five people, so there was room to add the six-member Reed family.

While dinner was being served, mini-conversations filled the room. Listening to Harmony, Pace kept his eyes on Kami. Accustomed to being the center of attention, he wondered how she felt about Pace dominating Harmony's attention and JC being attentive to Victoria.

What man would be brave enough to win her affections? He grunted to himself. Not his problem anymore. Besides, she seemed fine as the younger cousins, uncles, and aunties doted on her.

His uncle, Pastor Philip, gave thanks for the food and the occasion.

"I hope it doesn't take me long to get a job. My advisor helped me with my cover letter and résumé," Harmony said.

Pace didn't like her worry lines. "Your talent will open doors. I'm sure your portfolio is impressive."

Harmony blushed. "I think so. At least you don't have to find a job."

He rested his hand on top of hers on the table under suspecting eyes. "True. Not in St. Louis, but I like you and Chi-town, so I've decided to apply for positions in Chicago."

Even though chatter filled the room, forks clanged on China and heads turned. Harmony looked at him with wide eyes and her jaw slacked.

"You are?" Kami was the first to question his decision, followed by his mother.

Parke and the uncles didn't seem fazed. They knew he was attracted to Harmony and planned to go after what he wanted.

Harmony leaned closer and whispered, "When did you decide this?"

"I thought about it when I visited you in January. Recently, I've been praying about it, and today…" *When you looked into my eyes…* He cleared his throat. "It just makes sense."

Kami scratched her head. "You already have a job. Applying for something else doesn't make sense." His sister was so clueless when it came to matters of the heart. *Thank You, Jesus!*

That's because you haven't fallen for someone yet, baby sister. Pace held his tongue. He didn't want to rub it in if she was longing for companionship, but he definitely planned to find out.

"I'll still be close to home," Pace assured his mother.

Chicago was five hours by car and forty-five minutes by air. The cost of living was higher, but salaries were competitive, and the Black historical sites would make him a lifelong tourist.

This would be the best summer ever. Pace could feel it. *Come on, August*. He was ready to move.

Two weeks later, it was JC's turn to procession in with the Wash U band playing "Pomp and Circumstance." On his graduation day, his reconnected family from Chicago made their presence known when JC's name was announced.

His friends, church members, and every local Jamieson family showed up, but JC's mother, Diane, and ten-year-old brother, Henry, short for Hennessey, beamed with pride by his accomplishment.

Pace didn't know who cheered the loudest, JC's mother or Victoria, until Grandma BB yelled through a small megaphone, "That's my kinfolks—a nephew down the line."

With Victoria back at home and loosening her defenses around JC, it was about to become an interesting summer indeed for the Jamieson family.

Chapter Twenty

Unemployed. This wasn't how Harmony imagined her life after graduation, especially after her dad told her to start right away.

"I need a job." Harmony glanced out the kitchen window of her childhood home. Working freelance on one project that her oldest brother, Laurence Jr., helped secure through a friend of a friend didn't count.

Kimbrell had been unsuccessful at the television station for something but would keep her in mind. She felt helpless, like a child again, dependent upon family to supply finances for what she couldn't. After three weeks of celebrating adulthood, she had to find a job—a permanent one.

Her mother walked into the kitchen. "Good morning, honey. Thanks for making coffee. You're up early. It's good to have you home." She rested her head on Harmony's shoulder like Harmony used to do to her as a child.

However, the comforting embrace left her sad. "Yeah, I'm back home with a degree but no job. I don't want to take any position. I want to use my skills to build my career." She sighed.

Harmony thought her life would be set with a degree.

She thought being back home would make her happy.

She thought since surrendering her life to the Lord, God would make everything alright in her world.

Where is your faith in Me? the Lord whispered.

Lorna poured her a cup of coffee, took a sip, then turned around and faced Harmony. "Do you have any interviews?"

"I wish." Harmony groaned. "When I moved back home, I thought it was cool to sleep late, not have to study for an exam or run up my tab eating in the dining hall."

Her mother had no rebuttal, only a weak smile.

"How long do you think it will take me to get a job?" Harmony couldn't help but compare herself to Wade Post, who had an incredible opportunity. Even Pace had a job offer but was willing to turn it down to move to Chicago. Unbelievable…and unfair.

"You're praying, right?" her mother asked.

Harmony blinked and straightened her body. If she was going to be an example to her family that the Holy Ghost had changed her, she had to trust God in all aspects of her life. "I am."

"Good. Me too."

Seek first My kingdom, and all things will be added to you, God whispered. Read Matthew, the sixth chapter in your Bible.

I will, Jesus. Harmony needed that boost. She hugged her mother tight, then walked out of the kitchen as she heard another whisper from the Lord.

Take therefore no thought for tomorrow: for tomorrow shall take thought for the things of itself, God whispered. *Continue to read My Word, which is to help Your growth.*

In her bedroom, Harmony pulled out her laptop and Bible to locate the Scriptures connected to what God said. After 1 Corinthians 15:19, then she turned to Matthew. After reading several chapters, she closed her Bible and prayed. *Lord, I thank You. I know You will supply me with everything I need. Help me to trust You more and more, in Jesus' name. Amen.*

Taking a deep breath, she opened her laptop and got to work, looking for jobs for recent graduates. She refused to let "experience" in the job description instill fear in her where faith should reside. The more she searched, the more she battled discouragement. "There has to be something that's entry-level for graduates."

A small win was one company paid her minimum wage to proof and process graphic files in the final stages of production. She shrugged. It was not very challenging, but it was a start in the industry.

That afternoon, Victoria called her. "I've got good news."

Harmony grinned. "Okay. I can use some."

"You know I decided to enroll in nursing school. Maybe one day, my history, fashion design, and nursing degrees will come together. I'm still trying to figure out my purpose in life."

"You will." Harmony now understood how the brilliant twenty-year-old with a high IQ could whiz through college with two majors. Victoria was a genius. Now, her friend was restless, eyeing a third degree. "You got accepted on a full ride, I'm sure. So what else do you have to tell me?"

"Well, I'm going to stay in St. Louis and attend Wash U because my family is here."

That made sense but there had to be more, and Victoria was drawing it out. "You have a great family."

"And JC decided to attend Wash U's law school. He wasn't at first, but I think I inspired him." She sounded triumphant. "And he got a full ride, too."

Harmony snickered. "Interesting. I'm seeing a whole new Victoria. I'm used to you ready to claw any guy who showed interest… Now, I understand your disdain. I'm so glad God is helping you."

"Me too. JC is different. I've been watching how he treats Kami—the third wheel—when he's around me. He's kind and caring and makes me feel safe like my brothers and dad. Before I was adopted, I didn't think that was possible."

"I'm glad JC is a winner."

Victoria chuckled. "Yep. That's probably why he and Pace are best friends. He's like family to the Jamiesons, and we learned that he is a distant relative of Grandma BB. Who knew? But I have to feel safe, or I'll come out swinging." She made a growling sound.

Harmony shivered. She couldn't imagine the horror her friend endured by people who supposedly had her best interest.

"Okay. Enough about me. Pace is working and studying hard, so he'll relocate to Chicago after he graduates," Victoria said.

"Yeah." Harmony shook her head. "I still can't believe that. But I'm looking forward to him driving up this weekend. I have a picnic planned for us in Washington Park." She giggled.

"*Hmmm*. I guess that's love," Victoria teased and giggled too.

"Whoa. I don't want to move too fast and regret it later. It's just a weekend visit, not a Vegas wedding. When he told me he was applying to companies in Chicago, I was shocked."

"Me too." Victoria laughed. "But not the aunties in my family."

Harmony spied the time and looked at her progress on job hunting. "Well, I'd better go. I'm giving myself a daily goal of applying for five positions that really interest me, plus something part-time for now."

"Okay, sis. I'm praying for you and my sister to land something soon."

"I'll take all the prayers I can get. Most good companies want candidates with at least five years of work experience. They outnumber those that say no experience was necessary."

When they ended the call, Harmony prayed, *I'll take anything, Lord. Anything.*

Pace left for Chicago on Friday afternoon. He would arrive there before dark, rest, and be ready for a full day of whatever Harmony had planned for them. He expected this to be the first of many trips to Chicago to see Harmony until he moved there permanently.

He was entering Joliet, Illinois, when Harmony's ringtone made him smile. "Hello."

"Hi. How close are you?"

When he told her, Harmony became excited. "So you're less than an hour away. Factor in traffic to my house, and I should see you in an hour and a half."

Pace couldn't wait to see her, but he wanted to be fresh and rested. "I thought we were doing something tomorrow."

"We are, but I miss you, so I'll wait in the hotel lobby to get a hug, then I'll go home."

The laugh that ignited in the pit of his stomach tumbled out. "Okay. See you soon."

Harmony's calculations were on point when he parked at the Holiday Inn. He gathered his overnight bag and a bouquet he'd picked up at a gas station store. Pace walked in, and Harmony stood and opened her arms. He made a beeline to her instead of the clerk at the desk who greeted him.

Pace buried his head into her hair and relaxed. They said nothing as he was content to hold her. Although he was in no rush to release her, they were standing in the lobby, so he loosened his hold and presented his flowers.

Her eyes were bright. "Thank you." She sniffed and exhaled. "I got what I came for, and I'm thankful that God brought you here safely. "See you tomorrow."

When she tried to sidestep, he looped his arm around her waist. "Oh, no, you don't. You got your hug. I want a kiss."

They glanced around the lobby. Besides a couple walking out of the elevator and the clerk at the desk, they didn't have an audience, so he wiggled a brow in a challenge.

Harmony stood on her toes, pressed her soft lips against his, then ran toward the entrance. "See you tomorrow," she yelled over her shoulder and giggled.

At the counter, the woman blushed. "Your girlfriend is pretty."

Pace accepted the compliment. "Thank you."

"Morning, baby," Lorna said to her daughter. "You're singing, smiling, and look the happiest I've seen you all week. I guess this has something to do with Pace being in town." She chuckled.

"Yes, and I'm preparing a picnic basket, so we can spend the day at Washington Park in the Hyde Park neighborhood."

"That will be nice," her mother said as the doorbell rang.

Pace. Harmony liked a man who was never late. His baritone voice sent shivers over her shoulder as he chatted with her mother and appeared in the kitchen doorway. A coral polo shirt and tan shorts showed off his physique. She was tempted to change out of her denim shirt and shorts and raid her closet for something to match him.

"Good morning, beautiful." His eyes sparkled as if he was admiring diamonds.

"Morning." She smiled and lifted the basket. "Ready for a picnic."

"Yep." Pace took a couple of strides and lifted the basket with little effort.

"Bye, Mama." She scooped up the throw blanket.

"Bye, Mrs. Reed." Linking his fingers through hers, they left her house for a day filled with pure bliss.

"I can drive since I know where we're going. It's not far from the museum."

Pace opened her door. "I'm moving here, remember?" He grinned. "I might as well learn my way."

He stored the basket in the backseat, then slid behind the wheel and entered the park name, which came up as Washington (Harold) Park. Harmony verified that it was the one, and they were on their way.

While en route, they chatted about school, work, and family. The park overlooked Lake Michigan. In the distance, young children were engaged in a makeshift soccer game. A few young girls played volleyball while others lounged around with their pets.

"This is nice," Pace said as she tugged him toward one of many trees for their brunch.

Pace laughed as Harmony pulled out fruit—grapes, plums, cherries—and an assortment of cheese cubes.

"I have mini sandwiches, chips—" The rest of what she had packed was lost as Pace guided her closer and swallowed up her words in a kiss.

A sweet kiss.

A long, passionate kiss that made her want to faint.

When he released her, Harmony blinked. "Wow, I guess you're not hungry."

"It can wait," he said as he kissed her again.

Pace's presence, his kisses, and their contentment made it the best day, and every minute spent with Pace was seared into her memory.

Pace and JC chatted the following weekend as they crossed the parking lot to their cars after Sunday morning service. After Pace ate dinner at his parents' house, he planned to study at the campus library.

His best friend was in high demand. Since Grandma BB learned JC was related to her, she insisted he check up on her, so JC planned to stop and visit her before going to his house. He shook his head as he pulled his car keys from his pocket. "I can't believe you're moving to Chi-Town. Wow." He bit his bottom lip, thinking. "It's not going to be the same here without you, man."

"But Harmony is there, and we had the best weekend, which started with a picnic and ended with her church service last Sunday. I'm sold on Chicago." Pace nodded.

"The move is just as much about my personal life as my professional."

"Got it. When I can get away, I'll drive up to visit and bring two beautiful ladies with me."

Pace chuckled. Without knowing it, JC had committed to the role of their bodyguard because men always tried to get his sisters' attention. Since Kami and Victoria had a strong resemblance, their mother must have been beautiful but found herself in a situation that caused her to lose custody of her daughters.

"I'm going to miss you. That's for sure. We're like brothers."

"Always." Pace waved at some of his family and church members but kept in step with his friend. "Yep. I don't see any other way for Harmony and me to build a relationship. School and distance were standing in our way. I'm eliminating all barriers. I started applying to corporations in Chicago the minute I came back from her graduation. One recruiter reached out to me and thought my skills were a good fit, but the company needed someone right away. I think the closer I get to graduation, I should get some offers. I have almost two years of experience and two degrees."

"Cool. I've never seen you this confident in a relationship."

"That's because there wasn't a Harmony Reed in my life before. I've prayed for a wife…"

"Whoa." JC stopped in his tracks and gave Pace a dumbfounded expression. "A wife? Are you that serious?"

"I'm serious about dating wife material." Pace nodded and grinned. "Otherwise, I wouldn't have stepped back when she said she wasn't interested. She reminds me of my sisters, and I love the two Jamieson troublemakers."

"Your sisters have been everything but that. I've enjoyed getting to know them." JC grinned.

They had almost reached their vehicles when Pace's phone rang. He grinned, showing JC the caller: Harmony. "Hey… What?"

Pace frowned and looked at JC as he tried to make out what Harmony was saying before heavenly tongues filled her mouth.

Alarmed, JC stayed by Pace's side, ready to act if Pace needed him.

"My mom got it! We visited an Apostolic church this morning because I didn't want to go alone, and Mom repented and was baptized in Jesus' name. God gave her His Holy Ghost!"

Pace's heart settled, and he smiled at JC. "Harmony's mom surrendered to the Lord today and received the gift of the Holy Ghost."

Harmony ended the call while speaking to the Lord in heavenly tongues, and Pace smiled.

JC lifted his hands in praise. "Praise the Lord. There is still hope for my mother."

"It never gets old when I hear or see people surrender to the Lord. Never." Pace patted him on his shoulder, and they crossed the aisle to their cars, silently praising God for delivering Mrs. Reed out of the devil's clutches. He texted Harmony. **I'll drive up next weekend, and we can celebrate.**

Minutes later, Harmony responded with an **Amen.**

Once he was behind the wheel of his SUV, he sent his family a group text: **Harmony's mom received the gift of the Holy Ghost today!**

The *Amen*s, *Praise the Lord*s, and *Hallelujah*s came in rapid fire. Pace drove off, wishing he was in Chicago right now so he could praise the Lord along with Harmony. To be honest, Pace would be in Chi-town every weekend if he didn't have to work and study.

He had to stay employed—albeit part-time—to have the substance to build a future with Harmony. Pace alternated between the weekends he visited her and the ones he stayed and worked.

Harmony Reed better get ready for him because Pace wouldn't leave any obstacles in his way when the time was right to make her his wife.

Chapter Twenty-one

Thoughts of Harmony pushed Pace to work harder. Yet, with less than a month before the summer term ended, his coursework mounted as he prepared for his finals. He rubbed his neck and stretched.

He needed to get to the gym. First, he needed to hear Harmony's voice, so he called. "Hey, I won't be able to come this weekend." This would be the second time since she'd graduated.

"*Awww*." She didn't hide her disappointment, and that made him smile, knowing that she missed him as much as he missed her and was just as excited about their budding relationship.

Pace imagined she was pouting, which was an invitation to smother her with kisses until she giggled. It was impossible not to smile at how adorable she was when she did that.

"I was looking forward to taking you on a tour of some historic homes, including the one of Ida B. Wells-Barnett."

"And I would have loved to see it with you. I love our exploration trips, but…" Pace didn't want to say he needed to focus on his studies until the end because she might consider herself a distraction and pull away, and he didn't want her to retreat. They had switched places because instead of sending her morning Scriptures like he did when she was in school, she now enjoyed being the first to send the Scriptures, so he let her. "Put that on our to-do list."

"I will."

He could hear her smile through her voice on the phone. "I'll try to get up there before the month ends, but the Jamiesons have our back-to-school family game night the last weekend of July."

"I want to come." Harmony's voice was filled with longing.

"You sure? It will be similar to what you saw last Christmas Eve at the dinner, except the families are more competitive. Trust me. They were tame for the holiday. Some of our Kansas City Robnetts will come to participate as if it's a baseball rivalry between the St. Louis Cardinals and the Kansas City Royals. I'll get you a Team Parke T-shirt and send you a plane ticket." This made his day.

"I can drive or—"

"You will not," Pace said more forcibly than he wanted. They weren't officially a couple for him to have a say—he hoped that would change soon—nor was he her brother or father, so he softened his tone. "Harmony, please don't make me have to come get you and drive you back here." Pace would, and it would be madness on his end.

"Okay, but I can pay my way. I did invite myself."

Pace huffed. This woman right here… "There are so many reasons that isn't happening. I want us to be in a committed relationship despite the distance for now."

"I thought we were."

Her admission made Pace's heart leap. He exhaled slowly.

"I didn't want to assume your feelings had caught up with mine for us to be exclusive. That said, I can pay for my woman who I care about to visit me, and you didn't invite yourself. You expressed a desire, and I'm making it happen." He grinned. "Tell me your T-shirt size." Pace paused, tilting his head to recall how dainty she felt in his arms. "I would say a small."

"I'd say you're a smart one," she joked.

"Of course. You would never date a dumb man." They both chuckled. "Tell me when you want to come, and I'll get your ticket when I finish the call."

"Early. I can't wait to see you. Will you book me a hotel?"

Pace was slow in answering. "I can, if that is what you want, but I'm sure Grandma BB and my sisters would have something to say about that."

"I didn't want to assume." She giggled, teasing him with his own words. "I can't wait." Then for the first time, Harmony threw him kisses over the phone.

Her teasing emboldened him to could play along. "Save those for when you see me." He ended the call and booked her flight.

Minutes later, Kami called, screaming in his ear that Harmony was coming. "Whoa. I can't wait to take her—"

Word traveled fast between those three. "Hold it, sis. There will be no taking Harmony anywhere. She's my guest. Harmony will sleep at Grandma BB's house. Otherwise, her schedule is booked."

Kami *hmmmph*ed. "You forgot that she was my friend first."

Pace grunted. "Nope. I didn't forget that, and thank you for introducing us, but I've upped you. We're officially a couple now."

"I don't know what took you so long," she said, and suddenly, they were arguing like they had as children, each trying to get their way. Pace was seconds away from saying she should get her own boyfriend, but he didn't know if that would hurt her feelings since Victoria was getting closer to JC. "Okay. You win."

"I always do."

Pace squinted as if he could see her sticking out her tongue at him. "Only because I let you. She's coming on Friday evening. You've got two hours while she's here. That's it. Bye."

Pace grinned. His sister could never outsmart him. *Come on, Friday.*

Wednesday before her trip, Harmony stuffed her suitcase. Her mother entered her room and frowned at the clothes thrown across Harmony's bed. A conservative traveler, Lorna never overpacked.

"Honey, you're only going for three days." She folded her arms.

"Mom, I may want to change when I arrive on Friday evening."

"After a forty-five-minute flight?" Lorna rolled her eyes and shook her head. "And Saturday is game night, right? That's one outfit." She sat on the bed and examined the pile of clothes that didn't make the cut.

"Yes, and I'll need two for that day, plus an extra just because." In Harmony's mind, it made sense. Placing her hands on her hips, Harmony scanned her bedroom to make sure she wasn't leaving anything.

"You're coming back Sunday." Her mother counted on her hand.

"Mom, that's two. Church clothes, then a change of clothes for travel." She needed this trip. After weeks of applying for jobs, Harmony hadn't made any progress. If she got any response, it was a rejection email. At the moment, besides her walk with Christ, Pace was the only good thing happening to her.

All good things come from above from Me, God's voice thundered.

Harmony paused and repented as her mother left her bedroom. *Lord, I'm so sorry for complaining. I know Your timing is perfect. I prayed for a job, and I'm thankful for Pace, but can't I have the man and a job, too?*

When Shane dropped Harmony off at Midway Airport on Friday, he spied her luggage again. "Really? All this for a weekend?"

She jutted her chin. "Hair, makeup, and clothes. All the necessities."

He laughed and hugged her. "Have a safe trip. Tell Miss Kami I asked about her." Her brother had been infatuated with her since he'd met her at their college graduation.

"I doubt she would be interested."

"I'm a Reed man. Of course, she would be interested." He mimicked tipping a hat that he wasn't wearing.

Shane was the best-looking of her three brothers, and he knew it. If his brown eyes didn't get the ladies, his baritone voice or his physique did. He might be all that, but Kami would drain him mentally, making him work for her affections. Harmony had seen it firsthand. Once she rolled her luggage inside, the siblings waved, then Shane returned to the car and drove off.

After checking in, she cleared the security checkpoint. Harmony walked to her gate as if she didn't have a care in the world. She was literally leaving her cares behind. Once she boarded the plane and claimed a window seat, she stared outside. She hadn't been back to St. Louis since the Christmas break.

So much had happened since she'd first met Pace. There was some attraction between them, but Harmony tried not to entertain it, but Pace Jamieson wasn't one to ignore.

Less than an hour later, Harmony stepped off the plane. As she exited the terminal to the baggage claim, a group of Jamiesons awaited her. Everyone faded in the background as Pace stood out, then started toward her.

Pace held a sign that read *Home Where You Belong*. He grinned, then shrugged and nodded behind him where Victoria stood on one side holding welcome balloons. JC was beside her. Kami was on the other with a bouquet.

Grandma BB and her bodyguards held signs with her name on them.

She gushed as Pace's confident stride met her halfway. "Wow. What is all this?"

Pace brushed his lips against hers for a quick kiss. "You threw a lot of kisses, so I expect you to deliver."

Harmony had played with fire, judging by the intense stare in Pace's eyes. She exhaled to get her bearings.

"To answer your question, they wanted to come, so I put them to work to hold things."

Harmony laughed as Pace lifted her carry-on off her shoulder and linked their fingers—his touch was comforting. He guided her to the group where she squealed, hugged her friends, and then Grandma BB.

"Here are your flowers," Kami said, grinning.

"I'll see you back at the house," Grandma BB said, honking the horn on her scooter with her bodyguards at her side. They turned the opposite way to leave.

Pace stayed by Harmony's side as she, his sisters, and JC took the stairs to baggage claim.

Harmony's luggage couldn't be missed, she pointed it out. "It's black and white with Paris as the backdrop. I liked it because of the fashionably colorful dressed black woman that made it pop."

"That's so you." He kissed her quickly, then walked closer to the carousel. One touch and her lips felt numb. *Whew.* She exhaled as her friends snickered.

Once Pace retrieved her luggage, he returned to her side as she chatted with Kami and Victoria. JC stood nearby. Harmony leaned against Pace, missing his closeness, and he put his arm around her shoulders. It was a comforting gesture that made her feel loved, even though they were nowhere close to that emotion. They had just confirmed they were a couple.

Harmony didn't realize how much she'd missed Victoria and Kami as they talked about what had happened in their lives since their phone call last weekend.

"Ladies," Pace's deep voice sliced through their conversation, "you get to spend time with her later. This is my time, and we're on the clock." He squeezed her fingers.

She loved his polite possessiveness but what schedule? Frowning, Harmony looked at him. “We are?”

“Hey,” Kami protested. “You promised us two hours with Harmony.”

What was going on? Pace was on the clock, and his sisters got two hours. Whatever the reason, her being in high demand was comical and amusing. She liked it.

“And you get it tonight when I bring her back to Grandma BB’s because I’m sure you three aren’t going to sleep.”

Harmony wondered if she should have protested, too. After all, they were some of the first friends she’d met on campus, and they’d invited her to their home—or Grandma BB’s—when her flight got canceled. That was probably one of her best Christmases ever because she’d met Pace. She was fine with either company but preferred Pace.

Pace tugged her toward the garage exit, squeezing her hand gently. Harmony hugged them goodbye as they parted ways with JC and his sisters. At his vehicle, Pace opened the door and helped Harmony inside. Her mother would be as impressed with Pace’s chivalry as she was.

The drive to Grandma BB’s house was short as Harmony inhaled Pace’s cologne. She closed her eyes, content, until he came to a stop.

“Wait here, Harmony. I’ll drop off your luggage,” he said, parking his vehicle.

Minutes later, Harmony admired Pace’s swagger as he returned to his SUV. He slid behind the wheel. “If you’re hungry and delivery or takeout is okay, I’d rather relax.” Pace glanced in the rearview mirror before pulling off.

She liked his honesty. “I’m happy I’m here with you. Whatever you want to do is fine. You’ve been working and studying hard. I don’t want you to feel you have to entertain me. Tomorrow will be entertaining enough, I’m sure.”

Pace rewarded her with a smile that melted her heart. Clearly, she had given the right answer. When Pace stopped at the light, he leaned over and gave her a sweet kiss.

"Thank you. How about I order our hometown favorite, Imo's Pizza, and we chill at my parents' house? They'll be glad to see you, but we'll have privacy too."

"I like that." Closing her eyes, Harmony sighed. He was the guy she never knew she needed or would miss when he wasn't around. "I hate that you're leaving a job here to come to Chicago without one."

"You're there."

There was no further discussion for the rest of the ride.

At the Jamiesons' house, Harmony was smothered with attention from his parents and brothers. Pace seemed annoyed that he was in competition for her, but he remained polite. She liked the respect he gave to his family. It was an endearing quality.

Cheney's eyes sparkled as she studied Harmony with a welcoming smile. "Here's your T-shirt, sweetie. I hope it fits."

When Parke and Cheney sent their sons upstairs to their rooms, and they retired to their own bedroom, Pace exhaled. "Finally alone." He pulled her closer.

"Low key is good for me right now because I'm tired," he admitted, and his eyes backed it up.

"How about a movie?" Harmony suggested a romance or documentary. "Those are my favorites. I only watch action-packed adventures if I don't see blood."

He laughed and chose one. Before the first commercial, he had dozed off. Harmony nudged him. "Hey, you need your rest too. Take me to Grandma BB's house."

"I'm too weak to protest." He stood, stretched, and reached for her hand. "I'll make it up to you tomorrow."

Harmony shook her head. "There's nothing to make up. You forgot I went through the graduation stress three months ago."

"Good point." Pace grabbed his keys, and in less than ten minutes, he stood on Grandma BB's porch and kissed her good night.

Chapter Twenty-two

Pace couldn't believe he dozed while in the presence of his beautiful woman. To make matters worse, he overslept that morning when he planned to take Harmony to breakfast, but he was well-rested. He reached for his phone. There were two missed texts from Harmony. The first was a Scripture.

In everything, give thanks: for this is the will of God in Christ Jesus concerning you. 1 Thessalonians 5:18

Good morning to you, babe. He grinned.

Babe? I like that. I figured you were tired last night. You're the poor baby. Kami called your mom. She said you were probably still sleeping. Your sisters said they were getting their two hours in with me, and we were going shopping. Kisses.

Pace feigned a snarled, then laughed. His sisters had upped him anyway. **Enjoy yourself. I'm sending you money to shop. You don't have a job. It's my treat. I want you to enjoy yourself.**

He sent a hundred dollars electronically, then stepped out of bed and knelt to thank the Lord for another day and Harmony's safe arrival. He took his time petitioning God for all who had asked for prayer.

When he finished, Pace called JC.

"Hey. Why aren't you with Harmony?"

"She's with Victoria and Kami. I figure I could get a thirty-minute workout at the gym."

"I'll meet you there."

Harmony called seconds after ending his conversation with JC. "Pace, you're sweet for sending me spending money. Thank you. I didn't expect this."

"Surprise. This is the way a man treats his lady. Please tell my sisters that I'm picking you up at Grandma BB's at noon, and I told you about sending me kisses through texts. I only accept them in person."

She made ear-piercing smooches over the phone, then giggled before she ended the call.

Pace laughed and couldn't wait to collect.

Harmony felt like a celebrity when she entered the hotel ballroom at Pace's side. His family sported #TeamParke black T-shirts with white lettering. Each family had their own colors: #TeamMalcolm, #TeamDupree, #TeamKidd, #TeamAce, #TeamCam, and #TeamRobnett.

"Harmony." Queen Bee waltzed across the carpet with the grace of a swan with her arms open. "It's good to see you again. Welcome to game night." She was tall, elegant, and fashionably dressed in a bronze-ish T-shirt with #TeamRobnett in white lettering. Her white culottes seemed to be snatched off a model on a runway.

"It's good to see you again." Queen Bee grinned—a smile that captured her sincerity. "I'm glad my nephew has good taste."

"I'm standing here," Pace said, laughing and hugging her.

"It was meant to be heard." Queen Bee playfully scrunched her nose at him.

Next came Pace's uncles, other aunties, and young, teenage, and toddler cousins. JC showed up to Harmony's relief so she wouldn't be the sole outsider, although Pace's family made her feel at home. It was the same energetic atmosphere as at the Christmas Eve dinner.

More groups arrived until all the tables were full. Pace's grandfather, Papa P, stood at the head table where he sat with his wife, Charlotte, another individual, and Grandma BB, whose bodyguards were nearby.

"It's good to see family and friends." He smiled at Harmony, and she blushed as Pace squeezed her hand. "Will my nephew come and bless our gathering and food, so the games can begin?"

Pace's uncle, Pastor Philip, walked to the center of the tables, carrying his baby daughter. His wife, Queen, walked with a strut like Queen Bee to relieve him, but Philip held her hand, keeping her at his side. "With bowed heads. Oh, dear Lord, we thank You for family and extended family today. Lord, Your Word tells us if any man lacks wisdom, let him ask of You. We gather to exercise our worldly wisdom in a friendly—" he emphasized *friendly*— "manner, saints. Help us to increase in Your knowledge, too. Bless our food for the nourishment of our bodies. Let us not waste a morsel, remembering those who are hungry. We ask this in Jesus' name. Amen."

"Amen," everyone repeated, and the children raced to the buffet table, took a plate, then waited for their parents to come and assist them.

Pace stood. "Want me to fix your plate?"

"I'll go with you." He helped her stand, and he trailed her to the buffet.

"Does this remind you of anything?" Pace whispered in her ear.

She giggled because his closeness tickled. "Yes. First time we met."

They stacked their plates with finger food and joined Kami, Victoria, JC, and Pace's younger brothers, Paden and Chance, and his parents at the round table for ten.

They chatted while they ate, mostly about landing that first real job while the teenagers bemoaned the fact that they had less than a month before school started.

Grandma BB rang a cowbell about twenty minutes later to get everyone's attention. "I hate that thing," his dad complained. "I don't know why my father lets her use it."

Cheney tapped her husband's hand. "Parke, let her have her fun."

Papa P stood. "Let the games begin. Each family has submitted questions to test the others, and I have added some too."

Harmony turned to Pace. He gave her his complete attention. "Ready?"

"Yep." She nodded. "I don't know how many winning points I'll get."

"There are no wrong answers to me."

Kami *shush*ed them as the first question was read.

"This one comes from the Bible," Papa P said, and Harmony perked up and leaned forward. "Name five parables."

Buzzers went off. Harmony whipped her neck around to see who had the answer.

"There's a bonus point if you can name ten." Papa P pointed. "I saw your hand first after the buzzer. My second oldest grandson, MJ."

A teenager stood at #TeamMalcolm's table. His confidence showed in the lift of his chin and the square of his shoulders. Whereas Pace's family was mostly fair, everyone at #TeamMalcolm's table had satiny brown skin.

Harmony remembered him as one of the musicians at the dinner.

"The ten virgins, the wise and foolish, lost sheep, lost coin, rich fool…"

Harmony counted them off her fingers. She only knew about the ten virgins and the lost sheep.

"And for the bonus point: the persistent widow, the rich man and Lazarus, lamp under the bowl…" He paused as Harmony egged him on.

"Two more to go. You can do it," Harmony shouted as everyone at her table laughed.

"Babe, we're competing against them." Pace chuckled.

"Oh."

"New cloth and an old coat, hidden treasure," MJ finished to the roar of his family as his grandfather checked off his answers with the Bible open.

Parke and others showered the teenager with attention, and his confidence slipped as he blushed shyly.

"The question is Black history. Name at least ten northern states that were part of the Underground Railroad network."

A buzzer sounded from across the room. Duchess stood at Queen Bee's table.

"My niece from the Kansas City Robnett team. I love that our young people have been studying."

Duchess grinned. "Some northern states were Colorado, Connecticut, Illinois, Indiana, Iowa, Kansas, Maine, Massachusetts, Michigan, Nebraska, New Jersey, New York, Ohio, Pennsylvania, Rhode Island, and Wisconsin. There were southern routes, too."

"Wow." Harmony leaned back in her chair. School was out, but she had some more studying to do.

The questions kept coming, and the teenagers popped up. Harmony gnawed on her lips. She was determined to jump in the ring. At least no one would boo her, she hoped.

"Name all sixty-six books in the King James Version Bible."

Harmony slapped her hand on the buzzer at the same time as Pastor Philip's niece. She was a twin. Papa P looked from Harmony to the child.

The girl, who looked to be about six years old, said, "It's okay, Papa P. Mommy and Daddy said it's rude not to let our guests have a chance."

"Camille, that is sweet of you," Papa P said to the hearty applause from her relatives as if she had given the right answer.

Humbled by the little girl's gracious withdrawal, the pressure was on. Her heart pounded as she recited, "Genesis, Exodus, Deuteronomy…" Did they have to be in order? she wondered but didn't want to ask. There was Leviticus and Numbers, but she couldn't remember which was first. By the time she finished the Old Testament, she had the books out of order and probably mentioned some prophets twice.

Pace squeezed one of the hands she fumbled with. "Want some help?" he whispered.

"No." She swallowed and took a deep breath, then started with the Gospels as Camille ran to her table, took Harmony's other hand and displayed a missing-tooth grin.

"I can help. We can do it together and both win," she whispered loud enough for some adults to chuckle.

How could she turn away this precious child? Together, they finished to a standing ovation. Victoria, Kami, and Pace surrounded her and Camille in a celebration huddle.

The Jamieson family game night taught her a valuable lesson: It's more fun to work together, and she needed to be ready if there was a next time. No way would she let a six-year-old up her again.

Chapter Twenty-three

Two weeks later, Pace was a ball of nerves. He was about to receive his degree in the university's summer graduation ceremony.

"*Whew*." He exhaled.

Not only did Harmony return for it, but her parents and Shane accompanied her. Their mothers hit it off by talking about their salvation experience, and Mrs. Reed enjoyed hearing his mother's testimonies about being unable to have children, then giving birth. Cheney never mentioned adoption. She left that for her children's discretion.

They sat outside a cafe in the Delmar Loop, blocks away from the St. Louis city limits. Wash U's campus, where he would graduate that evening, was less than ten minutes walking distance.

He needed downtime first.

He needed private time with his lady.

He needed for realization to sink in. Like his sisters, Pace was about to become a college grad.

"I'm proud—I mean godly proud—of you." Harmony's words were filled with emotion, and Pace could see unshed tears in her eyes.

This was what he wanted—a woman who was happy about his achievements. Yeah, she was the one for him. Pace didn't want her to see him become emotional. He glanced away at the pedestrians admiring the brass stars on the sidewalk of the St. Louis Walk of Fame to regroup. They seemed in awe of St. Louis natives, including Chuck Berry, Scott Joplin, Charles Lindberg, Cedric the Entertainer, and Tennessee Williams.

"Hey." Harmony's soft voice ceased his drifting. "You look so intense. What's on your mind?"

He faced her again and studied her beauty. The floral gold sundress showed off her toned muscles and flawless brown skin. "I'm moving." He paused and let that tidbit sink in. "In two weeks, I will move into my Chicago apartment, with or without a job."

Harmony squirmed in her seat, then placed her hands, which were cold from holding her cup of cold lemonade, on top of his. "For the record, I'm against that. It's soooo hard trying to find a job. The freelance projects give me minimal experience, but not the kind I want or the pay I'm worth, and it's been three months. What if it takes you that long?"

"It won't, baby." The endearment always made her glow, and Pace liked saying it more. He grinned to reassure Harmony that he wouldn't go broke. "I've worked every possible hour without interfering with my studies. I've studied harder so as not to fall behind—"

"All this while you came to see me twice." She shook her head as if she was guilty of them sightseeing more of Chicago's historic places at his request.

"Visiting you was my weekend getaway that recharged me. But I've spoken to a few recruits who are on the lookout for me. I have two years of experience if I include my internship. God will open the door." He nodded.

"I hope He does the same for me, too." Harmony sighed.

Pace didn't want to say anything to discourage her, but some degrees were more bankable than others. She had chosen a career path with limited job options, but he would keep praying that God would open doors for both of them.

He stood and reached for their trash. "Come on. We'd better head back to your hotel and me to my house. It's my turn to walk across the stage."

Looping her arm through his, they strolled to his vehicle. Although the move was all his idea, Pace needed her to see the benefit and be an accomplice to what their relationship could become.

Hours later, the August temperature had cooled somewhat, and God gave them a gentle breeze ever so often. Harmony sat in the bleacher next to her family. Pace's supporters seemed to be a hundred strong. She saw Jamiesons and Robnetts she'd met at functions, then some people who had to be church members.

Harmony experienced a bout of melancholy. He had given up all this home support to pursue her in Chicago, and the magnitude of his feelings scared her. He was so determined in his goals.

The "Pomp and Circumstance" melody began the procession. Tears filled Harmony's eyes as the people in green gowns with black trim made their way to their assigned seats. She could see the school emblem patch on Pace's shoulder. Because he was graduating from the master's program, she noted the difference in sleeve shapes. His were oblong.

She learned that this school was considered the Harvard of the Midwest, and this was where Kami attended her freshman year before following Victoria to Oklahoma.

A veteran actor born in St. Louis delivered the keynote address about his career and taking chances. That's exactly what Pace was doing. It was bittersweet. *Lord, where are my chances to take?*

Her musing ended when those around her applauded. Harmony readied her camera to record the engineering degree candidates whose names were about to be called.

His siblings and cousins began to cheer as he stepped closer to the stage.

"Parke Kokumuo Jamieson the eighth."

Harmony stood and cheered. She cupped her hand to her mouth and shouted, "I love you, Pace!" before she realized those coveted words had escaped from her lips. Harmony blinked. Did she say that? She gave Kami a side-eye. Had anyone heard her declaration? Hopefully not. Harmony didn't say another word, preferring to clap instead.

When the ceremony ended, the Reed family—except Harmony—held back so Pace's family and close friends could congratulate him first. Kami and Victoria had looped their arms through hers and hurried toward their brother.

Neither mentioned anything about what she'd shouted through the crowd. Harmony exhaled. She thought her private musings were locked up until the appropriate time. Harmony had never been in love before, and she wanted to evaluate her feelings to make sure the emotion she had toward Pace was love.

As she inched closer to him, he turned his head as if to search her out. He started toward her, and when she was within reach, he wrapped his arm around her and buried his face in her hair. "I did it. I did it."

She lifted his face by placing a hand on each side of his hair-covered cheeks that were a thin beard and then kissed his lips. Mindful of their audience, they didn't linger. "Congratulations, Parke Kokumuo Jamieson the eighth."

"Pace is fine," he said with one arm around her shoulders as he introduced her to his church members, old neighbors, classmates—too many folks for Harmony to keep up.

The evening was long, but Harmony never left his side, even if she wanted to, and she didn't. Pace Jamieson had a hold on her that she didn't want to let go.

Chapter Twenty-four

On Labor Day weekend, Pace packed up his belongings. He was ready to get on the road. His family would trail him with furniture pieces his mother had given him for his apartment.

Parke pulled him aside while everyone was getting into their cars. "I'm proud of you, son—my firstborn son." He choked. "I've tried to be the best example as a black man, husband, and father to you, keeping God first to help me."

Pace didn't break his stare into his father's eyes. "Yes, sir. You have."

"Now, it's your turn to set the example for your younger brothers." His dad patted him on the shoulder. "Harmony is a sweet young woman who cares about you. I see it every time she looks at you. Remember to walk with the Lord and to listen for His directions. I had hoped you would have a job by now in Chicago, but your mother and I support you. If you need help with anything," he said, squinting, "anything, you let me know. I don't care if it's bill money, rent, or food."

"Yes, sir. I've saved up enough money for three months' rent. Chicago is expensive, but I've got this." Pace hugged his dad, and Parke hugged him tighter.

The two walked outside together. Parke locked up and got behind the wheel of his vehicle, where Chance, Paden, and his mother were waiting. Pace went to his SUV. Kami and Victoria were riding with him. After entering his apartment address into his GPS, he drove off with his father trailing him.

"I'm going to miss you," Kami said from her spot in the passenger seat.

"We're going to miss you," Victoria corrected from her perch in the back.

Pace smiled. "I'm going to miss you, too, like when you two decided the school in Oklahoma is where you wanted to go." He was quiet as he glanced in his rearview mirror to make sure his father made the traffic light. "When we were little, I couldn't wait to grow up and be on my own." His sisters nodded in agreement. "But being an adult is scary. I feel like I'm losing a part of me I can never get back."

"That's what I'm hoping for," Victoria said. "I wanted my childhood to be over fast. I had to grow up to survive, but when Mom and Dad adopted me, I could relax and at least be a teenager."

Kami sniffed and reached for her hand in the back, and Victoria grasped it. "I was so happy to have a sister."

"We know," Victoria and Pace said in unison.

They all laughed.

"Well, hopefully, that one company you interviewed with will hire you," Victoria said. After phone and virtual interviews, Kami received a verbal offer from a logistics company for their management trainee program. Now, she was waiting for the offer in writing.

Victoria had started the nursing program at Wash U, and JC would keep an eye on her. It was still mind-blowing that his best friend was serious about his baby sister.

A few hours into the drive, the car interior was quiet until Kami turned to him. "What's going to happen between you and Harmony?"

Pace gave his sister a quick side-eye. "Do you have information for me in exchange?"

"Not really." Kami shrugged. "Just wondering if you'll ever move back home."

"No."

"Boy, that was a quick answer."

Pace did not explain while Harmony called twice, wanting an update. Forty-five minutes out, he told Kami to text Harmony. "Give her our ETA."

As soon as all this was settled, Pace planned to profess his love to her. School was behind them, and a future was before them. He liked Chicago, with its diversity and history ready for him to embrace.

"Mom!" Harmony jingled the car keys. "Pace and his family are less than an hour away. We need to leave."

While giving Pace tours of Chi-town neighborhoods, she'd pointed out the University of Chicago. He said he liked the vibe of the area. She had no idea he would pick an apartment on East 52nd Street, six minutes from the campus. At the time, she didn't believe he was serious about moving.

But Pace Jamieson didn't bluff. He usually said what he meant. Harmony liked that quality in him since she was the opposite. She could change her mind based on the time of the month.

Harmony was excited and scared. Neither had secured full-time employment, so she kept praying for open doors.

"Let me get my purse," Lorna said, then kissed her husband goodbye.

"Tell your young man, 'Welcome to the Windy City.'"

"I will, Dad."

Minutes later, Harmony was steering her mom's car to the highway. She was glad her mother liked Pace and was involved in whatever was important in Harmony's life. Lorna Reed was a fierce supporter. Plus, they both received the Lord's Holy Spirit, so they had more in common.

Except for Harmony's two older brothers, her family liked Pace enough to attend his graduation. Shane had an agenda that had fizzled with Kami.

"The way you're driving, are you trying to beat him there?" Lorna asked, spying the speed on the dashboard.

Harmony pumped the brakes. She didn't need a ticket, which was an unexpected expense. "Guess I'm excited to see him and Kami and Victoria. Thanks for riding with me, Mom." Harmony smiled.

"In case you go missing, I need to know where to find you." Although her mother liked Pace, she was over-cautious about her children. "How serious are you two?"

"I love him." She glanced at her mother for a reaction. Lorna didn't seem surprised by the admission. "But I haven't told him yet."

Lorna chuckled. "Love is an action word. Pace has been there for you since you met him. He respects you and treats you like a lady."

Harmony bit her bottom lip, grinning. "Yeah, he does."

"Keep in mind, he's your first serious boyfriend. Don't move too fast. You may agree on things now, but take your time and pay attention to red flags that can creep up on you. I know you're grown, but you're still my baby, and no mother wants to see their child unhappy because of bad decisions."

"Mom, my brain is aching, and I am trying to read between the lines. Can you be straightforward, please?" Harmony was about ten minutes away, so they needed to finish this talk.

"Pace may be your first love, but sometimes first loves don't become the last love. Keep that in mind," she said as Harmony exited off the highway.

It was another of her mother's pearls of wisdom that she would tuck away, but Harmony doubted she would have to retrieve it. Lorna agreed that love was an action word, and Pace was big on showing it.

Chapter Twenty-five

Sunday morning, Pace's siblings and parents stopped by his new apartment after leaving their hotel to head home.

"Remember what I said," Parke gave his son a pointed look.

Pace nodded. "Yes, sir. He extended his hand, but his father hugged him and patted him on his back several times while rocking him. "I love you, son, and am godly proud of you. Walk with God, no matter what. Pray that you don't yield to the devil's temptation with Harmony or any situation." He squeezed Pace's neck tighter, released him, then stepped back.

His father's eyes were watery as he let the others have their turn. Kami and Victoria held on to him the longest.

His brothers were quiet. Pace tried to read their moods. When Chance, the youngest, looked away, sadness consumed him. Yesterday was fun and games. They'd moved stuff in and shopped for more things. Plus, Harmony was there, and Chance had a crush on Pace's girlfriend.

"Hey, buddy." Pace patted his shoulder. "You can always come and visit any time."

Chance fell into his arms, bawling. "But you're my big brother. I can't visit you on campus like at the dorm."

Now, it was Pace's turn to squeeze someone tight. He loved his brothers, who shared his bloodline, just as much as his sisters.

"I love you, Pace. I don't want you to leave us." Chance sniffed and wiped his nose with the back of his hand.

"Gross." Kami handed him a tissue.

"I'll come home as often as I can," Pace said, short of a promise.

"With Harmony, too?" Chance's eyes brightened. Hope filled them.

Pace chuckled. "If she can. Remember, I don't have a job yet, so it may be a while."

"I have money." Chance perked up.

"Me too!" Paden chimed in. He wasn't as emotional since he wasn't the baby and thought he could boss Chance around.

His parents turned away. Cheney walked into the kitchen and let Pace handle the goodbyes.

"Paden, I want you to take care of Chance for me. No pickin' fights. Act like the big brother." Pace grabbed both of them in bear hugs and kissed their heads like he often did to irritate them at first, but it became a sign of endearment.

Parke cleared his throat. "Okay, family. Let's pray so we can get on the road." He instructed everyone to form a circle and hold hands. "Father, in the mighty name of Jesus, we come boldly to Your throne of grace. Thank You for Your sacrifice on the cross for us. Thank You for my firstborn son. Thank You for saving him as a young boy. Thank You for his accomplishments. Please protect Pace as he begins life's journey. Keep his mind on You."

Instead of "Amen," his mother began her list of petitions before the Lord, "Jesus, You love Pace more than us, so we trust You to take care of him. Please give him favor with his superiors, his coworkers, and whatever he puts his hands on..."

Kami picked up the prayer, "God, thank You for all my brothers, especially my big brother. Thank You for the example he has set with You as the head..."

Victoria's voice was soft, then increased like thunder. "Jesus, dispatch Your angels to protect my brother. Please make sure he suits up his armor every day, taking the shield of faith so the wicked can't take him out or down."

"Yeah," Paden said, jumping in, "and, Jesus, don't let him leave home without his helmet of salvation and the sword of the Spirit."

"Which is the Word of God!" Chance shouted the rest of the Scripture in Ephesians six. "Please take care of my brother, Jesus. I love him."

A quietness fell on them, then a sudden boom shook the room as the power of the Holy Ghost surrounded them, and they worshipped the Lord in a heavenly language.

Tears streamed down Pace's cheeks, and he lifted his arms in surrender. Soon, they danced and praised God, christening his first apartment.

Monday morning after his prayer time, Pace sent Harmony a text: **Good morning from Hyde Park. But Jesus beheld them, and said unto them, With men this is impossible; but with God all things are possible. Matthew 19:26**

She called him right away. "Amen. Morning from the Sauganash neighborhood. It's Labor Day, so you're invited to my house for a barbecue."

"Reserve me a plate." He grinned. "What time should I come, and what should I bring?"

"Bring yourself any time after noon. Dad should be finished grilling by then."

"I'll be there." Another call came through from his parents' home phone, a landline that his mother refused to get rid of because of the hefty discount she received as a telephone company employee. He told Harmony goodbye and answered.

"Pace," Chance began, "Paden is not doing what you told him. He's being mean to me. I want to move in with you."

Pace smiled. He and Kami always argued like angels and demons until their parents intervened and scolded them to love one another. He missed those days, but not the fighting. "I need you to stand up to him and not let him intimidate you. Where are Mom and Dad?"

"They're at Grandma BB's house."

"Put Paden on the phone." For the next ten minutes, he had to referee their squabble. He was relieved when he heard his father's voice in the background.

"Who are you talking to?" his father asked Chance.

"Pace."

Seconds later, his father was on the line. "Hey, son. Everything alright?"

Pace chuckled. "Not at your house." He explained the nature of the argument and call.

"Chance misses you. Paden too. It's not like you haven't lived away from home on campus." They chatted a few minutes, then ended the call.

Pace showered and dressed. An hour later, he left his apartment and followed his GPS to Harmony's house. He made a stop at a store and picked up some sweet tea.

Harmony opened the door in a colorful floral romper.

They greeted each other with a kiss. "You're beautiful."

From the moment Pace walked inside, he felt he was home.

By mid-week, Pace and Harmony resumed their job search. "I'm waiting to hear back from a recruiter. I texted him this morning that I have officially relocated, so hopefully, that will accelerate the hiring process. Let me know if you have a favorite place you want to eat."

After breakfast, Pace sat at his table and opened his laptop. With his skills, letters of reference, and degree, it shouldn't be this hard to get a job, he thought, as the job market was strong.

It is a waste of time, the devil taunted him.

Before the lie could set into his mind, Pace gathered spiritual strength and rebuked Satan with the Word of God in

Psalm 84. The verse wasn't as important as the ammo to fire. *For the Lord God is a sun and shield: the Lord will give grace and glory: no good thing will he withhold from them that walk uprightly.*

Satan had no comeback as Pace signed into the online platform to search companies' job openings and track down the recruiters to contact.

A few days later, the call came. An official offer was made. Pace laughed at the devil as the recruiter told him to open his email to review the contract. "Congratulations, Pace," Rick Davis said. "If something's not right, this is your time to negotiate salary, vacation days, and other perks. Speak now or hold your peace until your yearly evaluation."

Rick was patient as they reviewed each clause. Everything looked good except for paid holidays. This was his first job. Should he be petty, or remain silent like it was okay not to be off on the holidays dear to his heart?

Son, stand up for what you believe is important and right. His father's counsel came to mind. "I would like Dr. Martin Luther King Jr. Day and Juneteenth to be paid standard holidays for me, not floaters."

"That's easy. I'll get the changes made, so expect the final version in a few days. Congratulations, Pace."

"Thank you." Praise started deep within Pace as he thanked the Lord for the job, earning six figures. Obtaining the dual degree had paid off. He called his family with the good news, then Harmony. He had to be quick about it before Kami or Victoria spilled the beans.

"Hey, babe. How's it going?"

"I'm having a good day. I may have a recruiter interested in matching my skills with companies."

"Then it sounds like we need to celebrate." Pace grinned, barely containing his excitement.

"Pace, it's not a job offer."

"But it's more than you had yesterday," he reminded her. "And I received a verbal job offer today."

Harmony screamed her excitement. “Pace, that’s wonderful. I’m so happy for you. Which job was it?”

“Mitchell & Drake Engineering. I requested a few changes, but I should have the print contract in a few days. My recruiter doesn’t see it as a problem. So, dinner tomorrow night, and I need you to take me shopping on Saturday.”

Pace was glad she agreed because he wanted to get her something special when he told her he loved her.

Chapter Twenty-six

Harmony was ecstatic that Pace had a job.

She was.

But when she ended the call, she cried, literally into her pillow so she wouldn't alarm her parents. *Lord, have You forgotten about me?*

Show me your faith, God whispered.

Harmony didn't know how to do that. She sniffed quietly. Harmony prayed, read her Bible, and attended church faithfully, so what was she missing? She wondered if she hadn't been saved long enough to earn points or favor.

Have you not read that I have no respect of persons? God asked. *Are you hoping for what you want or what I want for you?*

Harmony blinked and strained her brain. She thought it was the same thing. Getting up, she walked into the bathroom and washed her face. She returned to her bedroom and picked up her Bible, opened it to Hebrews, chapter eleven and began to read about the people who showed the Lord their faith.

She was still reading when there was a knock on her door. Her mother opened it after Harmony said to come in.

"Hey, sweetie. I saw your light on. Everything okay?" Lorna's voice was soft and comforting.

"Trying to get a break on that first job."

Lorna hugged her. "It will come, sweetie."

"Mom, will you pray with me? I really want to hear someone else pray. Maybe God will listen to you."

"Of course. What did the pastor say a few weeks ago about prayer?" She rolled her lips, thinking. "'*And it shall come to pass, that before they call, I will answer; and while they are yet speaking, I will hear.*' Isaiah sixty-five and twenty-four." Her mother took her hands and bowed her head. She began to pray like Harmony had never heard her before. There was comfort in her words.

When they whispered, "Amen," Harmony felt better.

"Thanks, Mom. I needed that. Pace got a verbal offer today. Now, he's waiting on the letter. I was feeling like a failure when you came in."

"Nonsense. You're a smart, talented, and beautiful young lady inside and out. Otherwise, Pace wouldn't be attracted to you. You have a gift to create images to tell stories. Your job is important. It may take more time, that's all. Sometimes, patience is the hardest part of life. Plus, you belong not only to the Reeds but also to Jesus, and no good thing will He withhold from you. I've been reading Psalm eighty-four." She grinned, stood, and kissed her cheek. "Good night, sweetie."

Harmony finished her bedtime regimen and drifted off to sleep. She was at peace with her life.

The next morning, splinters of sunlight teased her awake before Pace's morning text. She stretched and grabbed her phone. Prayer really did change things. She was in a better place today.

Good morning, babe. The Lord is not slack concerning His promise, as some men count slackness; but is longsuffering toward us, not willing that any should perish, but that all should come to repentance. 2 Peter 3:9

Amen. Good morning. Thanks for the reminder. Harmony had peace.

You're welcome, beautiful. I made reservations for 6 p.m. at Brinkley's.

Wow. Pace had picked a jazzy place. **I'll be ready at 5.**

Hours later, Harmony received two requests for graphic projects from a site where she'd signed up as a freelancer. One was a referral from a small public relations firm. This could be her opening, so she had to be meticulous.

It was going to be a good day. She could feel it.

And it was. She spent time with God in prayer and read her Bible, then got busy.

She worked nonstop for the new client to showcase her visual interpretation of the company's mission statement. She sent it to her old boss at the studio in Oklahoma where she worked for his input. He raved about the colors and fonts but suggested a few tweaks to make the graphic pop without overdoing it.

She took his advice, made the changes, then emailed the proof to the client. Harmony turned to the other project. This customer wanted a generic design with little creativity, but paid well.

Pace called a few hours before picking her up. "I haven't heard your voice all day. You must be busy."

"I am. I feel better working with a recruiter."

"Well, I miss you. See you soon."

She blew kisses over the phone to tease him and waited for him to say what she loved to hear. Harmony smiled in anticipation.

"I told you, I only accept them in person."

Harmony laughed, then went to primp for her dinner date. She was glad her mother prayed for her, too, so that tonight she could be happy for Pace and celebrate with him without being envious of his blessing.

Pace's jaw dropped and never recovered when Harmony opened the door. He could barely breathe as he stared at her.

"May I help you?" Harmony's tease freed him to recalibrate.

He inhaled, then smiled. "You look breathtaking."

She blushed. Pace liked to take credit for that. When Harmony moved back, Pace stepped into her house and towered over her a couple of inches, even with the heels she wore.

He scanned her bronze nail polish on her toes and the shape of her dress, then admired her thick hair, which was swept up from her face, exposing her distinct features. "Pretty."

"I thought so too," Mr. Reed said, coming into focus from the kitchen.

Pace tamed down his attraction and greeted her father. "Good evening, sir." They exchanged handshakes. Her mother, who was on the phone, waved and mouthed, *Praise the Lord.*

"Ready?" he asked Harmony.

He helped her into the car, then walked around the bumper and slid behind the wheel. Before driving off, Pace linked his fingers through hers, brought them to his lips for a kiss, then drove off.

Chicago's downtown skyline was a beacon as he followed his GPS to Brinkley's on Lakeshore Drive. "I don't know if I'll ever get used to this traffic. *Whew.*"

"You see why most people take the transit—easier to get around and most times faster. At least we're moving."

Pace glanced at her and noticed her eyes were closed. She looked relaxed with her thick lashes resting. A smile tugged at her full lips.

"Are you tired?" Pace frowned.

"No. Happy. I had a good day, and now I'm enjoying a great night with this incredibly handsome man who walks with God. That's why I'm happy."

"I have a lot to be happy about, too. The offer came back earlier than expected, and I'm officially a Mitchell & Drake Engineering employee. I report next Wednesday."

"Congratulations." She opened her eyes, leaned over, and blessed him with a soft kiss on his cheek.

I love her. Everything about her. And Pace couldn't wait to profess it over the candlelight dinner. Even though he had moved to Chicago to be closer to her, he still felt too far away.

"Tell me about your day and what you worked on."

Harmony came alive with excitement when she discussed a referral she'd received from a small PR company.

"I wanted to get it right—think outside the norm—so I called my old supervisor at the Oklahoma studio and shared my thoughts, and he brainstormed some changes. I tweaked it and liked the finished product. I'm hoping it can open the door for me."

"I'll pray that God will open the door so no one can shut you out."

"Thank you."

They arrived at Brinkley's, and the valet took the keys to his SUV, and Pace escorted her inside. Booked from the reviews online, the atmosphere didn't disappoint. The lighting was low to accentuate the tasteful decor of contrasting light and dark shades of green. Intimate and he hoped romantic for Harmony. A string quartet entertained patrons. Judging from Harmony's pleased expression, Pace had done well.

He gave the hostess his name, and they were shown to their table. Once they informed the server they did not want any drinks, he removed the stemware and told them about the specials.

Pace nodded for her to go first. "Babe?"

"The salmon wellington sounds delicious."

Their hostess nodded and, without a notepad, asked about sides, then turned to Pace.

"I'll take the steak—well done—with asparagus topped with the shaved Parmesan."

Left alone, Pace reached for her hands. "I have something very important to say."

She blinked and waited.

"I love you, Harmony Reed." He glanced away to make sure they weren't the center of anyone's attention. He wanted this moment to be private, just the two of them. Satisfied others were in their own worlds, Pace faced her again. His shyness made him choke. "I wanted to tell you sooner, and it was torture having to wait, but when a man professes his love to his woman, everything has to be in place, including a job and a plan for his intentions. We're set now for whatever the Lord has for you and me."

Harmony blinked. What more was there to say? Him loving her was momentous. When Pace shifted in his chair, Harmony caught her breath. Was a proposal coming? Now? Twenty-two was too young to be serious about her next thirty or forty years of happily ever after. She recalled her talk with her mother.

She stared into his clear brown eyes, which were intense and captivating. He looked back at her with such tenderness. Harmony admired the softness of his smile and the handsomeness of his features. His African American blood was equally matched with his Latino roots. His sincerity in walking with the Lord was the icing on any gourmet cupcake.

"On one of the most important days of my life, when you were there at my graduation, I heard your voice—I know your distinct pitch. I heard you say…" He broke contact and patted his chest. "You loved me. The degree took a backseat. All the gifts and money I received that night paled to having earned your love."

Pace's raw emotions spilled over to her. She never imagined those three words coming from the right person would fill her veins like a transfusion. "I meant it."

"I know you did." He nodded. "I couldn't wait for you to say it again."

As she whispered her love, he mingled his with hers.

When their dinners arrived, Harmony was already satiated as Pace gave thanks and blessed their food. He kissed the palms of her hands, then slowly released them.

Harmony's skin tingled as she tried to steady her right hand to eat.

The night moved in slow motion as she cataloged each smile, sigh, and twinkle in his eyes to dream about later.

After a lull in conversation, Pace rested his fork. He wasn't finished eating, but whatever he had to say was important. "I know you've been bummed about not having a job, but know I've been fasting and praying for God's will for you—your job, your happiness, and our relationship. I want you to have it all. If you need anything—anything—please ask me. Will you do that?"

It's coming, Harmony. Trust Me, the Lord whispered.

"I will." She smiled, then resumed enjoying her tasty meal.

"So," Pace said, leaning across the table, beckoning for her to meet him halfway, "are we in a happy place?"

She closed her eyes and enjoyed the touch of his soft lips, mumbling, "I'm definitely happy."

Chapter Twenty-seven

There was a promise, so Harmony hoped Design Express would permanently add her to the payroll since they liked her work. She was completing two projects a week for them anyway.

Still, the recruiter continued to search for companies that matched her job skills. Her college advisor encouraged her to expand her locations.

Every morning, the Scripture she and Pace exchanged inspired her, and every week, he asked if she needed money for gas, shopping, or fun.

She talked to Kami and Victoria about the development in her dating life and lack of movement in her professional life.

"Girl, he is husband material, and I'm not saying that because he's my brother. I see my dad and uncles treat their wives the same way," Kami said.

"But we aren't married or engaged."

"My brother can be so extra sometimes," Victoria chimed in on the video conference call. They giggled.

Friday nights were Pace and Harmony's way of kicking off the weekend with a romantic dinner. That seemed to be when he splurged on a meal for them because he said Fridays should always be special to them.

On Saturdays, they explored more of Chicagoland, some places she didn't know about. He even got the Reeds interested in their family roots. On Sunday, he and her mother got a kick out of Pace, who came to take them to service and then stayed for Sunday dinner at her parents' house.

Pace and Shane were becoming good friends.

Then it happened.

Her big break.

One Friday morning, while tweaking comps for Design Express, her recruiter sent an email: "Let's talk about one o'clock this afternoon. I have news—good news—exciting news."

Harmony didn't know if she was about to laugh or cry from the excitement at Wayne Taylor's message. Pace was in a meeting, and she didn't want to disturb him with the unknown until after one. But she was so happy she had to share it with someone. Kami was working, too, and Victoria had clinical rotations on Fridays. Her father was at work, and her mother was out. Home alone, she wondered who she could share this prelude to good news.

Talk to me. God reminded her of His presence.

Harmony lowered her head in embarrassment and repentance. *Lord, You are there when I'm happy and sad. I know all good things come from above. And I thank You for any good news five months after I graduated. Lord, I'm excited and don't even know what it is, but I hope You approve, and this is Your will. I love You, Lord, and thank You for dying for me on the cross. In Jesus' name. Amen.*

For the next three hours, Harmony hoped someone would call or text so she could tell them what she knew until she spoke with Wayne. Meanwhile, she attempted to concentrate on the project, but it was useless. She was glad it wasn't due until next Tuesday because it was complicated with many components for the client's upcoming mega concert. All the social media graphics needed to be coordinated with minor differences.

At twelve-fifty, Harmony's phone rang, and her heart almost leaped out of her chest. She grabbed her phone while inhaling and exhaling. "Hi, Wayne."

"Harmony! I'm about to make your day," he said.

Putting Wayne on speakerphone to free her hands, she clapped, wiggled in her chair, and grinned. "Okay. What is it?"

"Ever heard of Applesome and Hutch?"

Harmony's eyes widened. "Yes, absolutely. They are huge." They were one of the top public relations firms in the country and boasted an impressive list of international clients.

"Well, I'd never heard of them, but I've heard of their clients. Cereal brands, airlines, entertainment, shipping, and on and on. Wow, I was so impressed I wanted to apply myself," he joked. "Anyway, they were blown away by your education and the samples uploaded with your profile. They want to talk. They have offices in Singapore and London. Their headquarters is in San Francisco, but they are expanding to the Midwest."

Harmony practiced breathing techniques so she wouldn't faint before Wayne got all the details out as he rambled on about possible cities.

"Your strength is in brand architecture, brand engagement, and interactive and new media. They are willing to offer you training and an impressive compensation package. How does seventy thousand sound? I got you up from sixty-one thousand. The more you make, the bigger my commission."

Tears spilled from her eyes. Yes, some things were worth waiting for. She wouldn't have to move to the West or East Coast.

Perfect.

It made sense the company picked Chicago for its Midwest location. The city had two international airports and a transportation system to get people anywhere from the suburbs to the city, she mused about her hometown. "Thank You, God, and thank you, Wayne. I can sign the contract yesterday. When is the company setting up an office in Chicago?"

"They're not. Omaha beat them out, offering tax incentives and perks to lure their Midwest office there. If you can be in Omaha in two weeks, the job is yours, and there is a stipend for moving expenses. That's what the hiring manager said, but of course, you have to meet with him and the team you'll work with."

"Wow." The salary, the prestige, and the experience were a plus. The location gave her pause, but being associated with them would take her far in her career. "Please set up the interview."

"How about three-thirty today? You'll meet with Lynn Johnson, the hiring manager, and I'll forward you the link."

Harmony blinked. After a slow start, things were moving quickly. "Yes." Wayne ended the call, and Harmony breathed as her head spun.

Her mother walked in the door, and she ran to tell her the good news. Immediately, Lorna lifted her hands, praising God like Harmony should have, and together, they thanked the Lord.

"So should I take it, Mom? It's in Omaha." Harmony needed guidance. She didn't want to be a big girl and make this decision.

"Do you want it?"

"Yes. I was starting to doubt my college education, but it's about to pay off."

"What does Pace think about this opportunity and a move?"

"I haven't spoken with him yet, but he supports me. He wants me to be happy, and getting this experience would make me happy and more qualified."

"If God said yes, then go for it." She smiled, but her eyes held a touch of sadness. "God knows what's best."

"Thanks, Mom." They hugged, and then Harmony returned to her bedroom to prepare her mind. She put on a nice blouse and makeup for the video call and prayed for favor, God's will, His blessings, and every other phrase she had heard used in church.

Harmony signed in at three twenty-three and waited. Exactly at three-thirty, a black man appeared. Wow, a brother in charge of her department. She smiled, liking the company even more for its diversity.

"Harmony, I'm Lynn Johnson, the hiring manager. Your résumé seems to match the job skills we're looking for, and we'll help you hone them to become another superstar at our company."

"Thank you for this incredible opportunity. What about my portfolio stood out?"

He grinned. "That's easy. Your motion graphic sample and exhibition design. Impressive vision. We want to hire you and another recent graduate to round off the team of five because we want to give our new client fresh eyes on the campaign."

Four faces appeared on the screen, one by one. Harmony guessed the other graduate hadn't started yet. Another black guy who looked to be in his late thirties, way older than Laurence Jr. The other three were one man and two women. One seemed to be about Harmony's age, and the other woman was older. They introduced themselves as Jason, Kelli, and Yala.

They were pleasant and welcoming as they described their work and their length of time with the company. Most had transferred from the headquarters. The interview wasn't long. The next step is for you to meet our Vice President Donn Winters. He is waiting on my call because he has time to meet with you this afternoon. The job will be yours if you wow him like you did me. Good Luck." Lynn grinned, and the video meeting ended.

As expected, her mother hurried into the room. "Well?"

Harmony exhaled. "I impressed the hiring manager. Next, I'll meet with the VP. After a slow start to getting a job offer, Applesome and Hutch are making up for it in lightning speed to get me hired."

The two chatted until Harmony received an email with a link for another video conference in ten minutes. Her mother hugged her and said a quick prayer, then left the room.

Regrouping, Harmony prepared herself and signed in. VP Donn Winters appeared seconds later. His smile was warm, reminding Harmony of her father. After a few pleasantries, Donn got to the point. "As Lynn probably told you, this position is a fast-track management training program that lasts two years. Three if you receive a promotion within that time. We want to get a return on our investment in you. Lynn was impressed with you and your background. We will expedite your background check, and if that goes well, human resources will send you a written offer."

Her mother rushed back into Harmony's bedroom as Harmony said her goodbye.

"Well?" Lorna was giddy with excitement.

Harmony felt like she was dreaming. "Basically, I got the job if my background check clears."

"And it will."

"I'm so excited, Mom." Harmony jumped up and hugged her mother.

"When are you going to tell Pace?"

"Tonight at dinner." She danced in place. "He will be so happy for me."

Pace schooled his expression. He was happy for her until he wasn't. *God, how can You take her away from me?*

This is not about you but her growth. I am with her, God whispered.

"Congratulations, baby." He strained to get the words out.

"They see that they are getting a jewel—" *My jewel—* "but in Omaha."

"I know." She pouted. "But the cost of living and doing business in Omaha was cheaper than Chicago. This is an opportunity I can't pass up."

She was so happy, and this was her moment. He listened as she named their top clients.

"Some are actors, 2016 Olympics, Hulu..." She was breathless when she finished.

"That's impressive." Pace took advantage of the pause and asked, "What about us?"

Harmony blinked. "What do you mean?" Her big, beautiful eyes seemed clueless.

Do we have to go there? Are you going to make me say it? He exhaled. "Baby, I moved to Chicago to be close to you, to pamper you as we build our relationship."

She squeezed her lips as if she had something to say. "Pace, you said you want me to be happy, and this opportunity makes me happy. If I want the job, I have to move to Omaha."

"I know that." Pace nodded in defeat. He needed to tread ever so lightly. He didn't want her to feel like she had to choose, but in a sense, she did.

Suddenly losing his appetite, he pushed aside his plate and leaned across the table, and she met him halfway. "I can't move to Omaha, babe."

"I'm not asking you to." She pecked his lips softly.

"What are you asking me to do? Fly there every other weekend and send for you when I can't make it?"

She shook her head. "Some campaigns may require I work overtime, depending on the deadlines set by the clients and how fast I learn their expectations."

Pace rubbed his temples. "I need you to tell me what will happen to us."

"I love you, you love me. Can we put our dating on hold? Only for two years while I'm in the management training program."

What? his inner voice roared. Blinking, Pace fumed. "How do I do that, Harmony Reed? We're building a relationship so that one day we can talk about marriage, a family, becoming seniors together."

She sucked in her breath. "Marriage? Pace, we're too young to make a long-term commitment."

"Let me be clear, Harmony Reed. I know you're the one for me. If I didn't, I wouldn't have moved here."

He waited for her to say the same. Harmony didn't. That stung. "I get it…" No, he didn't. Pace couldn't convince himself he was okay with that. He wasn't.

She had discombobulated him. "Since we'll be 'on hold' the day you leave, I'll abide by your request, I guess." He shrugged. "Let me go on the record and say I don't like it. Two years, huh? Two years to put our emotions on hold. How is that possible?" He grunted again as his nostrils flared in frustration. That sounded ridiculous to his ears.

Harmony gritted her teeth in hesitation. "Ah, the management program could be three years, Pace," she said softly.

But she might as well have shouted it as far as his heart was concerned. Patting the table, he looked away to gather his thoughts. "Well, if you meet a man who meets your approval in that time, please give me the courtesy of letting me know so I'll cut my heartstrings."

"Pace, I told you from the beginning that my emotions work at a slow cooker speed, and I have to be sure with no doubts." Her eyes watered.

"You have doubts about our love?" Pace didn't know if he was ticked or crushed. Looking into her eyes, he could tell that both their hearts were breaking. The night was not going to end well. Pace sighed. "So, how much time do we have?"

"Two weeks." Harmony didn't look at him while she pinched her napkin.

Chapter Twenty-eight

Harmony called Kami when she got home, sniffing to contain her tears.

"Hey. Aren't you and Pace on a date night?" Kami cheerfully answered.

"I've got good news and bad news," Harmony said in a shaky voice, which cracked to keep her from bawling.

"What's wrong?" Kami's voice pitched on high alert. "Give me the bad news first."

"Is Victoria around?" Harmony didn't want to have to repeat the details as she dabbed her eyes with tissue.

"*Uh-oh.* It must be serious if Victoria needs to be here. No. Jamison took her to the Foundry's Art at the Arcade. So tell me what's going on."

At least Victoria was letting her guard down around JC. Harmony inhaled, then released. "I feel like Pace and I are breaking up."

"What?" she shrieked in Harmony's ear.

"That's the bad news that was the fall out as a result of the good news."

"Girl, stop with the jeopardy. Tell me."

"Well, I got a job through a recruiter. Good salary and perks."

"I'm happy because you've been looking for so long. Thank You, Jesus!"

Harmony smiled, knowing her friend would be happy for her. This was the celebration she had hoped for with Pace. "I start in two weeks."

"Okay, so why are you and my brother breaking up?"

"Because the job is in Omaha, and the breakup is in effect when I leave." Harmony sniffed. Her head was starting to pound.

"*Oooh.*" Kami was quiet. "So what happened? He gave you an ultimatum to stay and if you didn't, it was over? Wait until—"

"No, the bad news is I told him I wanted to put our relationship on hold."

"Huh? Why? Pace wants to marry you."

"Yeah, he told me that tonight, but he can't be serious. We just graduated from college. I'm only twenty-two. What would you do?"

"Well, number one, I wouldn't marry my brother."

That wasn't funny. Harmony sighed.

"You have to understand the men in my family. They go after the woman they want for life. I think it's an inherited gene for my uncles to love their wives." Kami paused. "But as for the job, I would say take it. You worked hard for this, but my brother has worked hard for you."

"Layer on the guilt trip. Thanks." Harmony twisted her lips.

"Sis, take the job if it's God's will. And I'll pray for the Lord to help you two figure it out."

"Thanks." Harmony was about to say goodbye when she heard Victoria in the background. Kami gave her a recap, then Victoria came on the line.

"I know how hard it has been to get a job, so I'm in your corner," Victoria said. "We were friends first, right? And we'll always be friends. Boyfriends come and go."

Wow, did Pace know his sisters were such traitors? But she needed to hear this.

"Yeah," the trio cheered, although Harmony wasn't sure there would be a Pace Jamieson again.

She was about to find out in two weeks.

After a sulky Friday night, Pace called his best friend and his parents Saturday morning. They were all happy for Harmony—until Pace told them about the devil in the details.

"Son, if you and Harmony are meant to be, it will work out," his mother said.

"Not if she doesn't want that," Pace said dryly.

"Slow down. Let her feelings catch up. You Jamieson men can be persistent and annoying if I remember correctly," she said.

"Hey, I got my woman—my wife," Parke said on speaker mode.

"Hush," Cheney fussed at her husband. "Pace, you both have been there for each other this year. Continue praying."

Pace nodded and spied the time. He owed Harmony a Scripture. Would that stop too? A Scripture came to mind—a long one. It was more for him than her, but he shared it anyway. **Rejoice with those who rejoice; weep with those who weep. Live in harmony with one another. Do not be proud but enjoy the company of the lowly. Do not be conceited. Do not repay anyone evil for evil. Carefully consider what is right in the eyes of everybody… Romans 12:16-17. I love you, baby.**

Amen. I love you too. Be happy for me, she texted back.

His heart softened. *Lord, help me to be happy.* He FaccTimcd her. "Babe, can we start over? How about I take you out for a celebration?"

"I would like that." Her voice was sad.

"See you soon."

"Okay." She blew him a kiss. "Bye."

Instead of his regular comeback, Pace caught it in his fist and held it tight. He never knew when it would be the last one.

One week before she had to relocate, Harmony had never cried so much. She would miss her family and Pace. Since accepting the position in Omaha, Harmony had stopped taking freelance projects. When she received her employee packet from Applesome and Hutch, she spent more time praying than ever before.

Pace wanted to marry her. That thought was never far from her mind. With their time together coming to an end, Harmony wanted to do something special for him. Every morning, she prepared Pace's lunch, rode the train downtown to Monroe, and hand-delivered it to his job.

Despite her leaving, Pace introduced her to his coworkers as his lady friend and invited her to stay as he ate with gusto.

One day, she asked him, "I'm leaving in three days, so why are you telling people that I'm your girlfriend?"

"Until you get on that airplane, you are Pace Jamieson's girlfriend." As he chewed on his sandwich, he asked, "Are you sure you don't want to change your mind?"

"About what?"

"Us." Pace rested a strong hand on hers.

Shaking her head, Harmony tried not to cry. "We can't do this for three years. It's not fair to either of us."

Pace stood from the table. His lunch was over. He looked at her with so much tenderness that Harmony wrapped her arms around his waist, and his strong arms trapped her. He broke away first when he realized they had an audience.

On Saturday morning, Pace came to her parents' house to say goodbye. "I have something for you." It was an oblong white box tied with a gold ribbon.

"Thank you." Why did she feel guilty about pursuing her dreams? Harmony couldn't look him in the eyes. Whew. Why was love so hard?

"Open it," he said gently.

Her parents and brothers left the living room to give them some privacy. She untied it and removed the lid. A tennis bracelet. The diamonds winked at her as Pace removed it from the box and fastened it around her wrist, then he took her hands in his. "I can't say goodbye, but I respect you and want you to succeed. But if you need anything—and I mean anything—call me. Agreed?" Pace searched her eyes until she nodded.

He wrapped his arms around her. The feel of his embrace made her sigh with contentment. Harmony squeezed him, then made herself release him. She sniffed and hurried to the bathroom for a tissue to dry her eyes and wipe her nose. Harmony couldn't do this.

She heard her father speak to him. "Thanks for the way you treat my daughter. I respect you for that."

"Don't make yourself a stranger. I expect to see you at church, and there will always be a hot meal at the table for you," her mother said.

"Thank you, Mrs. Reed. I'll leave you now."

A coward, Harmony couldn't come out to face him, or she would quit her first job before the first day. The pain of separation was real.

Seconds later, Harmony heard the alarm of the front door opening and then closing. End of the chapter. She sat on the commode for a good cry.

"Come on, Harmony. We don't want to miss our flight," her mother called from the other side of the door. "Your dad and I are ready to go."

"Okay. Just a minute." She blew her nose, took deep breaths, and patted her face with cold water. Harmony stared at her image, then opened the door. "Ready."

In the living room, her brothers hugged her. "We'll be up there to see you soon," Shane said, and the other brothers nodded. They didn't hide the sadness on their faces because they had prior commitments. This wasn't college where they knew she would return home during breaks. Omaha, Nebraska, could turn out to be a permanent relocation if her career depended on it.

This was too overwhelming. Her blessing was bringing sorrow to the people she loved.

Chapter Twenty-nine

Gone. Pace mused his new reality without Harmony. She was seven hours away by car, yet it felt like she was planets away. He prayed for her success daily and tried to give his best efforts at work as if he didn't have a care in the world. It was a lie.

God was his refuge for his broken heart, and Sunday's service was powerful at Harmony's former place of worship, Christ the Redeemer Church. The praise team's "When You Want to Talk to Jesus" resonated with his soul because that's what he had been doing since Harmony left.

Then he sat in a reflective state as Pastor Sam Marks preached, "Sometimes walking with God gets uncomfortable…but you still walk, trusting Him with every step of the way. The race wasn't given to the swift but he who endures to the end. Don't be in such a rush about things in life. Keep a steady pace and trust God. This applies to your job, family, your heart's desires—everything. Meditate this week on Ecclesiastes nine verse eleven: *I returned, and saw under the sun, that the race is not to the swift, nor the battle to the strong, neither yet bread to the wise, nor yet riches to men of understanding, nor yet favor to men of skill; but time and chance happens to them all.*"

God was speaking to Pace. Pastor Marks said so many things during his half-hour sermon, but hearing his name and trusting God in the same sentence reminded Pace that God knew his future.

The pastor called for anyone ready to surrender to Christ to come to the altar for prayer. Two souls walked down, repented, and requested water baptism in Jesus' name.

The benediction followed the offering, then Pace headed to the parking lot, where he saw Harmony's parents. Mrs. Reed waved at him. He crossed the parking lot to speak.

"Pace, it's good to see you," Mrs. Reed said.

"How are you doing, son?" Mr. Reed extended his hand for a shake. It was a bittersweet endearment that Pace had earned.

"I'm inspired after the message I heard." Pace didn't know how the man didn't respond to the Word of God and surrender, but Pace knew God had a different message for people to address their individual needs.

It was hard for Pace to look at them and not see Harmony in their features. Pity flashed on their faces, but Pace ignored the hurt. Asking about their daughter would be torture, and in the end, he had to recognize his birthright in Jesus was his comforter.

"If you're hungry, we have plenty and would enjoy your company," Mrs. Reed said with a genuine smile.

Pace nodded and slipped his hands in his pocket. "Thank you. Maybe another time."

"Sure, any time," her husband said, and they went their separate ways.

Maybe it was time for him to take a trip home. Suddenly, he had a taste for some of his mom's good home cooking.

Until then, Pace had tried some great eateries not far from his apartment. Once he arrived there, he changed and decided to walk to Bryan's Steakhouse and give JC a call.

"Hey, bro. Praise the Lord." His friend's cheery voice was a pick-me-up. "What's going on?"

Pace shrugged. "I got a little homesick."

"*Ummm-hmm.* You can't fool me. You're not thinking about home. I know you love and miss Harmony."

Pace stopped at a light and waited to cross the street with other pedestrians. "Between you and me, I never thought I'd be the one without the happy ending." He spied his destination a few blocks up. "I mean, I was sure my sister wouldn't give you the time of day, not with Kami as her bodyguard, but here you are. Victoria trusts you. You're together on campus. Basically, you're together, and I'm alone. I've got to get out of this mood and trust God."

"Honestly, bro, maybe Harmony did you a favor. Long distances are hard and expensive for a relationship, especially when you both are establishing your careers."

This was not the pep talk Pace expected, but he guessed he needed to hear. "I felt I could make it work, but you're right. That would be a lot of frequent flyer miles that I was willing to take, but I'm giving her the space, and it's killing me."

"Sorry, man. I feel for you." JC sighed.

I doubt anyone could feel what I'm feeling, not even Harmony.

Harmony was excited and scared. She was ecstatic because this was the job she had prayed for, but nervous that she was alone. There was no college campus where she could meet other newbies or incoming students…or a Pace Jamieson. Living in the heart of downtown Omaha was her reality now.

She and her mom had found the place online, and it had great reviews. They weren't disappointed when she and her parents arrived to move her in.

Harmony chuckled at the names of the floor plans: Lewis, Mo, Johnny, Clark, Buster. What was the deal with the male names? But she decided on Lewis, which was seven-hundred-plus square feet.

Unlike living in the dorm and at home, Harmony had to shop for everything besides furniture—hangers, towels, cleaning supplies. She had all the basic necessities and food.

Her living space was set. Harmony hoped after three months on the job, she could purchase a car. Otherwise, she would have to rely on Omaha Metro, which couldn't compare to Chicago, which had the largest public transportation system in the country.

Two days later, her mom and dad repacked their small suitcases to head home. She cried at another goodbye. This was so different from when they moved her across states to attend college.

"You're going to be okay, Harmony. We have confidence in your abilities, and they will take you far," her father said with watery eyes.

"Don't forget we're praying for your success and safety," her mother said after numerous hugs of goodbye.

Harmony stood on the sidewalk with them, waiting for their ride share. She watched until the car faded from her view. Her shoulders slumped. She was alone.

On the first day on the job, her boss, Lynn Johnson, or LJ, introduced himself again and then her team for the dedicated project. Jason was an incredibly handsome black man with an air that hinted he worshipped himself. Kelli appeared at least ten years older and had a no-nonsense personality. The three were veterans who had transferred to Omaha. She and Whitney were the only two recent graduates, and then there was Yala, who had come from Texas with two years of experience at a PR firm.

The diversity was split. She, LJ, and Jason were black, while the other three were white.

"I'll show you to your office, then we'll meet in the conference room to learn more about our client, see past samples from other agencies, and brainstorm innovative designs that can wow the client, bring them business, and win awards for us," LJ said.

"All of you were hired because of your individual strengths. Our combined talents should produce a brand everyone will rave about for years." LJ grinned, and that's when Harmony noticed his gap, which was not significant but slight.

He produced vintage images on the screen of a toy manufacturer that had thrived for almost one hundred years before being sold and disappearing. "Now, they want to get back in the game. We need to create a brand identity that will last another hundred years." He laughed at his joke, which only he got. "I'll take twenty-five."

Harmony was already thinking of a motion graphic with the "then and now" message.

Kelli nodded. "LJ, we have to target the right audience to get excited about this…" She scrunched her nose at the toy the client was introducing. "Looks like a drone replica to me."

The next three days were exhausting as they reviewed images, film, and motion graphics. They brainstormed what type of story they needed to tell for the returning toymaker.

"LJ," Harmony said as they sat around the conference table, "in my head, I'm seeing the progression from die-cast cars to transformers to robots to toy drones that retrieve objects and bring them back to the controller."

"*Ooh.* I can see that in a motion graphic with the right color." Whitney grinned and high-fived Harmony, and then they looked to LJ for his thoughts.

"I want to see a mockup before I celebrate." LJ tapped his pen on the table.

"Well, the trend is reds, oranges, and yellows," Whitney said.

"But do they want to follow the leader or become a trendsetter?" Harmony countered as they suggested one idea after another.

"Our mission is to create an eye-catching ad the first time," LJ told them. "Second chances aren't guaranteed in this industry."

Second chances aren't guaranteed made her think of Pace. She had wanted to hold on to their relationship, but it wasn't sustainable. They both knew that. The thought made her sad, so she dismissed it.

By the end of the first week, the group had clocked in almost fifty hours individually.

Friday evening, LJ offered to treat his team at a bar and grill so they could get to know each other outside the workplace.

He ordered a sampler platter with veggies, drumettes, meatballs, sauces, and more as an appetizer.

The waiter came to take orders. Harmony said, "I'll order when I come back from the restroom."

Rule number one, never leave food or drink unattended when going out, and who knows how fast the servers were or if she would have to wait for a turn in the restroom. *Best to overthink things*, she thought.

As the night progressed, LJ, Jason, and Kelli's language became offensive as the liquor consumed them. LJ began to step on her shoes, and when she tried to pull back, he trapped her feet until she yanked them free. He blinked and grinned. This was not a fun bunch.

On Saturday morning, she had survived the first work week. Her fast-paced job kept her mind occupied. All her furniture had been delivered, and she glanced out one of the two-bedroom windows, staring at her surroundings.

Across the street, an old mattress factory building had been converted into a bar and grill. She would eat there soon. There was more to explore with the arena nearby, home of the NCAA Men's College World Series. Impressive. Maybe she could attend a game next summer. Not that she was into baseball with two sports teams in Chicago.

She became nostalgic about anything college-related in Omaha, fueled by local chatter about an upcoming Creighton Bluejays basketball game at the CHI Health Convention Center. It was within walking distance from her apartment, another college sport to keep her connected to a world she thought she was ready to escape.

Oversized art sculptures posed in motion in front of a thirty-five-foot clock welcomed visitors to the convention center. The *Illumina*, it was the pride and joy of Omahaians. She could see herself sitting in its presence, drawing inspiration for her work.

She would have to find a church to attend on Sundays and not get comfortable with online service every week. Kami and Victoria had already called her several times inquiring about that.

Harmony stopped staring out the window and decided to get out and explore what she hadn't already seen during the week. Putting on her jacket, Pace's tennis bracelet dangled on her wrist, constantly reminding her how much she missed him. If he were there, they would explore the sights and sounds and what locals called the Old Market together.

"Just be happy for the time you had," she coaxed herself as she left her apartment and headed outside. As she strolled toward 10th Street from Howard, she spied Zio's Pizzeria, taunted as the city's best. She doubted any pizza could stand up against Chicago's Gino's on East Superior. Her mouth immediately watered for their deep-dish pan pizza. She passed on Zio's. Not today.

When she entered the Old Market district, Harmony fell in love. The street performers reminded her of home. She became an audience of one as other spectators stopped, then kept going. Right there, she knew this would be her hot spot. She settled at an outdoor cafe and wasn't bothered by the early October breeze, which the Lord had orchestrated.

Harmony took selfies and sent them to Kami and Victoria with the caption: **Enjoying the Omaha sunshine.**

Backtracking at the World Famous Spaghetti Works, where the smell of fresh pasta lured her closer, she climbed the stairs to the entrance. Harmony could customize her spaghetti with her choice of ingredients. She did and then took it outside to enjoy the view.

One sight that caught her attention was the horse-drawn carriage. The white globe reminded her of Cinderella's carriage. She people-watched for a good hour as she nibbled on the garlic parmesan cheese bread that seemed to melt in her mouth with the pasta.

After a while, Harmony decided to head back to her apartment but stumbled upon a passageway inside a building that opened to an outside narrow path. It appeared to be a back alley between brick buildings where green plants seemed to flourish inside the brick walls. This was like a hidden virtual world that beckoned her to uncover a treasure.

She strolled by cafe-style outdoor eateries and shops in between until the secret world ended at another set of stairs, which she had to climb to leave.

Once back on the sidewalk, Harmony set her GPS to get her on the right path to her apartment.

Twelve minutes later, she was back inside her cozy space, which lacked the warmth of being around people.

Kami FaceTimed her. “Hey. Cute photo of you earlier. So you like Omaha?”

Harmony shrugged. “I like exploring—your brother taught me that—but it’s lonely doing it by myself. I miss you and Victoria.”

“And I’m sure someone else,” Kami said. “Let me add Victoria.”

Moments later, both sisters stared back at her.

“You smiled in those photos you sent us, but your eyes say otherwise,” Victoria said.

“It’s lonely.” Harmony pouted. “I’ve got to make new friends all over again.”

“How’s your team?” Kami asked.

“Nice. We all went out to dinner to have, of course, Omaha steaks.”

They laughed.

Harmony wanted to know about Pace, but that would do her no good. She asked how Victoria’s nursing classes were going.

“Challenging, which is what I like.” She grinned.

Kami talked about her new job, then said, "We'll come up to visit you soon."

"Okay." Harmony genuinely smiled. "I can't wait."

Beginning week two at work, a magnificent bouquet of vibrant colors caught her eye on the receptionist's side desk. It stood boldly among coworkers' mail and packages waiting to be retrieved.

"Oh, Harmony," Sarah, a dark-skinned beauty at the receptionist's desk, stopped her. "These are for you."

"Me?" In awe, Harmony slowly reached for them. *Pace?* she wondered. Besides exchanging morning Scriptures, they hadn't spoken.

"They're beautiful." Harmony sniffed and admired the assorted yellow roses trimmed with, purple orchids, flowering branches, and another mix of colorful treats for the eyes.

She couldn't wait until she reached her desk to open the card. Her heart steadied as she read the message: *Welcome to the grown-up world, but we got this! Love, your sisters Kami and Victoria.* Disappointment struck her that there was no mention of Pace. She did not like the "on hold" relationship she'd requested. Then happiness settled back in her heart, and she realized she was loved and had friends who cared about her.

"Wow," some ladies—she had yet to recall their names from last week—said. Members on her team—Jason, Kelli, Whitney, and Yala—gave her lopsided grins.

Whitney applauded. "Go, Harmony."

"Boyfriend?" LJ teased. When she told him they were from her college friends, he nodded. "Maybe those colors will serve as our inspiration this week."

"I'm inspired already." Whitney smiled.

At the end of the week, the group talked about meeting up again.

"I'll pass," Harmony said. She wasn't going to ask for a raincheck.

As the others were heading out the door, Harmony decided to stay over to explore different concepts to mockup. Alone in her office, she heard footsteps and looked up and saw LJ approaching with an unreadable expression.

"Harmony, in the future, you might want to reconsider going out with us on Friday nights for drinks."

"I don't drink." Harmony felt uncomfortable with his closeness and tone.

"Then consider it a team-building event. Whatever you're working on tonight better be worth skipping out on us come Monday." He turned and walked out.

Pressure. *Lord, how am I going to get out of this every Friday night?* she wondered. Now she was under more pressure to dazzle him come Monday.

It was going to be a long weekend.

Chapter Thirty

St. Louis.

It seemed like forever since Pace had been home. Evidently, his younger brothers thought so as they held up large signs. Chance waved one that read: *My big brother is home!*

Paden, on the other hand, stood tall and tried not to show emotion as he held a generic welcome home sign.

His parents stood nearby with smiles, while Kami and Victoria, dressed like runway models, grinned from ear to ear. J.C. was there too.

After hugs and kisses, Pace followed his family to their SUV in the airport parking garage.

"It took you forever to come home," Chance said as they settled in the vehicle.

"Sorry, I'm here now." Pace grinned and rubbed the curls on his head then anchored his arm around Chance's shoulder in a bear hug. His youngest brother protested while laughing.

"Where's Harmony? She didn't come with you?" Chance asked.

His parents were quiet as Pace gave an answer that wouldn't crush his baby brother's heart like his. "Harmony got a new job and had to move to Omaha."

Chance scrunched his nose. He didn't like Pace's answer. "Well, she'd better come visit me."

Pace exhaled. His brother took it better than him.

It was Friday night, and usually, the family did their own thing, but Pace was treated as the main attraction. Kami and Victoria would spend the night at home instead of Grandma BB's.

It was like old times. The house was alive with love and laughter. This was what Pace needed. Chance and Paden didn't leave his side as Pace played a video game with them, to their delight. Victoria and Kami weren't as chatty as they seemed to think before they spoke, never mentioning Harmony's name.

Saturday morning, he was about to meet JC at the gym when he passed by his sisters' bedroom and heard Harmony's name mentioned. Victoria wasn't happy about whatever was being said.

"Girl, you need backup. I don't like your boss," Victoria said.

Pace wouldn't eavesdrop. If it was something serious, he hoped they would let him know or Harmony would call him. When he heard Kami promise not to mention whatever they were discussing with him, Pace knew no information would be forthcoming. *Lord, You know all things. Please watch over her.*

At the gym, he and JC greeted each other with a handshake and pat on the back, then started their routines while catching up. "It looks like you're taking care of my sisters. I appreciate that."

JC shrugged like it was no big deal, but it was. "I figure you wouldn't have it any other way. Both of them."

"I wouldn't." Pace rested from his first set of weightlifting.

"Any word from Harmony?"

"Nope. I think she means business by putting my affections on hold. I have a time limit, man. I love her to life, but before there was Pace and Harmony, there was Pace."

"I'm glad you can move on like that." JC shook his head in disbelief.

"I can't. Not right now, but God will open the door when the hold runs out, which I hope won't happen."

Saturday afternoon, back at his parents' house, it was quiet. His brothers went to a school game, and Kami and Victoria had their own agendas.

Parke and Cheney were cuddled up to watch a movie in their makeshift theater room. He smiled when he walked in on them. "Okay, lovebirds, your son is in the room."

His dad paused the movie and grinned but didn't unwrap his arm from around his wife. "What's up, son?"

Pace took a seat on the ottoman. "Back for more life lessons."

"If this is about Harmony…" Cheney paused and frowned with the same expressions his sisters had when they didn't want to say something. "Maybe you moved too fast by relocating to Chicago. That's a life lesson. Sometimes, being overly confident like your dad isn't a good thing."

"*Humph*," his father objected. "You see, I got my woman—the one God had for me." He smothered Cheney with a kiss on the cheek, and she blushed.

Cheney playfully scrunched her nose at him. "I wouldn't have it any other way. I knew he loved me."

"Harmony hinted that a relationship was not her priority in the beginning. I thought she changed her mind when I moved to Chicago."

"Son," Parke chimed in, "think of it this way: Do you think Kami and Victoria are ready for a serious relationship?"

Pace grunted. "Absolutely not."

"What about Harmony?"

"That's different because I love her." He lowered his voice to remain respectful.

"JC has strong feelings for Victoria, and after so many years of her avoiding men, I'm glad she feels safe around him. Women are sometimes in a different place in relationships than men, Give Harmony time to grow." Cheney smiled.

"JC is here to protect my sisters. What protection does Harmony have? I don't know if there's someone nearby to protect her." Pace puffed in frustration.

"Son," Parke jumped in, "your thoughts are all over the place. Remember, Harmony isn't alone. Jesus is her covering, but if it makes you feel better, we have kinfolks in practically every state, including the Robnetts, whose ancestors dotted the Oregon Trail. Queen Bee told me besides Kansas City, there are relatives in Colorado, Nebraska, and Iowa. It's a lot of Robnetts. If some are in the Omaha area, maybe they could befriend her."

That gave Pace an idea. "Thanks, Mom and Dad." He stood and kissed them, then headed to his room to make calls.

Queen Bee answered with cheeriness in her voice.

"Hey, nephew. How is everyone?"

"The family is good."

"And Harmony? You two make a cute couple. She surrendered to the Lord. Perfect! I think it's romantic you moved to Chicago to be with her," she rambled on.

"Well, it's not so perfect. She couldn't find a job in her field in Chicago, so Omaha came calling. She decided to take it."

Wow, Pace couldn't believe his family hadn't given Queen Bee an update. Maybe they were hoping, like him, that he and Harmony would grow closer, not apart.

"Oh, Pace, I'm sorry. I know that's heartbreaking. But long-distance relationships do work—for a while."

"That's what I told her."

Queen Bee *tsk*ed. "What did you expect her to do? Even though a woman would appreciate any man who would give it all up for love, Harmony is a beautiful, carefree soul who has to find her way in life. Give her time to realize you, my nephew Parke Jamieson the eighth is the catch."

This cousin, who he addressed as an auntie, always made him blush with her accolades. "Thanks, can you introduce me to the cousins in Omaha who can keep an eye out for her?"

"Let me put together a game night next weekend with the family. Can you make it?"

"Make it? I'll book my flight when I end this call." Was Queen Bee kidding him? Pace had expected an introduction through a phone call or video chat, not a meet-and-greet on short notice. "How can I go to Omaha without seeing Harmony?"

"I'll invite her. She's met me, Rejoice, and Duchess, so she might come."

"Me showing up unannounced wouldn't be giving her space."

"Nephew, she has to know that there is a possibility you might come. After all, we are your family. But I won't pressure her."

Pace grinned. He loved family. "That might work. See you next weekend in Omaha. Text me the address."

"I'm sure Kami and Victoria would want to come and see their friend."

"Just don't mention I had anything to do with it." If his sisters could keep secrets, so could he.

Harmony wasn't expecting a call from Kami and Victoria's cousin, Queen Bee, but she was happy to hear a friendly voice that was sultry and distinct, as if she were reading a movie script.

After a few minutes of chatting, Queen Bee said, "My nieces—young cousins—told me the exciting news about your job that brought you to Omaha. Although I'm sorry to hear about you and my nephew—I had to throw my opinion out there—I would like to invite you to a Robnett game night next Saturday."

"I'm not good at those game questions. One of the Jamieson twins came to my rescue to finish the books of the Bible, remember?"

Queen Bee laughed. "That was so sweet of Camille, and our family loves you, so there is no wrong answer you can give."

"Thank you for saying that, but I thought you lived in Kansas City, Kansas."

"I do, but we have Robnetts in about five or more states, including four cousins in Omaha."

"I would like that." Any reason to look forward to the weekends other than the awful Friday night team-building happy hour. She had already decided to visit Bible-teaching churches in the area. The online service from her Chicago church wasn't the same as being there.

"You'll get a chance to meet more of us. Besides, Rejoice and Duchess are coming with me. I'm sure it won't take much to convince Kami and Victoria to come. And…I'm sure Pace wouldn't want to be left out. I know he loves you—I had to give you my opinion again."

Harmony's heart fluttered. "If he wants to come, I won't stop him." *But If I look into his eyes, I'll miss him more.* Harmony had to stay focused on her first job, and that man was a distraction—big time.

"My cousins Esquire, Dame, Vaughn, and Lawson live there."

"I love their names."

"And I have to admit they are fine—Pace Jamieson fine—but I'm sure they won't cross the line, unlike one cousin, Frederic, who has been banned from family gatherings, or he'll get a beat down coming he deserves, but that's another story."

Harmony wanted to hear the details, but her mind was on Pace. "Pace and I aren't doing long-distance dating."

"Sometimes, honey, finding love is a long shot. I would take it. Enough about that." Queen Bee gave her the address but offered to pick her up so she wouldn't have to get a ride share. "Lock my number in, and if you need anything—doesn't matter how small—the Robnetts and Jamiesons gotcha."

Choked with emotion, she whispered her thanks before she said goodbye.

Harmony was riding a spiritual high Monday when she walked into the office. Besides the online sermon from her home church in Chicago, she spoke with each family member, checking up on her. The Jamieson sisters kept her on the phone, laughing at Kami's antics on her job, and then Queen Bee's invitation made Harmony feel loved and not so alone anymore.

She and Whitney had formed a strong bond at work, maybe because their status as recent college graduates with little experience connected them.

LJ began his morning meeting with all smiles. "The client liked the colors we chose for their toy product and can't wait to see how we use them in the branding. Harmony, your sketches are attention-grabbing, and the concept is outside the norm," he nodded, "but something is missing. I would like to see bolder expressions on the toys."

"Yes, sir."

"Yala," he said, rubbing his mustache and squinting, "I think you're on to something with your catchphrases, but I'm waiting for it all to come together. Remember, sometimes illogical phrases become catchy and logical to consumers."

She nodded.

Jason assured LJ he was committed to crafting compelling web designs.

And as part of the meeting, they studied award-winning designs from competitors and discussed their likes and dislikes about the ads.

When LJ dismissed them, he complimented Harmony's attire. "You're glowing too. I don't know if it's your makeup, hair, or that pantsuit you're rocking, but nice." His eyes twinkled in appreciation.

"Thanks, LJ. My glow is from the Holy Ghost." Harmony walked away, not wanting to read more into his praise.

Her boss grunted.

Harmony didn't care about his reaction. God gave her this job, and He would cause her to shine.

But it's about to dim, the devil taunted her.

Chapter Thirty-one

Mid-week, Uncle Philip's brother—Pace sometimes addressed him as the judge—texted him as he walked off the Red Line L-train on Garfield.

Hi, Pace. How is Chicago treating you? I've meant to visit you before now. I'm coming that way this weekend. I hope we can do dinner.

Although he enjoyed conversations with the judge, only the Lord could stop Pace from going to Nebraska that weekend under the guise of fun and games with the Robnetts. His uncle-in-law, Judge Drexel Dupree, would have to take a rain check.

What's up, Unc? Actually, I'm traveling to Omaha. Auntie Queen Bee is getting her family together so Harmony can meet them. Did you know she moved there for a job?

I'm sure you're not happy about that. I thought you two would get married before me. :)

Yeah, me too. Pace sighed. The tragedy of their relationship was they both loved each other.

Seconds later, Pace's phone rang. He grinned at the caller ID. "Good evening."

"Good evening, nephew. What's this about seeing Queen Bee?"

It was no secret that his uncle-in-law had a big crush on his auntie. Although Philip's wife, Queen Jamieson Dupree, and Queen Robnett, affectionately called Queen Bee, were distant cousins, they were as close as sisters.

"Actually, I reached out to her for the Robnetts to look out for Harmony. Kami and Victoria are flying there, too."

Drexel laughed. "That woman is a hoot. Are you thinking about driving or flying?"

"Flying." Pace was not about to waste time on a road trip. He wanted to get to Omaha and see Harmony.

"I'll book my ticket now." They chatted for a few minutes then the judge hurried off to make travel plans.

Pace walked through the door of his apartment. He had worked a few hours of overtime to complete a job for a major client. Pace wasn't hurting for money. He accepted the extra hours to fill the void of Harmony's absence.

On Friday evening, the judge waited for Pace to arrive at their terminal gate at O'Hare Airport. Instead of driving the three-and-a-half hours to Chi-town, he took a flight from Springfield, Illinois' state capital, with a stopover in Chicago to travel with Pace.

The two shook hands and exchanged pats on the back. "Have you ever been to Omaha?" Pace asked.

"I've never been to Nebraska, but I thought Queen Bee lived in Kansas. Did she move there too?"

"Oh no. I called her about Harmony, and she called cousins who live in the city."

The judge nodded as he stretched out and crossed one ankle over his knee. Two female travelers sat across from them. They appeared to be in their thirties. Pace caught them staring more than once at his uncle, a commanding figure even without his robe.

Harmony's name came up first as they chatted, then Queen Bee's.

"So what's the plan with your lady love?" He folded his hands and adjusted his body to study Pace to decipher whether he would tell the truth. They weren't in court.

"I don't have a plan. All the plans I thought we had were canceled." He twisted his lips as if there was a sour taste in his mouth. "Or put 'on hold' as she called it." Pace used air quotes.

He lifted a suspecting brow, reminding Pace of his brother, Pastor Philip. "Well, you two are young and have careers to establish."

"That could have been done in Chicago together, but I don't begrudge her for accepting the job. She tried diligently for months to get something here."

"So where's the compromise?"

"We don't have one."

The judge grunted. "Watch me. Let me show you young folks how to form a long-distance relationship if Queen Bee gives me a chance."

It was Pace's turn to laugh. He had seen many guys hit on Queen Bee, and she stung their egos. "Okay, Unc. I'm originally from the Show Me State, so show me."

The agent announced that passengers should begin to line up to board their flight.

The pair arrived at Omaha Airport an hour later. He texted his parents and Queen Bee: Landed. His sisters would be there in the morning and stay with Harmony. Pace secured a rental car, which the judge insisted on paying for, and then they headed to the hotel.

How would she respond to him after not seeing him for three weeks?

They checked in at Embassy Suites by Hilton, where Pace's job had a corporate account. The employees could use the discount anytime they traveled. They were early enough to see the city before tomorrow afternoon's Robnett game night. Pace was more excited to see Harmony again than the fun and games with family.

"Did you tell Queen Bee that I had come with you?" The judge seemed calm, but looked eager for his answer.

"Ah, nope." His mind had been elsewhere.

"Do it," he said in his no-nonsense judge tone.

Pace did as told when he stopped at a light since he was behind the wheel, and Queen Bee responded immediately. **Excellent. The more, the merrier.**

The judge frowned. "Does excellent mean she's good to see me, or is that a generic response?"

"I guess you'll find out, Unc." Pace accepted his key card from the desk clerk, then asked, "Where is the best place to grab a bite to eat and check out the city?"

"We're a few blocks from where the Old Market district begins. Check out the city's vibes and enjoy the food selections."

Pace glanced at the judge and then shrugged. "Why not? It's nice outside for a walk."

"How will we know when we're at the Old Market district?"

"Follow the red cobble street. Enjoy, gentlemen."

The men checked into their rooms then returned to the lobby. Ready, they left for their exploration. As they strolled, Pace noted the older buildings that had been re-purposed into thriving businesses.

A row of red brick two-story buildings, maybe three floors, reminded Pace of a scene from a Western movie. The cars parked at angles for easy zip-ins and outs. The sidewalks were sheltered by makeshift roofs covered by batches of flowers to absorb the sun.

They passed by coffee shops, candy stores, and clothing shops until dining places began to pop up.

Turning on Howard Street, the judge paused in front of the Twisted Fork. "My treat," he said, nodding to the restaurant.

"Why not?" Pace followed him to the entrance, where the sign read, *Wait to Be Seated.*

A petite hostess appeared with red pixie hair, small-rimmed glasses, and red lipstick. "Welcome. Would you like to dine in or on our patio?"

"Patio," Pace said.

As they'd walked through the city, his mind wandered. Where was Harmony? Was she happy? Did she like her job? What was she doing on a Friday evening? All questions he wanted the answers to.

Once he and the judge were seated and handed the menus, all conversation ceased as they considered their choices. The waitress appeared and introduced herself as she dropped off two glasses of water. "What would you like to drink?"

Both asked for lemonade, and she left to do their bidding. When she returned, they were ready to order.

"The Yukon Ribeye with asparagus looks good." The judge rubbed his chin, then folded his menu and handed it back to her.

"Good choice. And you, sir?" She turned to Pace.

"*Hmmm*. What do you suggest?"

She chuckled. "If you like meatloaf, then you've got to try the Pitchfork Ranch Meatloaf-N-Mac."

"Sold." He grinned.

After they received and blessed their food, both men ate with gusto, then patted their stomachs but made no rush to leave as the server tapped off their water. The judge paid the tab, and they planned to return to their hotel but made the wrong turn and stumbled upon what Pace could only describe as an upscale gangway with greenery dripping from second- and third-floor windows.

"Oh, wow. This is hidden," the judge said as he turned to explore.

Not having anything too urgent to do back at the hotel except think about Harmony, Pace followed.

"Man, can you believe we passed up a Mexican joint?" He pointed to Trini's as if he was about to step inside for a snack.

It wasn't crowded and one group at the table made Pace catch his breath. Harmony was with them. She looked bored, and a couple of them appeared drunk as they raised their glasses to make a toast.

Pace pulled his uncle back from entering.

The judge turned around and frowned. “Hey, I was just going to check out the menu.”

“Harmony is in there,” he whispered. “I just want to admire her from a distance.”

He indulged Pace by folding his arms and leaning against the brick wall before finally tugging on Pace’s sleeve. “That’s enough admiring, nephew. Come on before you embarrass her and get charged with stalking. For the record, I have no jurisdiction outside of Illinois to help you.”

Pace was about to step toward the entrance, but the judge blocked his path. “Whatever you’re thinking of doing, don’t. You’ll see her tomorrow. Be satisfied with that.”

That was the problem. Pace wasn’t satisfied with this situation at all—as they retraced their steps to the hotel. Yeah, he couldn’t wait until tomorrow.

Chapter Thirty-two

Harmony hated when people couldn't hold their liquor and felt liberated to say and do whatever they chose without taking accountability for their actions.

Not only was LJ drunk, but so was Kelli. Whitney exchanged turned-off looks with Harmony. At least, she knew better than to sit next to or in front of him in case LJ felt the urge to become playful. Harmony was so ready to go back to her apartment. The highlight of her weekend would be game night, meeting people who lived there.

She let her mind drift as LJ talked about his troubled childhood with his father in prison. There had to be something in her contract where she could opt out of these after-hours fake team-building gatherings on Friday evening.

"Well, I'm heading home," she said firmly, ignoring LJ's protest.

Whitney, in solidarity, got to her feet too. "See you all on Monday." She walked out of the restaurant with Harmony.

They hurried from the Old Market passageway to 10th Street.

"Girl, I am not going to another team-building anything," Whitney echoed, her tone mirroring Harmony's frustration.

"I'm with you. I'd rather work late on a Friday night." Harmony shivered with disdain. She didn't live far, but it was getting dark. Whitney stayed in apartments closer to Creighton University.

They split a rideshare fare. Harmony was dropped off first, then Whitney. She texted Harmony that she had made it home.

With two months to go, Harmony couldn't wait to purchase a car. Taking public transportation during the day was fine, but she didn't want to risk her safety at night. She tidied her apartment because Kami and Victoria would arrive from St. Louis in the morning. Harmony could barely wait to see her friends. She wondered if Pace would come or decline. Harmony hadn't left him much encouragement.

But she missed him so much it was as if she could feel his presence. With that thought, she drifted off to sleep.

The next morning, Harmony paced the lobby of her apartment as she waited for the Jamieson sisters to arrive. Their plane had landed, and they were in a rideshare on their way.

When they stepped out of the car, Harmony raced out the door. The trio screamed their excitement and embraced in a tight hug. Harmony didn't realize she was crying until she sniffed.

"You look great," Victoria commented as Harmony looped her arms through theirs as the sisters rolled their carry-ons into the building.

"Wow, this is nice," Victoria said, admiring the lobby's grayish-blue and black décor with peach accents.

"And it seems secure." Kami nodded. "Now, you're making me ready to move out on my own."

"It's neat and lonely at times. Being an adult isn't as glamorous as I had imagined. Harmony gave them a tour of her small apartment. "I'm still decorating. I have the basics."

"You have potential," Victoria said as she glanced out the window. "Wow. The convention center is almost in your backyard. You can attend events and walk back to your apartment."

"Yep, I have a bird's-eye view." She grabbed her keys. Come on. I'll treat you at the Table Coffee Company."

Their walk was two blocks. They ordered immediately and found a table near a window and chatted. Harmony was happy her friends were thriving with their professional and personal lives. "I've missed you two."

"And we're proud of you for taking that step toward the career you prepared for," Kami said.

"Even if I broke your brother's and my heart for it?" She searched Kami's and Victoria's faces for the truth.

"Our brother is strong and determined. He respects your decision. Who's to say you two won't find someone else?" Kami acted as if her statement wouldn't have a magnanimous effect on her.

"And that's going to be a problem for somebody." Victoria squinted.

"I know." Harmony bowed her head. She would definitely blame herself if Pace found his happily ever after with another woman worthy of his love. Yes, Pace would be the one she let get away. That was a possibility. Would she be okay with that? "But if it were you two, would you take the opportunity? Be honest, Kami and Victoria."

"Yep," the sisters said in unison.

"Well, Pace is here…" Kami began.

Harmony's heart fluttered. *He's here. He came?*

"And I guess when you see him, you'll know whether you made the right decision." Kami took a sip from her cup, eying her. "Only thing I can say is I'm glad I'm not in your shoes."

Hours later, the ladies decided to take a rideshare to the venue for the Robnett gathering at Haven 150, saving Queen Bee from coming out of her way to get them. Harmony was surprised when their driver turned onto a road that led to a farm with animals behind a fenced-in pasture. A rural setting.

"This will be different. We're accustomed to the Jamiesons hosting family game night at hotels. It's a little chilly for an outdoor family gathering," Victoria said.

Then the welcome sign came into view. "*This venue was founded to provide recreational therapy for persons with disabilities. Our property is open to businesses and private parties to help support our mission of serving the disabled community*," Harmony read silently, reflecting on the charity work this organization was doing. Suddenly, she didn't mind being here.

In the distance were two structures—a traditional three-story redwood barn with a gray metal roof and white-paned windows and doors, something she would see in a portrait. The other building, feet away, reminded her of a large wood cabin with a sloped roof. The area would be clean and deserted if it weren't for the cars already parked there.

The trio stepped out and tightened their jackets close against the cool air. Underneath, Harmony sported the extra Jamieson T-shirt Kami had brought her and felt pretty because the sisters did her hair and makeup like they used to do in college.

They looked around and walked inside. The large meeting room was rustic as the exterior with a cathedral ceiling with wood beams, concrete floors, and round tables. Despite the size, the place wasn't overpowering, as the unknown faces who looked at her.

About thirty or forty of Kami and Victoria's family wore a mix of Jamieson and Robnett T-shirts. They stood to welcome her as if she was the guest of honor at a surprise celebration.

Queen Bee strutted toward them with a flair in every step to give them hugs. "My nieces Victoria and Kami, and Harmony, my niece-in-waiting. My opinions are my own."

As she returned her embrace, Harmony didn't feel like an outsider. She never did at one of these family gatherings. Although all eyes were on her, one pair had a strong pull, and she turned to the right. One man stood out among the tall and handsome men in the room.

Pace Jamieson.

His black family T-shirt stretched across his chest. The cream blazer he wore over it couldn't camouflage his toned muscles. His hands were in his pockets as he stared at her. Pace didn't blink, and his expression was unreadable. Her heart screamed, *I miss you!* and then fell out in a temper tantrum because it wanted hugs and kisses from this man.

Duchess, Rejoice, and the others Harmony had met greeted her like they were welcoming an old friend. Pace hadn't moved, but something magnetic pulled her as the others parted a path until Harmony stood before him.

The room was silent as if everyone was holding their breath, including Harmony. Who would make the first move? When Pace slipped his hands out of his pockets and opened his arms.

She surrendered and collapsed in them. Cheers engulfed them like a whirlwind.

Harmony tried not to tear up, but her emotions overpowered her. "I've missed you." She looked into his eyes. She was foolish to think she could be okay without him.

"And I've missed you too." Pace gently rubbed her back. "We can work this out."

With her arms secured around his waist, Harmony snuggled deeper into his chest. "I want that."

Kami cleared her throat. "I think our job is done." She chuckled.

When reality hit, she and Pace noticed they were the center of attention. Pace squeezed her hand and pulled out a chair for her at his table. He lifted his arm at the small gathering. "Carry on, accomplices. Let your games begin. I've already won."

Chapter Thirty-three

Queen Bee stood in the front of the room. "Harmony, this gathering was meant as a meet-and-greet, but we see that my nephew has already greeted you. You two look good together—I thought I'd add that."

Harmony smiled and rested her back against Pace's chest, feeling at ease.

"Since you're on Robnett turf, I'm going to introduce you to my family, who have come to support you. Before I give you a brief overview of how the Jamiesons and Robnetts are related, let me make introductions," Queen Bee said.

"I feel loved that your family came here for me," Harmony mumbled.

Pace kissed her hair. "You are loved."

As Harmony tried to concentrate, Pace's closeness was making it difficult.

"Harmony, you already know my sister Rejoice, but I don't think you've met my youngest sister, Princess."

With all three together, let the photo shoot begin, Harmony thought, admiring their striking beauty.

"You've already met my cousin Duchess at Christmas. Here are her older sisters, Sapphire and Jewel."

All of them had light hazel eyes.

"Next comes my male cousins—or some of them." She waved for the occupants at the all-male table to stand. "Seth and Addam are brothers. They live in Kansas City." They raised their hands and nodded at Harmony. "Next are brothers Gold and Sterling."

Whoa. Fine and built like wrestlers. "I'd be afraid to meet them in the dark. Very afraid," Harmony mumbled to herself.

Pace kissed her forehead. "They would protect you."

"Daniel and Dillard are twins from Des Moines, and finally…" She squinted at the group that hadn't been mentioned. "You might as well stand. Keeping the best for last," she teased against the others' grumblings and protests. The bearded gentlemen were as good-looking as the others. Who were their parents?

Queen Bee laughed. "We're supposed to play a game, not have a testosterone competition, Robnett cousins. This smart aleck is Esquire Robnett. He lives here in Omaha and guess his profession…a lawyer."

"It just made sense." He shrugged and pivoted on his heel as if he was modeling his physique.

"Lawson is his brother who also lives here." The man lifted his glass for cheers toward Harmony and Pace. "This one is Vaughn, who managed to be an only child."

Vaughn pumped his fist in the air. "Who needs siblings when I've got these hardheaded cousins?"

Harmony blinked, trying to remember them all. "There are a lot of them."

"There's more, trust me, if the married ones had brought their children. Anyway, the only ones you need to remember are the ones here who are a phone call away," Pace said.

"Okay." She closed her eyes and accepted Pace's soft kiss.

"Well, Harmony," Queen Bee said, causing Harmony to jump to attention, "these are the ones who could make it on short notice to meet you."

"Don't believe our cousin," Esquire said. "We were threatened."

"Yeps," floated around the room.

"Let me give you a recap of how we're related to the Jamiesons. Hush," Queen Bee shushed her family into silence. "We're descendants of two sisters. The Robnetts are from Queen Pokou, born around 1767, and Princess Adaeze, who married King Seif—Jamieson's ancestors from their son, Paki Kokumuo Jaja. The Jamiesons track the men in their family. The Robnetts cherish the ladies as queens." She tapped the top of her head as if she was wearing a crown. "My eleventh great-grandmother Pokuo married King Kofi. They had Bolanie in 1786, Paki's first cousin, who married Prince Ekow. They had Princess Kadida, the mother of Queen, born in 1823. That is when our African ties were severed."

Esquire stood to pick up the story. "Not quite. Queen and Issa never married, but their offsprings found their way to each other while in American bondage and consummated their marriage in spirit."

When he began to pace the room as if he were arguing a case in court, Harmony and Pace chuckled.

"We've been able to pick up the trail in the Land of the Free," Esquire said sarcastically. "We were able to trace our lineage from Queen's daughter, Viney, a mulatto enslaved since birth in 1842. Her enslaver, Duncan G. Campbell, was her father. The irony is he died when she was three and promised her emancipation at sixteen and an inheritance of five thousand dollars. Due to inflation today, it would be worth about thirty-eight hundred dollars." He shrugged. "Anyway, she never received it."

Lawson stood and playfully nudged his brother aside. "Sorry, he's taking too long. A slave trader sold her in Missouri at six years old. She was housed in a slave pen, then Dr. John Sappington in St. Louis purchased her…"

Pace began to recite verbatim with his cousin, "When he died, Viney was sixteen. Slaveholder William Robnett traveled from Columbia, Missouri, to make purchases of human chattel at St. Louis' Old Courthouse. Unwittingly,

William Robnett had joined the descendants of the African groom and the bride."

"Unbelievable." Harmony shook her head. "I am so impressed with anyone who can trace their African roots when records were destroyed."

"That's why there's oral history, babe," Pace whispered.

"Okay, we've bored our guest of honor enough. Let's eat and get this party started," Esquire said.

I'm anything but bored, Harmony thought, then looked at Pace, who seemed to know what she was thinking when he brushed his lips against hers.

Ah, the kiss. That's what she missed most of all.

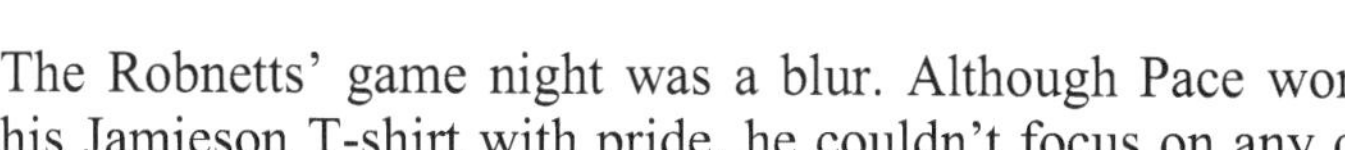

The Robnetts' game night was a blur. Although Pace wore his Jamieson T-shirt with pride, he couldn't focus on any of the questions. He let his sisters compete for Jamieson bragging rights.

Pace was more than content to opt out of playing as his arm rested on the back of Harmony's chair. His stomach growled as his appetite returned. He had been nervous all morning, not knowing what to expect.

Now, as she snuggled next to him, Pace thanked the Lord for this moment, although they didn't know what the future held for them.

"Hungry?" Pace whispered so as not to interrupt the Robnetts at his table on the edge of their seats, ready to claim the answer for another point.

Harmony faced him. "A little."

"I'll get us something to eat." He was about to untangle his arm, but she stopped him. "I'll go with you. I don't want to lose this closeness."

He understood and grinned. Pace loved this woman. They walked toward the buffet table at the end of the room. As they filled their plates, he asked, "So, do you like it here? The people? The job?"

"I haven't really explored it. I miss the L train and the META to get me anywhere and everywhere. Although I do like the charm of the Old Market district."

Pace waited for her to comment on the people as he recalled seeing her at the Mexican restaurant. He added a serving of meatballs to his and her plates.

"Thank you. I so missed eating out with you." Harmony leaned into him and let him continue to put appetizers on her plate.

"Me too, baby. Me too." He kissed the top of her hair.

"I like my coworkers and the challenges of the project I've been assigned, but…" She twisted her mouth.

"But what, baby?"

"We have these team-building happy hours every week at this Mexican restaurant. I like the food but hate some of the company. My boss, LJ, likes to drink and wants company while he does it."

That explained what he witnessed. He told her about seeing her when he and his uncle returned to the hotel.

"I wish you had come inside and rescued me, then I would have had an excuse to leave."

Pace shrugged. "I didn't know what liberties I had with an on-hold relationship." He scanned the room for the judge, thinking about him for the first time since they'd arrived. He chuckled because his uncle quietly studied Queen Bee.

"I don't know how to work a long-distance relationship, especially with the project I'm working on, which has a ridiculous deadline for a seasonal ad. In my opinion, the client is already too late. I don't want making plans and canceling them to become the norm."

"Babe, there is nothing normal about a man and his lady living in two separate cities."

"I'm not hearing any solutions. I tried to get a job in Chicago. You know that." Her voice held an edge of frustration. "The doors were closed."

Pace thought about the Scriptures in Revelation 3:7-8. "But God can open them where no man can shut them for you."

Harmony was quiet. If she didn't believe him, He knew she would believe God. "When I leave here tomorrow, I'll give you an open airline ticket to come home whenever you want for whatever reason, and I promise you won't regret it."

Chapter Thirty-four

Happiness bloomed inside Harmony three days later, causing her to smile at the memories of seeing Pace last weekend. He had left her with kisses, promises of his love, and his commitment to "them."

Maybe she was smiling too much because it irritated LJ. He was in a bad mood, as the client liked some aspects of the campaign but not all, and he wanted to launch the ads before Black Friday, which was less than thirty days away.

It was an unrealistic deadline, but LJ promised the client his team would do their best to have it in time for the holiday shopping period. Everyone was focused, while LJ was stressed and liked to pass on his frustrations. Harmony had learned he had a bit of a temper, with or without alcohol.

The team-building happy hour events ceased as everyone was required to work overtime. *Praise God* was Harmony's first thought that she wouldn't have to tolerate his behavior after hours in a drinking binge. She and the others mostly collaborated in the conference room but worked solo at their offices on Friday after work. Pace checked in with a text, and she let him know she was at work.

Call me when you leave. Love you.

After she responded with the same sentiments, Harmony tried to manipulate the daisy yellow's sharpness with fuchsia on the banner without it coming off as pink or purple. She glanced up as her door slowly opened, and LJ stepped inside and closed it quietly. Something was off about him. He seemed dark and savage. Immediately, a fight-or-flight instinct kicked in.

"What's up, LJ?" she asked, trying not to overthink his behavior.

He said nothing as he approached and peeked over her shoulder at her screen as if he were having trouble reading the large text.

This felt weird. He inched closer to her monitor, trapping Harmony in her personal space. One false move, and they would kiss. *Gross*. She looked away. "LJ, you're making me uncomfortable, so please give me some breathing room."

"Are you afraid of me?" LJ asked in a seductive tone.

Lord, rescue me! "You should be afraid of me," she said bravely, waiting for God to come through.

"I'm your boss. Why should I be afraid of someone who works under me and has to follow my commands?" LJ grunted.

When he placed his large hand on her shoulder, Harmony pushed her chair back with all the strength God had given her. Her heart raced as she attempted to go around to get out the door. "Whitney! Kelli!" she called out to her coworkers.

"I let them go home."

This was not good. "And why am I still here?"

"I thought we could talk. You know I've been attracted to you since I hired you—"

"To do a job for this company." As he inched closer, Harmony screamed with all her might, "Jesus."

That caught him off guard. She ran back to her desk and grabbed her purse. She pulled out her mace. "You've crossed the line, LJ. Get out of my office—now!"

He didn't move as he watched her. She stared him down until he snarled and, with an arrogant strut, walked out. "You've got to come out sometime, and I'll be waiting for you." He winked and closed the door behind her.

Now what? Once she left the room, he would likely ambush and rape her. Her friends and family couldn't help her.

I am here, God whispered.

As tears filled her eyes, Harmony sniffed. "God, he's stronger than me. I don't want to be a victim. I'm scared."

I have an army ready to dispatch, God whispered.

Harmony's heart pounded with hope. Her mind drifted to what one of Pace's cousins said: "If you have any trouble while you're here or need us, call." That came from one of the bodybuilder twins, but they lived in Kansas City. She needed someone closer. The lawyer's and his brother's numbers came up as she scrolled her phone. She called Lawson.

He answered right away. "What's going on, Harmony?"

"I'm trapped at work. My boss sent everyone home but me. He wants to seduce me." Her hands were shaking, but she refused to release the can of mace. "I'm in my office at…"

"I already have the address, and I'm en route. Don't leave the office. Call nine-one-one."

Swallowing hard, Harmony kept an eye on the door. Her fingers shook as she tapped in the three digits to the police for help.

"Nine-one-one. What's your emergency?"

"I'm at work—alone, and my boss attempted to assault me sexually. I'm in my office, but he says I have to come out sometime, so I'm trapped." Suddenly, the room went black. The outside streetlights illuminated shadows in her office. "Oh, my God, he's turned off the lights."

"Give me the address and stay on the line with me. Give me a description of the suspect."

Harmony did and whispered, "Hurry. Please."

"We're nearby. We're on our way."

She began to pray, recalling every Scripture about protection. "Jesus, help me. Send angels to protect me."

Tears streamed down her face as she heard sirens, then glass shattered somewhere. Harmony couldn't tell if it was inside or outside the building. Seconds later, the lights flashed on, and she scanned her office to make sure LJ had not snuck in.

"The police and a firetruck are on the scene. I'll disconnect now."

"No. Wait," she said, too late. The dispatcher was gone. Her phone rang back, and she answered without looking at the caller ID.

"Harmony, this is Lawson. I'm here. What floor are you on, and where's your office?"

She told him.

"Don't open that door until you hear a scratching on the door or if the police reach you before me. Got it?"

"Yes."

Voices grew louder, then she heard what sounded like someone clawing on the door. Harmony swallowed and cracked it open. Lawson walked in with a commanding presence, with his phone to his ear. "I've got her, cuz. Harmony is safe."

Lawson handed her his phone and squeezed her shoulder. He had on a fireman's uniform, and an axe was in his other hand. All the horror movies where an axe was the murder weapon came to mind. She was relieved to be on the winning side.

"Hello? Pace?" Her voice was as shaky as her hands.

"You sure you're okay, babe?"

She nodded, then answered as an officer stood in the doorway. "Yes. I think LJ wanted to rape me."

"He's a dead man," Pace snapped.

"Don't say that. Vengeance is the Lord's. I don't want you to get in trouble."

"Not only me. My sister Victoria has a conceal-and-carry permit. Grandma BB took her to shooting ranges, so she's loaded and ready to fire. If she gets to LJ before any of us, Victoria will pay him back for every man who touched her. She's a pit bull, Rottweiler, and shepherd rolled into one."

Harmony now understood why no man could survive Victoria's wrath after what she'd endured. "I'll call her and tell her to stand down." As Lawson looked outside her large window at the street below, her nerves were frazzled. "Pace, I'm ready to use that open ticket and come home."

The officer chatted with Lawson as if the two knew each other, then looked at Harmony and cleared his throat. "I need your statement, ma'am."

"Pace, I've got to go. The police want to talk to me."

"Catch the first flight out, baby, and I'll be waiting for you."

Handing the phone back to Lawson, she thanked him over and over. Harmony collapsed in her chair. All her strength was gone as she recalled what had almost happened and what LJ had said he would do.

"We got a call from Lawson after the dispatcher took your information. Were you harmed?" Officer John Friendly asked.

"I was threatened after I rejected his unwanted sexual advances, and when I told my boss, Lynn Johnson, he said I had to come out of my office sometime and he would be waiting for me." She shivered, recalling his smug expression. "I had no idea I was alone in the office with him. I want to press charges, whatever they are."

The officer nodded, and he asked more questions. "So far, we haven't located anyone else in the building. You're safe."

This time, Satan taunted her.

Pace was hot! The thoughts of bodily harm that went through his mind were ungodly. *Lord, I'm having a hard time repenting on this one. Help me out.*

He couldn't wait until tomorrow to see if Harmony was okay. JC called him as he was about to book the next flight out of Chicago.

"What's the plan? What do you need me to do? I can get on the road now...Kami and Victoria insist on coming, too, and Grandma BB is about to pack her guns."

Pace groaned. Harmony must have called his sisters. "Thanks, bro, but I need you to keep my sisters at home. Victoria takes no prisoners when she's worked up, and I can barely contain my anger. Thanks for having my back. I love you as a brother." He was glad he'd eventually listened to the Lord concerning not discouraging JC's attraction to his sister. "I was about to book a ticket tonight."

"Okay, I'll keep praying. Let's pray first." JC began, "Father, in the mighty name of Jesus, we thank You for Your protection tonight. Your Word says in all things, give thanks. We don't understand what the devil's plan is, but we're thankful You canceled it, in Jesus' name. Amen."

"Amen." Pace appreciated JC's petition to God while he struggled to find the words. "Love you, man."

"Love you back, bro." They ended the call.

Pace exhaled and opened his app to book a flight tonight and escort Harmony home Saturday morning. Nobody messed with a Jamieson woman. His heart dropped when there were no more flights available that night. Although he wasn't surprised, he had hope.

This is not your battle. You love her, but I loved her first and always, God whispered.

Pace paused his emotional overdrive. The Lord left him with no comeback, so he praised Him.

"Lord, I thank You for mercies. Thank You for sending angels to protect her until help arrived. I praise You..." He was thankful that Esquire, Lawson, and Vaughn were willing to take Harmony's number and be there for her when he couldn't. His prayer of thanks soon became worship as he thought about what could have been. "And Lord, please keep me, my family, and the Reed family from seeking revenge, in Jesus' name. Amen."

In perfect timing, Harmony finally called him back.

"Baby, are you home?"

"Yes." She sounded tired.

"Okay, from the beginning, tell me why I want to—if God would let me—strangle this man."

She told him everything, including that her boss was nowhere to be found. Her voice was still shaky. As far as Pace was concerned, Lynn Johnson, aka LJ, was a piece of trash.

I died for his sins, just like yours, God reminded him. *Pray for him.*

Pace would only do so because God told him to, knowing God was no respecter of persons when it came to salvation, but Pace couldn't look past the man's deeds to see a soul worthy of deliverance.

Harmony's voice pulled him out of his mental retribution against her boss.

"The thing about it was the police searched the building and there were no signs of LJ—none—while Lawson stayed to protect me. I didn't realize firefighters have access to buildings without a key."

Lawson was a fire captain, while Esquire was the attorney. "Yep. If firefighters don't have access to a lockbox, they will knock the door down to gain access by any means necessary."

"I've never been so scared. Why did I think the hashtag MeToo movement wouldn't affect me in the workplace? I love my job and new opportunities, but this guy makes me uncomfortable, and I did nothing to encourage his advancement. The coward either left or was hiding well. I hate to go back to work, but I need to file a complaint with human resources about his unwanted sexual advances. When I told my coworker Whitney about what happened and what I planned to do, she asked me if that was a good idea because I could lose my job," Harmony rambled, and he didn't interrupt her.

"I'd rather you be safe, but I support your decision, babe."

She exhaled. "Thank you. I'm glad you didn't suggest I quit and come home like I'm sure my family will demand."

You have no idea how I wanted to, but had no right, which was why she was there, and he was in Chicago.

Before ending the call, Pace prayed for her like never before until they both shed tears, then he called Esquire. "Hey, cuz. What's the plan with Harmony?"

"Well, she wants to file a complaint with human resources, which she should do in writing. Her boss should be reprimanded, but honestly, when those things happen, the environment can become hostile. She could get labeled a troublemaker and not be taken seriously until she quits."

"Harmony loves that job."

"Yeah, most people do. I'm glad I don't have sisters but plenty of female cousins. You know, I practice personal injury cases, but I can ask a colleague who specializes in all types of workplace harassment."

"Make the call," Pace said. LJ was going to pay for upsetting his woman and a child of God.

Chapter Thirty-five

Exiting the O'Hare International Airport terminal, Harmony didn't want to experience this kind of homecoming.

Her welcome party didn't wave signs or hold balloons. Concern plagued their faces. Pace stood before her family as if he led the delegation. She would have admired his handsome features, build, and stylish clothes at any other time. Those material things paled compared to the relief that caused his shoulders to slump.

Her parents didn't hide their emotions. Sadness overpowered their happiness to see her.

Laurence Jr., Kimbrell, and Shane's serious expressions and stance conveyed they were ready for war.

Pace began his stride to meet her halfway. With pure gentleness, he retrieved the weekender bag from Harmony's shoulder as he looked at her.

They didn't exchange words as his hug shielded her from the jostle of travelers around them. His strength made Harmony feel safe as he whispered, "You okay?"

"Yes." She nodded, taking his hand. Together, she approached her family, who inspected her for bumps, bruises, and scars.

"I'm glad you're safe." Her mother teared.

"You need to quit that job and move back home," Shane was the first to voice what was probably on everyone's mind as he folded his arms. "Because somebody's going to get hurt, and it won't be my sister."

"I'm not quitting." Harmony's fear turned into defiance.

Shane flexed his muscles and cracked his knuckles like he did when he was mad—hot.

Pace squeezed her hand. "I've got her covered."

"You do?" Harmony asked, along with her family, as they looked between the two of thcm.

"Yes. Now, if you don't mind, I'll drive her to your house in my car." It wasn't a question, yet Pace waited for her family's consent.

None seemed happy about his offer but conceded, but not without Shane mumbling, "You better be glad we let you back into the family."

"He was never kicked out." Her dad nodded at Pace as they were about to split directions in the parking garage. "She's in good hands."

Alone in the car with Pace, Harmony was numb. "I was so afraid," she confessed, "and I know fear disappoints God. I wasn't expecting that. I barely slept last night. It was a nightmare."

"I know, babe." Pace squeezed her hand. "*Shhh*. We don't have to talk about it."

"Thank you." And Harmony didn't want to think about it, but what had happened was stuck on replay in her head. Yet, she did feel safe now. Relaxing, Harmony yawned, closed her eyes, and drifted off for a nap.

When they reached her parents' house, Pace helped her out of the car and kept his arm around her waist as if she needed support to walk. Maybe Harmony did need his strcngth.

The front door to her childhood home was open. Her family stood inside the living room waiting for her, They watched her and then all at once, peppered her with questions.

Physically and mentally exhausted, Harmony sat on the loveseat and pulled Pace down next to her, encouraging her family to take a seat. They all did—except her mother.

"Are you hungry?" Lorna asked.

"Not really." Her appetite had deserted her.

Pace nudged his leg against hers. "Babe, try to eat something…for me."

His brown eyes pleaded with her, and Harmony couldn't resist. "Okay."

She was rewarded with a gentle hand squeeze, and minutes later, a cup of hot chocolate and a bagel smothered with cream cheese was placed before her on a dinner tray. Everyone else declined. Suddenly, the spacious living room seemed like a war room with the testosterone staring at her.

"Harmony, like I told you last night when you called us, it's not safe for you to be there by yourself," her father said in a tone not meant for disagreement. "It took a lot of praying from your mother to keep me from getting in my car last night for Omaha."

"As our little sister—" Laurence Jr. began.

"Grown sister," she corrected.

Her brother growled as if he had fangs. "Don't play with me, Harmony Lela Reed. I will hurt some man over you." He eyed Pace, then her again. "I think you should come back to Chicago."

The hot chocolate on her tongue awakened her taste buds, and she nibbled on the bagel. "Dad, I can't hide from bad people. The devil is everywhere, out in the open and hidden in shadows in every city, including Chicago. But I was scared. I called Pace's cousin, and help was on the way. I had nine-one-one on the phone and my can of mace in my other hand."

Rehashing the nightmare was draining. While her family brainstormed ways to protect her, the hot chocolate relaxed her as she rested her head against Pace's shoulder and closed her eyes. The last thing she heard was, "It's time for Harmony to upgrade from mace to a gun."

The next day, Pace and Harmony caught a midday flight back to Omaha. He had convinced the Reed family that Harmony's safety was the most important thing to him and his cousins there would watch out for her, and she didn't need to own a gun without proper training.

That morning when he arrived to take Harmony to the airport, her father met him at the front door. "Pace, I like you, son, and I believe you, but..." he said, pointing to Harmony, "she is daddy's little girl, and I have no problem going to jail over some low-life who wants to take advantage of my baby."

"Understood." Pace nodded. "We're praying that isn't God's option for you." Once Pace had reassured her family that he would take the lead in safety precautions for his lady, they calmed down a little, and he and Harmony left.

She was quiet on the short flight back to Omaha, and Pace wondered what she was thinking. He didn't ask but decided to watch her body language and read her expressions.

Once they landed at Omaha's airport, Pace rented a car and drove them the short distance to her apartment, which wasn't far from where he and the judge ate. Suddenly, her safe surroundings turned dark because of what could have happened.

He didn't disagree with everything her family suggested. Pace preferred a taser over a gun. One of her brothers moving to Omaha, escorting Harmony to work as if it was her first day of kindergarten to put bullies on notice, wasn't realistic.

The stakes had changed. This bully had the potential to ruin her career and violate her. Pace made sure his cousins had their eyes on the target—Lynn Johnson.

"You okay?" he asked, glancing at her when he stopped at the light. He wasn't an expert in trauma, but she had to be feeling some type of way.

Harmony had been quiet as she looked out the window. She shrugged and faced him. “In college, I never worried about date rape because your sisters and I didn’t drink and were careful when we attended parties.” She sighed. “This type of behavior wasn’t on my radar to be part of my experience on my first job. I guess I was naive.”

“No, baby.” He covered her hand with one of his. “We all let our guards down, which is what the devil is hoping for. That’s contrary to what the Lord tells us to do. This is a wake-up call for all of us to be prepared for the unexpected.”

“Yeah,” Harmony mumbled.

“Be alert, prayerful, and ready in case the police don’t scare him off.” Pace entered the building’s underground parking garage using her access card to lift the gate. The entry was so quick that another car couldn’t sneak in. A person could try but would be spotted, as a security guard was inside. Pace was okay with this setup.

They got out on her floor and used her access card again to get inside the building. The hall was clean, well-lit, and he spied a security camera. Pace squeezed her hand. She appeared calmer than him. He didn’t want to leave her.

Once inside her apartment, he scanned her furnishings and decor and smiled. “This is nice. I feel better knowing where you live and that the building is secure. While she took her weekender bag into the bedroom, Pace sat on her sofa. Minutes later, she joined him after he declined anything to drink. He held her close as she pointed the remote to her screen to watch a movie.

Pace had so many questions about how she was feeling, whether she was still afraid, and what he could do, but she didn’t appear to be in a talkative mood, so he remained quiet as they watched a movie until she nodded off.

“Okay, sleepy head, you need to get some rest. I’m going to check into the hotel down the street. I’ll be close in case you need me.” He stood and tugged her to walk him to the door.

"Thank you for everything." Harmony hugged him tightly around his waist, and he held her close. They shared a gentle kiss before he left for the night.

Pace didn't like being away from her. Neither one of them would cross the line to sin against God with an appearance of evil if he stayed. The hotel, which was five minutes away, was still too far.

Once he was checked into his room, he called his Omaha cousin, Esquire. "I'm here. What's the plan?"

"I don't trust the man," Esquire said. "He didn't succeed. He will probably retaliate to make Harmony miserable unless management reprimands him. I think he'll try it again when nobody's around, especially if she has to work late. She needs to hire an attorney—"

"I told you I'll pay for it."

"No need. Alan will accept the case pro bono as a favor to me. All she needs to do is initiate contact. I told him Harmony is family. She has to be strong-willed and fearless as a case is built against him."

Pace rubbed his forehead. "She is, but I don't like her being in harm's way."

"We got this. Lawson and I called in favors for some undercover work. He knows a friend of a friend whose nineteen-year-old needs a job. I know the owner of the business that has the cleaning contract for that building. It's a perfect setup to keep Harmony safe."

His cousin made it seem like there was no risk involved.

Esquire continued, "The young man's name is Derek Gray, and he'll work undercover as part of the janitorial crew. As long as Harmony is at work, he will look out for her. He will stay on his shift as long as Harmony is there. I also reached out to the property management and suggested they hire a security guard as long as someone is in the building. The guy didn't want to, but I told him that based on the recent incident, his company could be liable for not providing security."

Pace felt better. “Wow. Esquire, you have been busy. You’re alright, even if you are a Robnett.”

“Hey, we can get the job done.” His cousin laughed. “You don’t have to do anything.”

“Wrong.” Pace stood. “It’s praying time because everything you put in place is earthly. My woman needs spiritual intervention.”

“You handle that from your end and leave logistics here for me.”

When the call ended, the Lord scolded Pace. *You should have come to me in the beginning, and I would have given you peace. This is not your battle but Harmony’s.*

Pace groaned. He prayed that Harmony would come out unscathed.

Chapter Thirty-six

Omaha police had tracked him down at the home address Lawson had obtained. When they questioned him, LJ seemed surprised by her allegation, so it was her word against his.

Harmony didn't trust LJ after his stunt last week. Spiritual constraint kept her from confronting him when they crossed paths at the office.

Fuming inside at the snake, Harmony diligently worked on the campaign after she emailed human resources and copied the company's vice president. When she wasn't in the conference room, she camped out in Whitney's office, awaiting a response from the company's higher-ups.

It had been a week, and Harmony hadn't received a response to her urgent incident report. Her family, friends, and Pace were as irate as her. Pace reminded her not to let her guard down. She'd experienced firsthand what evil felt like.

Let not your heart be troubled. In the world you shall have tribulation: but be of good cheer; I have overcome the world, God whispered. *Read John 16.*

The Lord was her bodyguard. She had to keep reminding herself of that. Besides, her family, Pace, Kami, Victoria, the Robnett cousins, and the local Robnett men also checked up on her.

Victoria called more than once about different tactics of self-defense, from blinding him to giving him diarrhea by adding something to his drink. "Since I'm in nursing school, I can instruct you on how to dissect him, then stitch him up."

It felt good to laugh. "Now you want me to get charged with assault."

"I know a good lawyer," Victoria said, speaking proudly of JC, "or he will be once he takes the bar."

"Thanks, your cousin has me covered here." Harmony was in awe of how protected the Robnetts were of her.

"I plan to visit once I'm on winter break and put the fear of God in him." She paused and laughed. "But I'll want a tour of your company. Kami won't be able to come, but JC said wherever I'm going, he's coming, too, to keep an eye on me."

Harmony snickered and shook her head in disbelief. As long as she had been friends with the Jamieson sisters, Victoria had been the quiet one, but this had roused her up, and she wanted revenge for every child and woman who had been a victim in the world.

"Please be careful. I know I'm talking big—and I can back it up—but the Lord doesn't want us to fight our battles like that. I'm praying God will give you supernatural strength to defend yourself, in Jesus' name."

They both said, "Amen."

Once they ended the conversation, Harmony felt brave, empowered, and equipped with the Holy Ghost to protect herself.

Three weeks after the incident, Vice President Donn Winters responded to her via email and copied the human resources director.

I had a conference call with Lynn Johnson, who advised me that he wasn't on the premises when police and firefighters responded to an emergency call, so I can't reprimand him if he wasn't there. He says you are doing great work and is concerned that your accusations could create a hostile working environment. Please note that you are still on probation.

Harmony sat frozen, staring at the email. She reread it three times to make sure her brain was processing the words correctly. Then she called Pace. "Now what?"

"Pray. Esquire's attorney friend is trying to see if there was any surveillance video from that night. I don't like you being threatened. My cousins are on standby, and Derek is there undercover."

"Yes, I met him. He's buffed. I'm glad he's on my side." Harmony sighed. That was little comfort, knowing LJ had his tracks covered—this time.

LJ informed his team of a last-minute change on the Monday before Thanksgiving. "The pressure is on, people. Enjoy your turkey feast, but on Friday, I need everyone to come in for a half-day to finish the touches on the presentation for Monday. We missed Black Friday, but hopefully, we can jump in the ring next week."

No one seemed pleased, and they voiced their displeasures while Harmony remained silent. Without management behind her, she had to watch her back with LJ because he probably thought he was untouchable.

Harmony had done her best not to be in close proximity to LJ, but her Holy Ghost flashed "Warning, warning" whenever he was near.

That evening, she gave Pace the bad news. "I won't be home for Thanksgiving. I have to work the day after."

"What?" His roar seemed to echo from Chicago to Omaha. "Then I'm coming to you."

Harmony smiled because she felt loved but became sober in thought. "This is my fault. Maybe if I had waited longer for a job in Chicago—I mean, I did have freelance projects—maybe something would have come up, but Pace, I honestly thought this was God's will."

"Babe, no guilt trips. I believe the move was God's will, and He is with you. I can't be there every moment, but God can. The Lord also has boots on the ground ready to prevent anything from happening to you." He told her to call Esquire with this information.

She did.

Esquire wasn't surprised when Harmony told him about what LJ had requested. "But we might have something on him. As fate would have it, the Omaha PD was testing drones in the area over the convention center that night, monitoring the streets for suspicious behavior but not the buildings. Alan has requested they check their footage to see if it picked up any movements in buildings around the time the call came in. They are doing so now." He paused. "Just in case, I think you should set up a camera in your office."

Harmony gnawed on her lips, thinking. "Yeah and go live on social media. The company might turn a blind eye, but the world won't. That would teach him a lesson from trying to make me out to be a liar."

"That's not a good idea. Putting the company on social media could ruin future opportunities for you. All companies have dirt, and to hire a brave woman like you who has no problem exposing flaws would not make you a good candidate, regardless of your qualifications."

She didn't like being bait to prove her innocence. That frightened her as she counted down the day after Thanksgiving.

Chapter Thirty-seven

Pace arrived in Omaha the night before Thanksgiving. Harmony's family wanted to come, too, but only to confront LJ, and Mrs. Reed knew that wouldn't end well.

"I trust God and I trust you, Pace, to listen to God to keep my baby safe," she said when he joined them for Sunday dinner after church service.

So here he was. Once he checked into his hotel, he and Harmony strolled through the Old Market district, even taking a carriage ride. He did what he could to keep her mind off work.

The only thing that seemed to be happening that evening was the Grateful Gobble Drinksgiving Bar Crawl.

Pace didn't know how many times their horse trotted around the district. Harmony seemed content, snuggled next to him, sharing a blanket.

The next morning when Pace arrived at her apartment, Harmony was cheerful in her festive fall colors—gold and green. She had already spoken to her parents for the holiday, and they were relieved Pace was there.

They laughed, having dressed in matching colors. "I guess great minds think alike." He brushed a kiss on her pouty lips. "You look well rested."

"Knowing you were close by, I slept through the night." She graced him with a smile.

They made noon reservations for Thanksgiving brunch at Big Mama's Kitchen and Catering.

The drive from her apartment to the Highlander Accelerator took just twenty minutes, and there was very little traffic. They arrived on Patricia "Big Mama" Barron Street.

Walking inside hand in hand, Pace admired the cleanliness and spacious seating. The open ceiling exposed black-painted pipes and structures, matching the black chairs and tables.

The soul food restaurant buzzed with patrons and servers catering to them. Glass floor-to-ceiling walls surrounded them, providing plenty of lighting, except for the black wood wall that boasted pictures of the owners with celebrities and dignitaries.

A cheerful young hostess showed them to a table for two, decorated in brown and gold accents.

"This is nice." Harmony grinned and relaxed against her chair as jazz music serenaded guests. The owner, Big Mama, worked the room, greeting customers. "Thanks for coming. How's the food?" Pace overheard her ask diners nearby.

Within minutes, Pace and Harmony enjoyed the tasty Southern cooking everyone else raved and moaned about.

"Your dad seems to be enjoying church with your mom," Pace said as he was about to sample his apple pie with sculptured whipped cream.

Harmony bobbed her head, and her curls danced from side to side. He had an exquisite lady. "Mom likes him going and hopes he will surrender to the Lord one day. Thanks for accepting her invitation for dinner sometime."

"You don't have to thank me. Even though we're apart, I feel I'm close to you when I'm there."

That earned him a kiss as she leaned across the table. "I've only joined them a few times. My parents taught me not to wear out my welcome. Plus, when your brothers come for dinner, they act like they don't like to share."

The atmosphere was relaxing and unrushed. They planned to go to the theater and call it an early night since she had to work in the morning. Pace tried not to think about it.

Harmony's phone rang, and Pace thought another family member was checking up on her. "Hey, Whitney."

Pace stared as Harmony frowned.

"No, LJ hasn't called me."

The sound of that man's name caused Pace to ball his fists as he listened, ready to act and call for backup if necessary.

A smile tugged on Harmony's lips. Hope shone in her eyes. "I hope he does. Okay. Happy Thanksgiving to you, too. See you on Monday." She ended the call. "That was my coworker. She doesn't have to go to the office in the morning. Talk about abuse of power… He tells us we have to work, and now he's calling us to tell us not to come in."

"Well, let's hope you get that call too." He covered her hand with his.

Harmony shook her head. "The worst boss can make the best job in the world miserable."

A double-minded man is unstable in all his ways. God reminded Pace of James 1:8.

Pace was suspicious. Her boss wasn't trustworthy. *Lord, how can I protect her?* Pace had asked this question many times.

The answer was always the same. *You can't. I can.*

By the end of the evening, after seeing a movie and exploring Omaha until sunset, Harmony hadn't received "the" call. Pace suspected a setup but didn't want to mention it as they returned to her apartment, but she did.

"I have a bad feeling about tomorrow. Why didn't LJ give me the day off?"

Should he tell her his thoughts? Pace sighed. "Baby, I think he wants to ambush you, and that won't happen." He fumed. "I'm going to the office with you."

Harmony rubbed his cheek, and he kissed the inside of her hand. "You can't. All visitors have to be cleared."

"I can't have you walking in there alone." Pace's nostrils flared.

"Hopefully, Jason or Kelli will be there."

"And if they're not?" He grunted. "Let me call my cousin. If I can't go inside with you…" He started to say she wasn't going, but Harmony needed his support, not his control.

While they were brainstorming, Esquire called him. Pace told his cousin about the call Harmony didn't get.

"Put Harmony on speakerphone," Esquire said. "We'll make sure Derek is there tomorrow with his broom and trash bin to run surveillance and put a small camera in your office. That way, you can activate it to record any time someone comes in. You'll need evidence of this bad character's behavior. If the police's video footage from its drones didn't pick up anything, we'll get him on audio and visual."

Harmony told Pace when the call ended, "I don't like being the bait." She shook her head as worry lines crossed her forehead. "This is no longer my dream job."

"I'm sorry this is happening, babe. God knows what the devil is up to. I wish we did too." Pace cringed as he reluctantly stood to leave her apartment.

The next morning, after a night of prayer and fasting, Pace left his hotel in his rental car to take Harmony to work.

"Morning." Pace greeted her at the door with a kiss.

It didn't brighten her face.

"Hi." Her shoulders were slumped in defeat as she turned around to lock her door, then slipped her hand in his. "Maybe I'm worrying over nothing. Maybe all this is in my head, and I'm letting the devil make me paranoid."

Pace rubbed her back, then pushed the button and stepped into the elevator for the lobby. "The devil is a liar. The Bible says to be strong in the Lord and the power of His might. We are going into a spiritual battle every day wherever we go, so don't let the enemy trick you to drop your guard. '*Put on the full armor of God so that you can stand against the devil's schemes.*'" For the saints of God, Ephesians 6 was the golden text for their salvation walk.

Once she was comfortable and strapped in her seatbelt, Harmony faced him. "Why do I feel like I'm walking into the lion's den whenever I go to work? It's not fair."

He heard her frustration. It wasn't fair to her or any woman who had to put up with harassment because they were the weaker vessel of an already weak fallen man. Thinking of the attacks from the spiritual realm made him want to snarl, but he masked his emotions so as not to upset his lady.

He parked in front of the building, which looked foreboding because most of the businesses were closed for the holiday, and whatever vehicle was in sight was headed in the opposite direction toward the shops.

Pace stepped out and opened the door for her. "Are you sure I can't come in?"

Harmony shook her head. "I don't want to break any rules and give LJ a reason to threaten my job more than he already has."

Walking back to his car, Pace sat behind the wheel and looked through the two-story glass building. He watched Harmony walk up the stairs to the second floor.

A cleaning crew mop bucket and trash could be seen in the distance. Derek was in the building but out of sight. That gave him some relief.

No one else had entered the building, so Pace could only pray. His family and JC also prayed this would end soon, giving Harmony the victory and LJ a major defeat.

Chapter Thirty-eight

I give power to the faint, and to them that have no might, I increase their strength, God whispered Isaiah 40:29 as Harmony settled at her desk.

It was eerily quiet on the floor. She hadn't seen Derek, only his trash bin. Getting down to work so she could leave, Harmony felt LJ's presence before she looked up and saw him entering her office. Wearing jeans and an oxford shirt, he boasted a grin.

"Where are the others on the team?" she asked, acting surprised as she discreetly clicked the remote for the camera to begin recording.

"Not coming. It's just you and me." He lifted a brow.

"Why? You told us we had to work half a day after Thanksgiving." Harmony's heart pounded with her bogus bravery.

"I changed my mind. You and I can work together on this. Don't try any stunts. No calling the police or be assured I'll fire you. You're new. This is how it works in this business."

Harmony fumed. "This is not how it works with me. I am not sleeping with you, LJ, so forget it, and don't even think about touching my personal space."

"Ha! Big threats from a woman who has a promising career." LJ approached her and was centered on the camera's view. "Now, this will be between you and me."

"I have a boyfriend."

"Where is he now? Dude can't help you." When he reached for her breast, Harmony came out clawing, swinging, kicking, biting, screaming for Jesus. She was going to show no mercy.

"Jesus can't help you now." He tightened his grip around her waist.

Suddenly, her door opened, and Derek stood there.

What took him so long? she wondered.

"Let her go," he ordered calmly.

LJ laughed. "You're not supposed to be here. Look away if you know what's good for you, or I'll have your job!"

Derek used his mop stick as a bat and struck LJ's head like a baseball.

"Ouch!" LJ released her and went after Derek, who ran circles around her boss, taunting him with the mop stick.

She called Pace and the police, and this time, Harmony would make sure the snake didn't hide, escape, or whatever he did last time to disappear. Pace busted into the room, nostrils flaring, fists balled, and teeth gritted in a snarl. He looked fierce.

"Are you okay?" he asked, smoothing her hair and top.

"What took you so long?" Harmony demanded as the police arrived and looked from her to Pace to Derek and LJ who moaned and held his head.

"Esquire said we had to get Lynn Johnson's attempted assault on video, so it wouldn't be your word against his." Pace pleaded with his eyes for her to understand. "I didn't expect my baby to go ballistic. I watched it unfold on camera, along with Esquire and the police. I knew Derek was nearby."

Harmony crossed her arms and jutted her chin. "I broke a nail. You owe me a fresh manicure."

Pace wrapped his arms around her, laughing as the police approached for her statement.

"You can have whatever you want."

Monday morning, Harmony strolled into the office feeling victorious. Word had spread that LJ had been arrested on alleged assault charges.

Whitney ran up to her. "Are you okay?"

"How did you know it was me?"

"Girl, that security guard in the lobby gave us the scoop when we came into work," Whitney said.

"Where was he when I needed him?" Harmony waved her hand as if she was shooing a fly. "Doesn't matter. God gave me strength to fight back."

"Weren't you afraid? LJ is a big guy."

"I know. But I had to be like David in the Bible and not be intimidated by a Goliath man. My God is awesome. He's stronger, He's greater…" She felt like breaking out into a praise dance as she recalled the words of the gospel song "Our God."

She walked into her office, which Derek had restored after the incident, like a real janitor. It wouldn't be business as usual as Harmony waited for the legal process to work in her favor.

This past weekend, she and Pace met with Esquire's attorney friend, Alan, to sign a contract to formally appoint him to represent her in a sexual assault case against LJ.

With a copy of the initial police report, Alan covered all the bases. He drafted an email for Harmony to file a formal complaint with the Equal Employment Opportunity Commission against Applesome and Hutch while copying the company's vice president and human resources director.

By the end of the day, Donn Winters, the company's VP, had flown in from headquarters and called her into the conference room for a private meeting. His demeanor was different from their last conversation. “Harmony, please accept my apology for not taking your complaint seriously. A lot is riding on this project, where LJ was the lead, but you are incredibly talented, and we want to nurture your skills.”

Get to the point, Harmony thought, admiring her recent manicure.

“LJ has been terminated because he violated the company’s code of conduct. Gladys Wright from our San Francisco office will arrive in a few days to step in.”

Harmony nodded at the unknown. At least she wasn’t losing her job too. She liked the company and her team. “Donn, the next time you profess to want to nurture an employee’s talent, give us a safe workplace.” Harmony stood and walked out of the room, feeling empowered. Despite the fresh manicure, she would break a nail again if she had to.

Hopefully, there won’t be a next time, not with a sexual assault lawsuit pending against Lynn Johnson and arbitration between Harmony and Applesome and Hutch to keep the company out of the courtroom.

Epilogue

Two days before Christmas, Pace was a happy man. Harmony's eyes sparkled as she snuggled next to him on the plane ride to St. Louis.

Since it was almost the one-year anniversary of their first meeting, Pace asked and hoped she would be open to spending Christmas Eve with the Jamiesons in St. Louis and then flying to Chicago the next day so they could spend Christmas with her family, mimicking last year's series of events.

"We have survived a year from St. Louis to Oklahoma City to Chicago to Omaha. I hope you can see that we can make our relationship work. I'm in this to hear you say, 'I'm ready for something permanent.'"

Harmony closed her eyes and leaned in for a kiss, mumbling, "It may be sooner than you think."

Right. This was not the end of their love story. Pace would make sure of it. Their happily ever after was coming.

BOOK CLUB DISCUSSION QUESTIONS

1. Discuss whether Victoria should have disclosed her past to Harmony. Why or why not?
2. Discuss the emotional toll on Harmony from losing her close friendships.
3. What are your thoughts on Pace moving to Chicago to be close to Harmony without her asking him?
4. Did Harmony make the right decision to take the Omaha position? Why or why not?
5. Harmony was in a dangerous situation on her first job. Discuss how you think you would have handled it.

About the Author

Pat Simmons is a multi-published Christian romance author of forty-plus titles. She is a self-proclaimed genealogy sleuth passionate about researching her ancestors and casting them in starring roles in her novels. She is a five-time recipient of the RSJ Emma Rodgers Award for Best Inspirational Romance: *Still Guilty, Crowning Glory, The Confession, Christmas Dinner*, and *Queen's Surrender (To A Higher Calling)*. Pat's first inspirational women's fiction, *Lean On Me*, with Sourcebooks, was the national library system's February/March Together We Read Digital Book Club pick. *Here for You* and *Stand by Me* are also part of the Family is Forever series. Her holiday indie release, *Christmas Dinner*, and traditionally published, *Here for You*, were featured in *Woman's World*, a national magazine. *Here for You* was also listed in the "7 Great Reads That Help to Keep the Faith" by Sisters From AARP. She contributed an article, "I'm Listening," in the *Chicken Soup for the Soul: I'm Speaking Now* (2021). Pat is the recipient of the 2022 Leslie Esdaile "Trailblazer" Award given by Building Relationships Around Books Readers' Choice for her work in the Christian fiction genre.

As a Christian, Pat describes the evidence of the gift of the Holy Ghost as a life-altering experience. She has been a featured speaker and workshop presenter at various venues nationwide. Pat has converted her sofa-strapped sports fanatical husband into an amateur travel agent, untrained bodyguard, GPS-guided chauffeur, and administrative assistant who is constantly on probation. They have a son and a daughter. Pat holds a B.S. in mass communications from Emerson College in Boston, Massachusetts, and has worked in radio, television, and print media for over twenty years. She oversaw the media publicity for the annual RT Booklovers Conventions for fourteen years. Visit her at www.patsimmons.net.

Other Christian Titles

The Jamieson Legacy
Book 1: Guilty of Love
Book 2: Not Guilty of Love
Book 3: Still Guilty
Book 4: The Acquittal
Book 5: Guilty by Association
Book 6: The Guilt Trip
Book 7: Free from Guilt
Book 8: Sandra Nicholson's Backstory
Book 9: The Confession
Book 10: The Guilty Generation
Book 11: Queen's Surrender (To a Higher Calling)
Book 12: Contempt: Grandma BB's Shenanigans
Book 13: Christmas Takeover (The Next Generation)
Book 14: Accomplices in Love (The Next Generation)

The Intercessors
Book 1: Day Not Promised
Book 2: Day She Prayed
Book 3: Days Are Coming
Book 4: Day of Salvation

The Carmen Sisters
Book 1: No Easy Catch
Book 2: In Defense of Love
Book 3: Driven to Be Loved
Book 4: Redeeming Heart

Love at the Crossroads
Book 1: Stopping Traffic
Book 2: A Baby for Christmas
Book 3: The Keepsake
Book 4: What God Has for Me
Book 5: Every Woman Needs a Praying Man

Restore My Soul
Book 1: Crowning Glory
Book 2: Jet: The Back Story
Book 3: Love Led by the Spirit

Family is Forever
Book 1: Lean on Me
Book 2: Here For You
Book 3: Stand by Me

Making Love Work Anthology
Book 1: Love at Work
Book 2: Words of Love
Book 3: A Mother's Love

God's Gifts
Book 1: Couple by Christmas
Book 2: Prayers Answered by Christmas

Perfect Chance at Love series
Book 1: Love by Delivery
Book 2: Late Summer Love

Single titles
Talk to Me
Her Dress
House Calls for the Holidays (short story)
Christmas Dinner
Christmas Greetings
Taye's Gift
Waiting for Christmas
House Calls for the Holidays
Anderson Brothers
Book 1: Love for the Holidays (Three novellas):
A Christian Christmas
A Christian Easter
A Christian Father's Day
Book 2: A Woman After David's Heart (A Valentine's Day Story)
Book 3: A Noelle for Nathan

In *Crowning Glory*, Cinderella had a prince; Karyn Wallace has a King. While Karyn served four years in prison for an unthinkable crime, she embraced salvation through the Crowns for Christ outreach ministry. After her release, Karyn stays strong and confident, despite society's stigma on ex-offenders. Since Christ strengthens the underdog, Karyn refuses to sway away from the scripture, "He whom the Son has set free is free indeed." Levi Tolliver, for the most part, is a practicing Christian. One contradiction is that he doesn't believe in turning the other cheek. He's steadfast that there is a price to pay for every sin committed, especially after the untimely death of his wife during a robbery. Then Karyn enters Levi's life. He is enthralled with her beauty and sweet spirit until he learns about her incarceration. If Levi can accept that Christ paid Karyn's debt in full, then a treasure awaits him. This is a powerful tale and reminds readers of the permanency of redemption.

Jet: The Back Story to Love Led By the Spirit, to say Jesetta "Jet" Hutchens issues is an understatement. In Crowning Glory, Book 1 of the Restoring My Soul series, she releases a firestorm of anger with an unforgiving heart. But every hurting soul has a history. In Jet: The Back Story to Love Led by the Spirit, Jet doesn't know how to cope with losing her younger sister, Diane. But God sets her on the road to a spiritual recovery. To ensure she doesn't get lost, Jesus sends the handsome and single Minister Rossi Tolliver to guide her. Psalm 147:3 says Jesus can heal the brokenhearted and bind up their wounds. That sets the stage for Love Led by the Spirit.

In *Love Led By the Spirit*, Minister Rossi Tolliver is ready to settle down. Besides the outward attraction, he desires a sweet, humble woman who loves church folks. It sounds simple enough on paper, but when he gets off his knees, praying for that special someone to come into his life, God opens his eyes to the woman who has been there all along. There is only a slight problem. Love is the farthest thing from Jesetta "Jet" Hutchens' mind. But Rossi, the man, and the minister, is hard to resist. Is Jet ready to allow the Holy Spirit to lead her to love?

In *Stopping Traffic*, Book 1, Candace Clark has a phobia about crossing the street, and for a good reason. As fate would have it, her daughter's principal assigns her to crossing guard duties as part of the school's Parent Participation program. With no choice in the matter, Candace begrudgingly accepts her stop sign and safety vest, then reports to her designated crosswalk. Once Candace is determined to overcome her fears, God opens the door for a blessing, and Royce Kavanaugh enters her life, a firefighter built to rescue any damsel in distress. When a spark of attraction ignites, Candace and Royce soon discover more than one way to stop traffic.

In *A Baby For Christmas*, Book 2, yes, diamonds are a girl's best friend, but in Solae Wyatt-Palmer's case, she desires something more valuable. Captain Hershel Kavanaugh is a divorcee and the father of two adorable little boys. Solae has never been married and longs to be a mother. Although Hershel showers her with expensive gifts, his hesitation about proposing causes Solae to walk and never look back. As the holidays approach, Hershel must convince Solae she has everything he could ever want for Christmas.

In *The Keepsake*, Book 3, Until death us do part…or until Desiree walks away. Desiree "Desi" Bishop is devastated when she finds evidence of her husband's affair. God knew she didn't get married only to one day have to stand before a judge and file for a divorce. But Desi wants out no matter how much her heart says to forgive Michael. That isn't easier said than done. She sees God's one acceptable reason for a divorce as the only opt-out clause in her marriage. Michael Bishop is a repenting man who loves his wife of three years. If only…he had paid attention to the red flags God sent to keep him from falling into the devil's snares. But Michael didn't and fell. Although God forgives him instantly when he repents, Desi's forgiveness is moving as a snail's pace. In the end, after all the tears have been shed and forgiveness granted and received, the couple learns that some marriages are worth keeping.

In *What God Has For Me*, Book 4, pregnant or not, Halcyon Holland is leaving her boyfriend. When her ex makes no attempts to reconcile their relationship, Halcyon begins to second-guess whether or not she compromised her chance for a happily ever after. But Zachary Bishop has had his eye on Halcyon since he first saw her. What one man doesn't cherish, Zach is ready to treasure. He's on a mission to offer her a second chance at love that she can't refuse: unconditional love for a ready-made family. Halcyon will soon learn that her past circumstances won't hinder the Lord's blessings for them.

In *Every Woman Needs A Praying Man*, Book 5, first impressions can make or break a business deal, and they definitely could be a relationship buster, but an ill-timed panic attack draws two strangers together. Unlike firefighters who run into danger, instincts tell businessman Tyson Graham to be weary of a certain damsel in distress and run. Days later, the same woman struts through his door for a job interview. Monica Wyatt might possess the outward beauty and the brains on paper, but Tyson doesn't trust her to work for his firm, or maybe he doesn't trust his heart around her.

In *Guilty of Love*, when do you know the most important decision of your life is the right one? Reaping the seeds from what she's sown; Cheney Reynolds moves into a historic neighborhood in Ferguson, Missouri, and becomes a reclusive. Her first neighbor, the incomparable Mrs. Beatrice Tilley Beacon aka Grandma BB, is an opinionated childless widow. Grandma BB is a self-proclaimed expert on topics Cheney isn't seeking advice—everything from landscaping to hip-hop dancing to romance. Then there is Parke Kokumuo Jamison VI, a direct descendant of a royal African tribe. He learned his family ancestry, African history, and lineage preservation before he could count. Unwittingly, they are drawn to each other, but it takes Christ to weave their lives into a spiritual bliss while He exonerates their past indiscretions.

In *Not Guilty*, one man, one woman, one God, and one big problem. Malcolm Jamieson wasn't the man who got away, but the man God instructed Hallison Dinkins to set free. Instead of their explosive love affair leading them to the wedding altar, God diverted Hallison to the prayer altar during her first visit back to church in years. Malcolm was convinced that his woman had loss her mind to break off their engagement. Didn't Hallison know that Malcolm, a tenth-generation descendant of a royal African tribe, couldn't be replaced? Once Malcolm concedes that their relationship can't be savaged, he issues Hallison his own edict, "If we're meant to be with each other, we'll find our way back. If not, that means there's a love stronger than we had." His words begin to haunt Hallison until she begins to regret their break up, and that's where their story begins. Someone has to retreat, and God never loses a battle.

In *Still Guilty*, Cheney Reynolds Jamieson made a choice years ago that is now shaping her future and the future of the men she loves. A botched abortion prevented her from carrying a baby to term, and her husband, Parke K. Jamison VI, is expected to produce heirs. With a wife who cannot give him a child, Parke vows to find and get custody of his illegitimate son by any means necessary. Meanwhile, Cheney's twin brother, Rainey, struggles with his anger over his ex-girlfriend's actions that haunt him, and their father, Dr. Roland Reynolds, fights to keep an old secret in the past.

In *The Acquittal*, two worlds apart, but their hearts dance to the same African drumbeat. On a professional level, Dr. Rainey Reynolds is a competent, highly sought-after orthodontist. Inwardly, he needs to be set free from the chaos of revelations that make him question if happiness is obtainable. To get away from the drama, Rainey is willing to leave the country under the guise of a mission trip with Dentist Without Borders. Will changing his surroundings really change him? If one woman can heal his wounds, then he will believe that there is really peace after the storm.

Ghanaian beauty Josephine Abena Yaa Amoah returns to Africa after completing her studies as an exchange student in St. Louis, Missouri. Although her heart bleeds for his peace, she knows she must step back and pray for Rainey's surrender to Christ so God can acquit him of his self-inflicted mental torture. In the Motherland of Ghana, Africa, Rainey not only visits the places of his ancestors, will he embrace the liberty that Christ's Blood does set every man free.

In *Guilty By Association*, how important is a name? To the St. Louis Jamiesons, tenth-generation descendants of a royal African tribe—everything. To the Boston Jamiesons whose father never married their mother—there is no loyalty or legacy.

Kidd Jamieson suffers from the "angry" male syndrome because his father was absent in the home, but insisted his two sons carry his last name. It takes an old woman who mingles genealogy truths and Bible verses together for Kidd to realize his worth as a strong black man. He learns it's not his association with the name that identifies him, but the man he becomes that defines him.

In *The Guilt Trip*, Aaron "Ace" Jamieson lives carefree. He's good-looking, and respectable when he's in the mood, but his weakness is women. If a woman tries to ambush him with a pregnancy, he takes off in the other direction. It's a lesson learned from his absentee father that responsibility is optional. Talise Rogers has a bright future ahead of her. She's pretty and has no problem catching a man's eye, which is exactly what she does with Ace. Trapping Ace Jamieson is the furthest thing from Talise's mind when she learns she is pregnant, and Ace rejects her. "I want nothing from you Ace, not even your name." And Talise meant it.

In *Free From Guilt*, it's salvation round-up time and Cameron Jamieson's name is on God's hit list. Although his brothers and cousins embraced God—thanks to the women in their lives—the two-degreed MIT graduate isn't going to let any woman take him down that path without a fight. He's satisfied with his career, social calendar, and good genes. But God uses a beautiful messenger, Gabrielle Dupree, to show him that he's in a spiritual deficit. Cameron learns the hard way that man's wisdom is like foolishness to God. For every philosophical argument he throws her way, Gabrielle exposes him to scriptures that makes him question his worldly knowledge.

In *Sandra Nicholson's Backstory*, Sandra has made good and bad choices throughout the years, but the best one was to give her life to Christ when her sons were small and to rear them up in the best Christian way she knew how. That was thirty-something years ago and Sandra has evolved from a young single mother of two rambunctious boys: Kidd and Ace Jamieson, to a godly woman seasoned with wisdom. Despite the challenges and trials of rearing two strong-willed personalities, Sandra maintained her sanity through the grace of God, which kept gray strands at bay. But there is something to be said about a woman's first love. Kidd and Ace Jamieson's father, Samuel Jamieson broke their mother's heart. Can Sandra recover? Her sons don't believe any man is good enough for her, especially their absent father. Kidd doesn't deny his mother should find love again since she never married Samuel. But will she fall for a carbon copy of his father? God's love gives second chances.

In *The Confession*, Sandra Nicholson had made good and bad choices throughout the years, but the best one was to give her life to Christ when her sons were small and to rear them up in the best Christian way she knew how. That was thirty-something years ago and Sandra has evolved from a young single mother of two rambunctious boys, Kidd and Ace Jamieson to a godly woman seasoned with wisdom. Despite the challenges and trials of rearing two strong-willed personalities, Sandra maintained her sanity through the grace of God, which kept gray strands at bay.

Now, Sandra Nicholson is on the threshold of happiness, but Kidd believes no man is good enough for his mother, especially if her love interest could be a man just like his absentee father.

In *The Guilty Generation*, seventeen-year-old Kami Jamieson is so over being daddy's little girl. Now that she has captured the attention of Tango, the bad boy from her school, Kami's love for her family and God have taken a backseat to her teen crush. Although the Jamiesons have instilled godly principles in Kami since she was young, they will stop at nothing, including prayer and fasting, to protect her from falling prey to society's peer pressure. Can Kami survive her teen rebellion, or will she be guilty of dividing the next generation?

In *Queen's Surrender (To a Higher Calling)*, Opposites attract...or clash. The Jamieson saga continues with the Queen of the family in this inspirational romance. She's the mistress of flirtation but Philip is unaffected by her charm. The two enjoy a harmless banter about God's will versus Queen's, who prefers her own free-will lifestyle. Philip doesn't judge her choices—most of the time—and Queen respects his opinions—most of the time. It's perfect harmony sometimes. Queen, the youngest sister of the Jamieson clan, wears her name as if it's a crown. She's single, sassy, and most of the time, loving her status, but she's about to strut down an unexpected spiritual path. Evangelist Philip Dupree is on the hot seat as the trial pastor at Total Surrender Church. The stalemate: They want a family man to lead their flock. The board's ultimatum is enough to make him quit the ministry. But can a man of God walk away from his calling? Can two people with different lifestyles and priorities cross paths and continue the journey as one? Who is going to be the first to surrender?

In *Contempt (Grandma BB's Shenanigans)*, Grandma BB, the unofficial matriarch of the Jamieson clan, is getting her house in order for the perfect homegoing celebration. After all, she's eighty-something. She summons Parke Jamieson VI, his brothers, cousins, and their families to play a part in the practice funeral program—only if they follow her instructions to the letter. Since the Jamiesons are at her house with bodyguards Chip and Dale, they might have an impromptu family game night. The evening is full of surprises, especially when an unexpected visitor shows up to steal the show. With more work that needs to be done, Grandma BB plans to put her funeral on hold and stick around for a couple more generations.

In *Accomplices in Love*, Parke "Pace" Jamieson VIII knows something is special about Harmony Reed, his sister's college friend who was almost stranded in St. Louis for Christmas. She checks all his compatibility boxes: looks, charm, a great sense of humor, and strong attraction. Plus, the Jamiesons love her.

When not at school, Harmony lives in Chicago with her three overprotective brothers. She is not interested in a relationship with her best friend's brother.

Pace, who lives in St. Louis, is not deterred by the distance, her objections, or her brothers. He's a Jamieson, and they play to win.

In *Fun and Games with the Jamieson Men*, The Jamieson Legacy series inspired this game book of fun activities: • Brain Teasers• Crossword Puzzles• Word Searches •Sudoku •Mazes •Coloring Pages. The Jamiesons are fictional characters that put emphasis on Black Heritage, which includes Black American History tidbits, African American genealogy, and strong Black families. Relax, grab a pencil and play along.

In *No Easy Catch*, Book 1, Shae Carmen hasn't lost her faith in God, only the men she's come across. Shae's recent heartbreak was discovering that her boyfriend was not only married, but on the verge of reconciling with his estranged wife. Humiliated, Shae begins to second guess herself as why she didn't see the signs that he was nothing more than a devil's decoy masquerading as a devout Christian man. St. Louis Outfielder Rahn Maxwell finds himself a victim of an attempted carjacking. The Lord guides him out of harms' way by opening the gunmen's eyes to Rahn's identity. The crook instead becomes an infatuated fan and asks for Rahn's autograph, and as a goodwill gesture, directs Rahn out of the ambush! When the news media gets wind of what happened with the baseball player, Shae's television station lands an exclusive interview. Shae and Rahn's chance meeting sets in motion a relationship where Rahn not only surrenders to Christ but pursues Shae with a purpose to prove that good men are still out there. After letting her guard down, Shae is faced with another scandal that rocks her world. This time the stakes are higher. Not only is her heart on the line, so is her professional credibility. She and Rahn are at odds as how to handle it and friction erupts between them. Will she strike out at love again? The Lord shows Rahn that nothing happens by chance, and everything is done for Him to get the glory.

In *Defense of Love*, Book 2, nothing in Garrett Nash's life has made sense lately. When two people close to the U.S. Marshal wrong him deeply, Garrett expects God to remove them from his life. Instead, the Lord relocates Garrett to another city to start over, as if he were the offender instead of the victim. Criminal attorney Shari Carmen is comfortable in her own skin—most of the time.

Being a "dark and lovely" African American sister has its challenges, especially when it comes to relationships. Although she's a fireball in the courtroom, she knows how to fade into the background and keep the proverbial spotlight off her personal life. But literal spotlights are a different matter altogether. While playing tenor saxophone at an anniversary party, she grabs the attention of Garrett Nash. And as God draws them closer together, He makes another request of Garrett, one to which it will prove far more difficult to say "Yes, Lord."

In *Redeeming Heart*, Book 3, Landon Thomas (In Defense of Love) brings a new definition to the word "prodigal," as in prodigal son, brother or anything else imaginable. It's good that God's love covers a multitude of sins, but He isn't letting Landon off easy. His journey from riches to rags proves to be humbling and a lesson well learned. Real Estate Agent Octavia Winston is a woman on a mission, whether it's God's or hers professionally. One thing is for certain, she's not about to compromise when it comes to a Christian mate, so why did God send a homeless man to steal her heart? Minister Rossi Tolliver (Crowning Glory) knows how to minister to God's lost sheep and through God's redemption, the game changes for Landon and Octavia.

In *Driven to Be Loved*, Book 4, on the surface, Brecee Carmen has nothing in common with Adrian Cole. She is a pediatrician certified in trauma care; he is a transportation problem solver for a luxury car dealership (a.k.a., a car salesman). Despite their slow but steady attraction to each other, neither one of them are sure that they're compatible. To complicate matters, Brecee is the sole unattached Carmen when it seems as though everyone else around her—family and friends—are finding love, except her. Through a series of discoveries, Adrian and Brecee learn that things don't happen by coincidence. Generational forces are at work, keeping promises, protecting family members, and perhaps even drawing Adrian back to the church. For Brecee and Adrian, God has been hard at work, playing matchmaker all along the way for their paths cross at the right time and the right place.

Lean on Me, Book 1. No one should have to go it alone... Caregivers sometimes need a little TLC too.

Tabitha Knicely believes in family before everything. She may be overwhelmed caring for her beloved great-aunt, but she would never turn her back on the woman who raised her, even if Aunt Tweet's dementia is getting worse. Tabitha is sure she can do this on her own. But when Aunt Tweet ends up on her neighbor's front porch, and the man has the audacity to accuse Tabitha of elder abuse, things go from bad to awful. Marcus Whittington feels a mountain of regret at causing problems for Tabitha and her great-aunt. How was he to know the frail older woman's niece was doing the best she could? As Marcus gets to know Aunt Tweet and sees how hard Tabitha is fighting to keep everything together, he can't walk away from the pair. Particularly when helping Tabitha care for her great-aunt leads the two of them on a spiritual journey of faith and surrender.

Here For You, Book 2. Rachel Knicely's life has been on hold for six months while she takes care of her great aunt, who has Alzheimer's. Putting her aunt first was an easy decision—accepting that Aunt Tweet is nearing the end of her battle is far more difficult. Nicholas Adams's ministry is bringing comfort to those who are sick and homebound. He responds to a request for help for an ailing woman but when he meets the Knicelys, he realizes Rachel is the one who needs support the most. Nicholas is charmed by and attracted to Rachel, but then devastating news brings both a crisis of faith and roadblocks to their budding relationship that neither could have anticipated. This beautifully emotional and clean story contains a hero and heroine who are better at taking care of other people than themselves, a dark moment that shakes their faith, and a well-earned happily ever after.

Stand by Me, Book 3. An uplifting story about embracing love and giving others—and yourself—one more chance. When it comes to being a caregiver, Kym Knicely has been there and done that. Then she meets Charles “Chaz” Banks and soon learns that every caregiving situation is different. Chaz takes care of his seven-year-old autistic granddaughter, Chauncy. Although Kym’s attraction to Chaz is strong, she has to decide whether a romantic relationship can survive and thrive between two people at different stages in life. It’s a journey with a different set of rules that Kym has to play by if she and Chaz are to have their happily ever after and the faith and family they envision.

About *Waiting for Christmas*,
A chance meeting. An undeniable attraction.

And a first date that starts with a stakeout that leads to a winner takes all shopping spree. It's the making of a holiday romance. While philanthropist Sterling Price believes in charitable causes, he and licensed social worker Ciara Summers have a difference of opinion on how to bless others. Ciara is a rebel with a cause and a hundred reasons why helping those less fortunate is important. Sterling is a man of means who believes there is a financial responsibility that comes with giving.

The Lord will make sure everyone's needs are met, and He has something extra for Sterling and Ciara that can't wait until Christmas.

About *Christmas Dinner*,
How do you celebrate the holidays after losing a loved one? Take the journey, beginning with Christmas Dinner. For months, Darcelle Price has suffered depression in silence. But things are about to change as she plans to celebrate Christmas Eve with family and share her journey. Darcelle invites them via group text, not knowing she had included her ex. Evanston Giles is surprised to hear from the woman he loved after months following their breakup. Seeking closure, he shows up on her doorstep for answers. A lot can happen on Christmas Eve. Restoring family ties, building her faith in God, and falling in love again is just the beginning of the night of miracles.

About *Taye's Gift*,
Welcome to Snowflake, Colorado—a small town where wishes come true! When six old high school friends receive a letter that their fellow friend, Charity Hart, wrote before she passed away,

their lives take an unexpected turn. She leaves them each a check for $1,500 and asks them to grant a wish—a secret wish—for someone else by Christmas. Who lays off someone before the holidays? Taye Thomas' employer did, so instead of Christmas shopping, she's job hunting. More devastating news comes when an old high school friend passed away. Could God be answering her prayers for help when she learns that Charity Hart left a $1500 check? No, the caveat is it's more blessed to give than receive. Taye has 30 days to find someone else in need to bless. To complicate matters, she's lives in Kansas City, which is more than eight hours away from Snowflake and she can't do it alone. Keeping a secret has never been so much work.

About *Couple by Christmas*,
Holidays haven't been the same for Derek Washington since his divorce. He and his ex-wife, Robyn, go out of their way to avoid each other. This Christmas may be different when he decides to give his son, Tyler, the family he once had before they split. Derek's going to need the Lord's intervention to soften her heart to agree to some outings. God's help doesn't come in the way he expected, but it's all good because everything falls in place for them to be a couple by Christmas.

About *Prayers Answered By Christmas*,
Christmas is coming. While other children are compiling their lists for a fictional Santa, eight-year-old Mikaela Washington is on her knees, making her requests known to the Lord: One mommy for Christmas please. Portia Hunter refuses to let her ex-husband cheat her out of the family she wants. Her prayer is for God to send the right man into her life. Marlon Washington will do anything for his two little girls, but can he find a mommy for them and a love for himself? Since Christmas is the time of year to remember the many gifts God has given men, maybe these three souls will get their heart s desire.

About *A Noelle for Nathan*,
A Noelle for Nathan is a story of kindness, selflessness, and falling in love during the Christmas season. Andersen Investors & Consultants, LLC, CFO Nathan Andersen (A Christian Christmas) isn't looking for attention when he buys a homeless man a meal,

but grade schoolteacher Noelle Foster is watching his every move with admiration. His generosity makes him a man after her own heart. While donors give more to children and families in need around the holiday season, Noelle Foster believes in giving year-round after seeing many of her students struggle with hunger and finding a warm bed at night. At a second-chance meeting, sparks fly when Noelle and Nathan share a kindred spirit with their passion to help those less fortunate. Whether they're doing charity work or attending Christmas parties, the couple becomes inseparable. Although Noelle and Nathan exchange gifts, the biggest present is the one from Christ.

One reader says, "A Noelle for Nathan makes you fall in love with love…the love of mankind and the love of God. You cannot read this without having a desire to give and do more, all while being appreciative of what you have."

About *Christmas Greetings*,
Saige Carter loves everything about Christmas: the shopping, the food, the lights, and of course, Christmas wouldn't be complete without family and friends to share in the traditions they've created together. Plus, Saige is extra excited about her line of Christmas greeting cards hitting store shelves, but when she gets devastating news around the holidays, she wonders if she'll ever look at Christmas the same again. Daniel Washington is no Scrooge, but he'd rather skip the holidays altogether than spend them with his estranged family. After one too many arguments around the dinner table one year, Daniel had enough and walked away from the drama. As one year has turned into many, no one seems willing to take the first step toward reconciliation. When Daniel reads one of Saige's greeting cards, he's unsure if the words inside are enough to erase the pain and bring about forgiveness. Once God reveals His purpose for their lives to them, they will have a reason to rejoice. *Come unto me, all ye that labor and are heavily laden, and I will give you rest. Take my yoke upon you, and learn of me; for I am meek and lowly in heart: and ye shall find rest unto your souls.* Matthew 11:28-29

About *A Baby for Christmas*,
Yes, diamonds are a girl's best friend, but unless the jewel is going on Solae Wyatt-Palmer's ring finger, they hold little value to her.

When she meets Fire Captain Hershel Kavanaugh, their magnetism is undeniable and there's no doubt that it's love at first sight. Since Solae adores Hershel's two boys from his failed marriage, she wouldn't blink at the chance to become a mother to them. But when it seems as if Hershel doesn't have a proposal on his agenda, she has no choice but to cut her losses and move on. But Christmas is coming. And in order to win Solae back, Hershel must resolve some past issues before convincing her that she possesses everything he wants.

About *A Christian Christmas*,
Christmas will never be the same for Joy Knight if Christian Andersen has his way. Not to be confused with a secret Santa, Christian and his family are busier than Santa's elves making sure the Lord's blessings are distributed to those less fortunate by Christmas day. Joy is playing the hand that life dealt her, rearing four children in a home that is on the brink of foreclosure. She's not looking for a handout, but when Christian rescues her in the checkout line; her niece thinks Christian is an angel. Joy thinks he's just another man who will eventually leave, disappointing her and the children. Although Christian is a servant of the Lord, he is a flesh and blood man and all he wants for Christmas is Joy Knight. Can time spent with Christian turn Joy's attention from her financial woes to the real meaning of Christmas—and true love? A Christian Christmas is a holiday novella to be enjoyed any time of the year.

In Every Day is Christmas, A Christmas ornament
A Christmas ornament, an ailing grandmother, and a match-making sister are all ingredients for a holiday romance.

Landon Michaels is on a mission to fulfill this grandmother's request for a one-of-a-kind Black angel ornament. With dementia setting in, this might be the last Christmas she remembers.

Gina Christmas is the gatekeeper of unique handcrafted ornaments. It's tax season, and the accountant is too busy crunching numbers to track down an ornament, especially since the holiday is months away.

When Granny Lonna wants something, Landon, her favorite and only grandson, is determined to make it happen. But what she really wants for Christmas is for Landon to find the perfect love.

Pat Simmons introduces a new Christian fiction series that reminds readers that the bad guys don't always win, especially when the Lord fights our battles.

In *Day Not Promised*, Omega Addams thought it was a typical workday until a detour on the way home changes everything. She's almost killed, but an innocent bystander, Mitchell Franklin, takes a bullet for Omega during a gas station robbery. In the aftermath, Omega has no idea that God expects her to "pray it forward" until a spiritual battle unfolds before her eyes. Another innocent bystander is in trouble; unless Omega gets her prayer life together, others will die without Christ. It's a chain reaction that highlights the responsibility of a Christian--hot, cold, or lukewarm. It's time to get our acts together. We are our brother's keeper.

In *Day She Prayed*, New Christian convert Tally Gilbert knows the power of prayer and the pain of walking away. She's witnessed family and friends' healing, salvation, and deliverance. There's one holdout, and he's at the top of her prayer list. The love of her life, Randall Addams, won't surrender to the Lord, so Tally ends the relationship. What will it take for Randall to turn to God? Will Tally's prayers be answered or will Randall—and their love—be lost forever?

Don't underestimate a woman who knows how to pray, has backup, and believes "The Word of God is quick, and powerful, and sharper than any two-edged sword, piercing even to the dividing the soul from the spirit, and of the joints and marrow, and is a discerner of the thoughts and intents of the heart." Hebrews 4:12.

If the devil wants a battle, he picks the wrong woman to fight.

In *Days Are Coming*, I'm coming for the children.

Minister Jude Morgan has a strong relationship with the Lord but doesn't know what the latest message means. He is determined to intercede for his young mentee, Carlton Oliver, and children worldwide.

Nine-year-old Carlton wants to get to know his estranged dad, but at what cost? He's about to discover many things he doesn't know about the man who fathered him, and he's on a mission to worship the Lord.

Sinclaire Oliver regrets getting her ex, Harrison Wakefield, involved in her life and that of his son Carlton. He's more trouble than the monthly child support payments she had to sue for. She knows he's angry but never expects it to take a dark turn. Sinclaire learns that God makes no mistakes, even when things don't make sense.

As God sends His judgment on the earth, the devil plants decoys to distract the saints from their mission to be on guard. Is the world doomed, or is there room for redemption?

In *Day of Salvation*, Mother Kincaid, from Christ Is For All Church, has been fervently praying, along with other prayer warriors around the world, for Jesus to return and rescue His saints from this wicked world.

One day, God answers her with a list of unknown individuals who need salvation and a commission for the intercessors and prayer warriors to find and draw them to Christ. Then He will come to redeem His saints, and judgment will begin on the earth.

The caveat to the Lord God's edict: the timer has been set, and if the intercessors don't witness to them, those people will be lost forever.

God thunders, "Get set, get ready, GO!!!!!"

Made in the USA
Columbia, SC
25 September 2024

43028549R00169